Praise for *The Dogs of Winter*, BOOK TWO in the
Russell and Leduc Mysteries:

"*The Dogs of Winter* is as much an exploration of a city and
its communities as a traditional crime novel. It's about power
and powerlessness in the dead of winter. And more than that,
it's a rollicking good read."

—ANN CLEEVES, author of the *Shetland* and *Vera* series

"Marie Russell makes her triumphant return in this
compelling and irresistible sequel to *The Birds That Stay*.
Moving the story from the Laurentian mountains to the
heart of the city of Montreal, Lambert's second Russell and
Leduc mystery features the welcome return of old favourites
and a new cast of fascinating characters. *The Dogs of Winter*
builds on the crackling chemistry between Professor Marie
Russell and Detective Roméo Leduc, propelling them into
a new investigation lined with unsung heroes and unseen
villains. Marie is truly a great Canadian character, and we see
her pitted against not only a sinister and elusive killer, but an
equally insidious structural inequity that stifles the course of
justice at every turn. Like its predecessor, *The Dogs of Winter*
does not shy away from the darker side of Canada's history—
nor its present—and makes for compulsive reading. With
Lambert's characteristic blend of humour, pathos, and vivid
prose, *The Dogs of Winter* should fly off the shelves."

—ANNE LAGACÉ DOWSON,
Montreal commentator and activist

D0841916

# THE DOGS OF WINTER

*A Russell and Leduc Mystery*

# THE
# DOGS
# OF
# WINTER

## Ann Lambert

Second Story Press

**Library and Archives Canada Cataloguing in Publication**

Title: The dogs of winter / Ann Lambert.
Names: Lambert, Ann, 1957- author.
Description: Series statement: A Russell and Leduc mystery
Identifiers: Canadiana (print) 20200209159 | Canadiana
(ebook) 20200209167 | ISBN 9781772601404
    (softcover) | ISBN 9781772601411 (EPUB)
Classification: LCC PS8573.A3849 D64 2020 | DDC C813/.54—dc23

Printed and bound in Canada

*Second Story Press gratefully acknowledges the support of the
Ontario Arts Council and the Canada Council for the Arts for our
publishing program. We acknowledge the financial support of the
Government of Canada through the Canada Book Fund.*

 ONTARIO ARTS COUNCIL
CONSEIL DES ARTS DE L'ONTARIO

 Canada Council    Conseil des Arts
for the Arts      du Canada

Funded by the Government of Canada
Financé par le gouvernement du Canada |  Canada

Published by
Second Story Press
20 Maud Street, Suite 401
Toronto, ON M5V 2M5
www.secondstorypress.ca

*For David, Alice, and Isaac, always.*

We have to be able to imagine a future
in which we matter.

# One

SHE KNEW it was stupid to go out in that storm. She knew it was dangerous. When Rosie Nukilik had first started out that afternoon, the city looked like the inside of the snow globe that she used to have, the kind that you could buy on Ste. Catherine street at souvenir shops—the sparkly skyline of Montreal with two skaters twirling in a plastic circle. But now, that gentle, snow-globe winter had transformed itself into a howling wolf.

The wind was blowing her sideways, and she struggled for traction on the narrow sidewalk. As she slid inside, the tunnel offered a blessed reprieve, and she briefly considered hiding there until the worst of it was over. She'd also lost one of her cherished mittens, the sealskin ones her *aana* had made for her when she turned twelve. She couldn't feel her fingers at all anymore, so she tucked her right hand inside her jacket and then squeezed it under her armpit in the hopes of restoring sensation. She'd had frostbite last winter, when one fingertip had to be amputated from her left hand. She stopped to catch her breath. He said he would meet her in the bus shelter on the other side of the tunnel. He promised. But now she realized he wouldn't be there. Not in this. Rosie knew she couldn't stay in the tunnel and continued carefully along, palming the wall with her covered left hand for guidance. Her right hand held her coat tightly, to protect him as much as she could.

As she emerged from the shelter of the tunnel, shards of icy snow cut into her face and a blast of wind almost blew her off her feet. The storm was so powerful now that almost everything was obliterated. She'd never seen that in the city before. There was no skyline, no trees, no cars. She remembered those whiteouts at home, where in seconds you couldn't know which way you were heading. You didn't even know if you were up or down. Her uncle died in one of those, trying to get her baby cousin home after a party. The baby had somehow been found alive, but no one could imagine how. Her *aana* said it was his spirit animal who had carried him back to safety.

Rosie leaned back into the tunnel and watched as the waves of snow tumbled overhead. She and Maggie had dreamed of having a big house in the city, where they and all their friends could live. Where they would eat country food all day, and she would play the piano for them, singing all their favorite tunes. He had promised her a piano. She looked back into the tunnel behind her but could see nothing—it had become like the black bottom of the bay in early winter. She tucked her face deeper into her jacket and pulled the bits of scarf over her head tighter, but her right hand felt frozen like a stone. She peeked into her coat. Amazingly, he was still asleep.

She stepped over the rail to make a run for it, but her feet skidded out from under her. She struggled to one knee, using her free, frozen hand for purchase in the snowdrift. Suddenly a light appeared through the tunnel like a phantom, like a revenant. She got unsteadily to her feet and tried to run. He had promised her. He had promised her.

# Two

IT HAD BEEN a fantastic day. It was one of those days where everything could have gone wrong, but nothing did. Everyone showed up. No one had a breakdown. She had navigated the needs and egos of the several high-maintenance guests who had nearly driven her crazy with their idiosyncratic demands. Her own keynote speech was inspiring—she knew it—and her *Women Smash the Glass!* conference was a resounding, exuberant success. And it was *her* baby. She was the germinator—but she was more than that. She was the *terminator* as well. If anyone knew anything about Danielle Champagne, it was that she could see an idea, a concept, *a way of life*, and see it to full actualization. Yes, today was a great success. She killed it, as her daughter would say. At one point, taking in the entire conference hall from her lectern on the enormous stage and seeing her giant image projected behind her, she had felt dizzy with joy and satisfaction. There was the mayor, in the front row, flanked by Michelle Obama and Reese Witherspoon. There were young women from across the entire spectrum, from every walk of life, looking up at her like she had the answer to all their questions. She, little Danielle Payette from

La Pocatière, had brought all these disparate groups of girls and women from all over North America together to find a common voice in the struggle against the glass ceiling that thwarted so many women the world over. If conferences like this could be held in every country, especially those where women were seen as barely more than chattel, they could change the world. In two years, she wanted to see simultaneous conferences in Mumbai, Los Angeles, Frankfurt, Cape Town, Jakarta, Sao Paolo, and Moscow. They had already asked her to organize next year's, and she would be sure to at least double her fee. One of the main lessons she had learned over the many years was know what you are worth, and don't be afraid to ask for it. She could hear her mother's voice commenting bitterly on her success—*Tu te prends pas pour du Seven Up flat, anh?* Danielle smiled as she wondered how she'd translate that one for her American friends—it means *you're getting so full of yourself.* She often entertained them with stories of her mother's uniquely Quebecois expressions that even the French from France (FFFs as they were called here) couldn't understand. Her mother's other favorite was *t'étais pas né pour un petit pain,* which literally means *you're not born for a little bread.* As an idiom, it means the small life is not for you. But the connotation is pejorative, like being an ambitious woman is unseemly. Unattractive. Danielle had resisted that kind of attitude her whole life. It started when she legally changed her last name to *Champagne,* the symbolic snipping of the cord to her childhood self. Now she really wished her mother was still alive to see just how big a life she'd created for herself. Not her mother's life, bitter about a husband who left her with five kids, a shitty old car, and a house with a mortgage that would take her three lifetimes to pay off.

Danielle smiled as she beeped off the alarm on her car and slid into the buttery leather seat of her white Lexus. But as she pulled out of the underground parking lot, her smile disappeared. The entire day's experience had left her feeling so magnanimous that she'd told her assistant, Chloé, to go home early, as it was her father's sixtieth birthday party and she was already late. But Danielle hated driving at night, and she was already regretting the gesture. She'd also had two glasses of wine—under the legal limit, she thought. Her regret turned to rage when she pulled out of the underground parking lot and onto Viger by the Convention Centre. The snow was falling so furiously that she couldn't make out whether the traffic light was green or red. The few cars on the road were crawling along, and one was already stuck in a snowdrift, its wheels spinning and whining with futility. She considered going right back into the safety of the lot, but she too wanted to get home and into the evening she had planned—a bottle of wine and a piping hot bubble bath. Danielle soon found herself at the entrance to the 20, the highway that in the old days would take her home on a Saturday evening in twenty-five minutes, but over the past two years Montreal had been replacing its entire infrastructure, after years of using subpar materials in its construction. In broad daylight, the entire area looked like Beirut circa 1974. But this was no war—this was simply Montreal fixing what should have been built properly in the first place. In a snowstorm, with all the construction and detours, it was impossible to even know where she was. She peered at the road sign that loomed at her, too late for her to react. She was just trying to get home to Beaconsfield, but it seemed that every possibility had been closed by orange cones. She slid slowly over to the left lane, where a truck loomed out of the swirling tornadoes of snow like some avenging fury. He blasted her with his horn. Danielle was redirected to the right lane and had no choice but to follow wherever it led. Maybe she could pull over into a parking lot or a McDonald's or something and wait for the storm to abate. Her Google maps app was calmly suggesting another route for the third time—her GPS could not keep up with the road closures that plagued Montreal. She screamed at it to shut up, and then punched it off. She inched along at about thirty kilometers an hour, clutching the steering wheel and peering out at the darkness, her windshield wipers swishing frantically and uselessly. The snow was just too thick, too relentless. She gasped at another sign that was briefly illuminated by someone's headlights: 20 Est Centre-Ville. Somehow, she had turned herself around and was heading east, *back* to the Convention Centre. There were no cars out. No snowplows. No police. It was like one of those end-of-the-world movies where the hero is utterly, irrevocably alone.

She pushed the button to put a call though to her daughter and got her voice mail. Then she called Chloé but ended the call immediately. What the hell was Chloé supposed to do?

Danielle followed the road signs as best she could, but this was *terra incognita*—she could end up on a bridge and heading off the island at any minute. Or she could even drive into the St. Lawrence river itself, she thought. That would be a fucking ironic ending to her perfect day—not the kind of bath she was hoping for. Then, as the wind abated for a few seconds as though catching its breath for another blast, the sign for the Atwater Tunnel briefly appeared. Her relief was so palpable she felt like she was going to cry. If she could get through the tunnel and up the Atwater hill, she could just dump her car somewhere in a snowbank and go see a movie at the Cineplex there. That's what she'd do. Or she could call her friend Monique and ask to spend the night in her condo in Westmount Square. This was just a snowstorm, and she'd survived many before, but the wind was now blowing so ferociously that Danielle could feel her car bouncing. As she entered the tunnel the wind stopped and for a few seconds, she could see. She considered just waiting it out in the tunnel, but it was much too dangerous. She could get rear-ended by a monster truck. Even if she locked herself in her car, she wouldn't feel safe in that part of town at night. She sped up on the dry, protected surface and unclenched her fingers from the steering wheel—her hands were aching with tension. She slowed down a bit as she exited the tunnel, but the wind came up and swirling snow blinded her instantly. And then out of nowhere, a hunched, dark *shape* just materialized in front of her, and Danielle slammed the brake to the floor. She felt the Lexus starting to spin out, and then a sickening thud. Her car skidded off whatever she hit, slid perilously close to the concrete barricade, then righted itself and shot forward at greater velocity. Oh my God, oh my God, oh my God. What the fuck was that? Was it a dog? Or a coyote? They are all over Montreal now, she read somewhere. It must have been a dog—she had seen it lurching in front of her, trying to get across the road but mistiming its run.

Danielle was finally able to pull up at the traffic light a few hundred meters ahead. It was swaying in the storm's wind as though any minute it might detach itself and plummet to the ground. What should she do? *What should she do?* The dog might be badly hurt. Or dead. Should she go back?

What if it was a coyote and now it was injured and dangerous? She couldn't just leave it there. But she couldn't go back.
She couldn't. She could call someone. Who? The SPCA? The
police? But what would she say? She hit an animal and she
didn't stop for it? What kind of person *does* that? She tried
to think clearly. This situation could be managed. She would
call the SPCA as soon as she got inside somewhere safe and
sound. Danielle clutched at the steering wheel and began the
long, very slow ascent of the Atwater hill, her car barely visi-
ble in the whiteness that seemed to swallow it whole.

# Three

MARIE FINALLY SETTLED back into her beloved old armchair and picked up the stack of papers she had been studiously avoiding for several hours. She had washed the dishes, restacked the firewood, brushed both dogs, and rearranged one kitchen cabinet. Supper was already chopped and waiting to be thrown into the pan for a stir-fry. The salad was washed, dressing prepared. Dessert was thawing in the fridge. She had showered and washed her hair. Unless she needed to start picking the lint off her sweaters, Marie had no choice now but to start marking the first assignments of the semester. It was the third week of classes of the winter term at Dawson College, where she was back teaching after a one-year sabbatical. It was also when students and teacher realize that the honeymoon is over. Marie was starting to figure out who the keeners and slackers were, the grade grubbers who'd do anything for a high mark, and their opposite—those who had never encountered an A in their lives and wouldn't know one if it attacked them and etched itself into their foreheads.

Marie didn't pick up her green pen though, the one she always corrected with. She stared into the fire, now roaring mutely behind the tempered glass of her wood stove. Barney, her Puggle, was curled up in a tight little fur circle by her feet, snoring softly. Her other dog, Dog, was lying on his back, his hind legs immodestly splayed, his ridiculously long front legs stretched over his head just begging for someone to scratch his belly. Marie loved her life here in her little house in the woods. After her ex-husband, Daniel, had walked out on their twenty-two-year marriage, it had taken her a long time to accept it. But Marie had finally sold their Montreal home and the life that went with it and moved in full time to their cottage, just outside the village of Ste. Lucie in the hills of the Laurentians. She kept a cramped and not cheap enough *pied à terre* in Montreal, so she didn't have to drive the hour or so up to Ste. Lucie on her three teaching days. But all that was possibly about to change.

Marie forced herself back to her students' papers and selected the first one on the pile. She picked up her pen and began to read the introduction: "There is only one species that kills for pleasure. There is only one species that has destroyed the multiple whales that used to roam the oceans. That is the human species…the cereal killers of the planet." Yes, we stabbed the *Rice Krispies* to death. We shot the *Shreddies*. Marie circled the spelling mistake and wrote (sp)! next to it—the millionth time she had done so. She continued reading: "Whales, especially humback (sp)! whales, long to be free. Free of hunting. But in countries like Norway, Japan and Ireland, they are always looking over their shoulders, scarred (sp)! a whaling harpon (sp)! is pointed right at them." Marie sighed. This was not a good start. Marie was teaching a course about whales—specifically the interaction of humans and cetaceans—and it attracted a lot of students. But many of them had no idea what they were doing in college, and much of their work was half-baked opinion based on Wikipedia research. Marie resorted to the age-old technique of marking survival: abandon the depressing one and move on. She read the beginnings of three more papers, but all of them had major spelling mistakes in the opening paragraph.

Marie picked up a fourth. This student was examining the anthropomorphism of whales, and how this has both served to protect and endanger them. She used several sources—including the gutting documentary story of orcas in captivity in *Blackfish*. The writing was lucid, her argumentation well-documented, effective, and thoughtful. Most importantly, the paper was concise. Marie hadn't read anything this good in a *very* long time. She took note of the student's name: Michaela Cruz. Which one was she? Marie closed her eyes and mapped out the class in her head. Michaela. Right. Second row, two chairs out from the wall. When she first saw her walk into class wearing six-inch heels and a crop-top that accentuated her voluptuous breasts on her tiny frame, Marie thought she had to be a ditz—the kind of girl you see lined up outside a club in sub-zero temperatures in thigh-high hooker boots and a crotch-grabbing mini-skirt. Marie recalled that Michaela had one of those breathy, little-girl voices that Marie couldn't help but think was an affectation. Affecting what? Weakness? Stupidity? Is that little girl stuff still considered sexy? But her paper was brilliant. Once again, Marie was reminded never to judge someone by her appearance. She returned to the paper, wrote "Thank you for this!" in green pen on the cover page, and gave it an A-plus. She leaned in to grab another paper, but her concentration was broken by the scene outside her living room window. The few meandering snowflakes that were falling earlier had apparently transformed into a blizzard. When did this happen? She got up to flick on the radio, and the disturbance caused Dog to change his upward dog yoga position ever so slightly. Barney, almost twelve years old, didn't hear her at all and didn't even budge. She turned on the radio and hit the weather report at precisely the correct moment. The weather channel was forecasting thirty to forty centimeters of snow, and dangerous roads because of high winds. They were warning of whiteout conditions. Marie flicked on her outdoor floodlight and returned to the window. She peered out into the night. Was Roméo still coming, or was the storm a perfect excuse? Not excuse—a good reason to stay home and safe. She decided to call.

"Hi! Are you still coming?"

There was a slight hesitation, then, "Absolutely. I'll be there in forty-five minutes."

"They're forecasting Snowmageddon. Again. What do you think?"

Roméo's baritone voice was as reassuring as a hot bath on a cold night. "I think that I will be about one hour ahead of the storm before it hits its full stride, and I will be at your place in…forty-three minutes."

When Marie had at first told some of her old friends she was dating a *cop*, they howled with laughter at the irony of it. Back when they were college activists, the police were the enemy, the fascist enforcers of a corrupt capitalist state. Marie smiled at the memory of their implacable certainty and tried to return to her work, but she couldn't focus on anything anymore.

Hearing Roméo's voice reminded her that tonight was the night. Again. The Decision deadline that Marie and Roméo had postponed twice already. After almost two years in a relationship, were they going to move in together? In Quebec, most couples started living together well before the two-year mark. But Marie and Roméo weren't most couples. They both guarded their independence ferociously. She kept her little apartment and house, and he kept his flat, because as head of homicide for the Sûreté du Québec in the St. Jerome district, he preferred to maintain his residence in the area. Despite Marie being sixty-one years old and Roméo fifty-one, their relationship was very physical. The best part was that Marie also felt no pressure at all if she wasn't feeling like having sex, and neither did he. There was a kind of shorthand in their communication, probably from their many combined years running around the romantic track. Roméo seemed content with whatever she wanted, and she with him. Yes, things were good between them—very good in fact. But Marie worried their moving in together could upset the delicate emotional ecosystem they each inhabited separately. Not to mention the many demands on their lives from work and children. Marie's two kids were finally sorting themselves out after a few years of twenty-something existential angst and agony. Ruby was in her second year of law school at McGill after giving up the acting dream and she didn't seem to hate law school for it. Ben was the father of her delicious two-year-old grandson, Noah, and might even be thinking of the next one with his partner, Maya.

Marie was also wary of moving in with Roméo and the greater proximity it would bring to the tempest of Sophie, his twenty-year-old daughter, a drama queen. She smiled at the irony of Roméo siring such a child—she must take after her mother, whom Roméo didn't discuss much. He was a discreet, honorable man who never gossiped, and it drove Marie crazy. As much as she would like him to, he would not expose the mother of his only child to Marie's scrutiny. Once again, Marie felt a *frisson* of joy at the thought of Roméo. The idea that she might have missed out on him altogether was horrifying to her now. Marie had felt so lonely in the early years after her divorce that she would actually go to a hairdresser to get her mop of curls tamed once every few weeks just so someone would touch her. Just so she could feel someone's hands on her with no expectation of reciprocation. The first few times Marie and Roméo had made love, her appetite for him, the wonder of his skin on her skin overwhelmed her. But still, she was ten years older, so she always got under the covers first and dimmed the lights so he couldn't see the roll of fat on her belly, the dimples of cellulite on her thighs and legs, the road-map her body resembled after almost sixty years around the track. One night, he gently asked that he be allowed to look at her. At every inch of her. She couldn't quite believe how thrilling it was. To have a man actually *see* her again. But they were both of *a certain age* as the euphemism goes and set in their ways—another euphemism for wanting to do what they want to, when they want to, where they want to, and how they want to. Neither Marie nor Roméo liked to give ground. So now it came down to this: Marie wanted them to live in her little house—this one right here. Roméo wanted them to buy a new place together, so they could start fresh, no baggage, no tracks behind them—only looking forward. They couldn't afford to do both. Marie would not give up her house. Marie remembered Ruby, her daughter, warning her that she might end up a cat lady if she didn't seize this chance to deepen the journey with Roméo. A dog lady, actually. Marie didn't like cats. And Roméo did. Reason enough to slow things down.

Marie glanced at the clock on her stove. Twenty minutes had passed, and she hadn't marked a second assignment. She thought of the stir-fry waiting on the stove and sighed. Roméo was a vegan, Marie an omnivore with strong carnivorous tendencies. She felt an impulse to shelve the stir-fry and pull out one of those T-bone steaks from her freezer. Add a pat of herbed butter to it, then a wallop of mashed potatoes and butter. Lots of salt and pepper. She had a few asparagus she could steam with butter and lemon. Her gastronomic reverie was interrupted by her cell phone. The opening notes of Debussy's "Clair de Lune." It was Roméo.

# Four

MICHAELA CRUZ HAD NEVER, ever seen anything like it in her life. Except in old movies, maybe. A guy about her age wearing a tuxedo and white gloves took her crappy old coat and faux-leather boots like they were precious, placed the latter in a clear plastic bag with her name on it, and then tucked them into a coat check area the size of a small apartment. He then gently handed her off to another guy about her age who escorted her into the most dazzling room she had ever entered. He whispered a soft *"Bonne chance, mademoiselle,"* as he released her near a table covered with more food and alcohol than she had ever witnessed in one place at one time, and that included her *nonna*'s Sunday afternoon family meals. There was a ziggurat tower of every imaginable fruit. There were cheeses of every possible configuration, bowls of jumbo shrimp, a mountain of lobster claws and tails, with small, personal-sized jars of garlic butter for dipping. A gorgeous man was cutting into a side of beef that fell away into pinkish perfection at the touch of his knife. There were martini glasses filled with *saumon tartare* or *caviar russe*. Michaela turned to her friend Brittany and said, "What's the dessert table going to look like?"

Brittany just squeezed Michaela's hand and whispered, "Don't do anything I wouldn't do!" Michaela didn't even have time to respond before Brittany disappeared into the throng of talking, laughing, eating, dancing people.

She would have liked to check her hair and makeup before she exposed herself to this crowd, especially after the snowstorm had done its worst, even in the few short steps from the Uber to the building's entrance. She figured she was still looking pretty good though, until she saw the bevy of Amazon women in the room. Each one towered over Michaela. Each one was effortlessly gorgeous. She spent the first few minutes of the party at breast-level of almost every woman in the room. Suddenly, Michaela felt very short and dumpy, and hated herself for feeling that way.

She hastened to the man standing by the Pur Vodka bottles embedded in a frozen igloo (cultural appropriation, or what?) and ordered a Cosmo. He shook one up in a matter of minutes and handed it to her with a knowing smile that she did not appreciate. She hovered near the bartender, though. The idea of stepping out into the party was terrifying. She scanned the room trying to spot Brittany, whose bright auburn updo was usually a beacon at any party, but in this world she just faded into the crowd. Michaela was trying not to feel resentful for being talked into this and then abandoned so abruptly. She hated big parties, especially full of people twice her age and a world away from her actual life. But Brittany had insisted. She explained that *everyone who was anyone* would be there, especially *vedettes* from the film and TV scene, and Mika had to start networking. Brittany was convinced that Mika was a genius—it was one of the reasons Mika liked her so much. Brittany sincerely believed that Mika's talent would make her a huge star one day, and talked her up to anyone who'd listen, without a trace of jealousy. Mika couldn't help but be drawn into her grandiose plans.

Suddenly, Michaela's drink splashed onto her neck and down her dress. It was shockingly cold. An enormous man loomed over her, swaying slightly, and started to dab at her chest with his napkin.

"I…I am sooooo sorry. Here. Lemme—"

Michaela swatted his giant paw away and gasped as the icy liquid trickled lower. "Get off of me!" When she looked way up to meet his eyes, she recognized him at once. Dimitri Golikov—The Flying Russian—the new superstar left-winger for the Montreal *Canadiens*. In spite of herself she smiled back at him goofily. "It was an accident. It's okay—I got it."

He returned the smile—all his teeth amazingly intact and dazzling in their whiteness—and tilted dangerously backwards when a woman as tall as he steadied him with a firm arm. "Dima. Time to go." He turned to Michaela and tried to wink. Then he put his arm around the tall woman's shoulders and nuzzled her neck. She gave Michaela the once-over, hovering very briefly at her breasts as though assessing if they were real or not, and then looked down at her with very yellow-green wolf eyes.

"How old are you?"

Michaela was not expecting that. She folded the wet napkin and dropped it on the bar. "Older than you think."

Wolf Eyes smiled without baring her teeth. Then she turned away and taking Dimitri Golikov by the hand like a little boy, steered him deftly through the throng and out of sight.

On her way to the bathroom to clean up her dress, Michaela was grinded on by two guys old enough to be her grandfather, smacked on the back of her head by the wayward hand of a woman dancing some weird sixties thing, and then accosted by a schlubby guy in a bow tie who kept insisting he was George R.R. Martin. She squirmed away from him and fled to what looked like a promising direction, but found herself in an enormous industrial kitchen, packed with frantic waiters who didn't even notice she was there. As Michaela retreated from their brutal efficiency, she found herself wandering down a cavernous hallway lined with black and white photos of female movie stars, each in an old-fashioned glamour pose, each signed by the star herself. She didn't really know who most of them were, but there were definitely a few she recognized and found mesmerizing. She peered closely at the inscription on one. It was from an ingénue Jane Fonda. "Dear Jean Luc, Here's one of me from many lifetimes ago! Love, Jane." Michaela only knew Jane Fonda from this show on Netflix she'd watched once or twice, about two old ladies whose elderly husbands fall in love with each other. She had no idea Jane Fonda had been a sex symbol.

"An inspiring woman."

Michaela startled to a man standing right behind her.

"Oh, *pardon mademoiselle*. I am sorry. I thought you saw me."

Michaela took a step away from him and hastened towards the door at the end of the hall. "I was just looking for the bathroom. I need to—" She gestured towards her dress. "Do you have any idea where it is?"

He didn't answer. Instead, he bowed his head as if to ask her permission, and gestured for her to follow, which after a moment's hesitation, she did.

The bathroom was twice the size of Michaela's parents' living room, but did not contain a sofa covered in plastic, or little bowls of stale mixed nuts strategically placed. It had a huge sunken marble tub, with steps leading down into it like a Roman bath. There was a giant three-way mirror, so she could check herself out from every angle. There were hand towels monogrammed with *J.L & M*, as well as thoughtful little baskets containing everything a woman might need: hand wipes, individual tissue packs, cotton swabs, tampons, and condoms. It took Michaela a while to figure out how the faucets worked—but when the water came it fell into the wide shallow sink like a waterfall. She slipped off her high heels and nestled her toes in the thick, silky carpet that she felt like having a little nap on. It was the most gorgeous carpet she'd ever seen, and it was in a bathroom. Not *the* bathroom. Just *a* bathroom. She touched up her mascara and lipstick, and poofed her hair up a bit. She would give this party fifteen more minutes, then she was dragging Brittany out by her red hair if she had to.

As she stepped into the adjoining room, she was startled a second time by the man, who was sitting in an armchair swirling a bit of ice in his glass. She realized she was in some kind of office or study. One of the walls was just one enormous window. Through the snowstorm that raged mutely outside she could just make out the spire lights of Notre-Dame-de-Bon-Secours, the church made famous by Leonard Cohen, and beyond that, the lights along the St. Lawrence river. The remaining walls were covered in photographs and framed diplomas. She also noticed several trophies on a glass display table, and the man caught her eye doing so.

"Emmy Awards. Seven of them. That's just this year."

Michaela nodded and smiled, but she wasn't stopping here. "I've got to go find my friend."

"Don't you want to know what I won them for?"

"No, thanks. I'm sure there's no shortage of women here who'd love to, though."

The man laughed so hard he sprayed the liquor in his mouth back into his glass, and all over his hands. He wiped them first before extending one. "Let me introduce myself. Jean Luc David. That was my bathroom you were admiring."

Michaela tried not to smile. It came out as a smirk. She shook his dry, soft hand.

"It's ostentatious. And a bit obscene. I did appreciate the carpet, though."

"Everything tasteful and classy is my wife's choice. Everything over the top and vulgar is mine. What can I say? I am *nouveau riche* boy from Terrebonne. What do I know?"

"You're not really Jean Luc David—?"

"Yes. I am. I'm better looking in the flesh though, aren't I?" He tilted his head into a pose. He had thick, salt-and-pepper hair, deeply blue eyes, and two long dimple lines down his cheeks that did in fact, make even an average face quite handsome. "What is your name?"

Michaela refused to smile but was dying to talk more to this man. When would she have the chance again?

"Oh, sorry! Michaela Cruz. And I am a *huge* fan of your show. I know, you must hear that from everyone—but I mean, you changed the entire playing field. Finally, you know, we have a story full of complex female characters who don't have to be superheroes or, or morally righteous. Flawed women who sometimes make poor choices with little…redemption. No apologizing, no moralizing, just real fucking…authentic women. With *Nasty Women*? You are one of the great feminist producers, Mr. David." Michaela tipped an imaginary hat in his direction. *Chapeaux!*

"Please call me Jean Luc. Mr. David was my father."

"There will be a season two? And three? And four?"

Jean Luc David eased out of his chair and approached Michaela. He wasn't much taller than she was, but he had an authority that made him seem so. He reached behind her and gently lifted the hair that had gotten tucked inside the back of her dress. "There." Then he turned abruptly and announced he had to get back to the party. Michaela just stood there, still feeling where his hand had touched her neck.

When Michaela finally found her way through the labyrinth of halls and back through the kitchen to the dance floor, Brittany had resurfaced. Michaela snaked her way across the dance floor and held onto both of her friend's hands, as she was very drunk and stumble-dancing. Her updo was down in ragged ringlets. She had lost an earring, and the heel on one shoe was gone. In a slurry voice she yelled into Michaela's ear that she had to pee and started to lift her skirt up right then and there. Michaela half-dragged her towards the room where they had checked their coats, managed to gather all their stuff, and dressed Brittany back into her winter gear as best she could. Before Michaela could stop her, Brittany wobbled back into the main hall. Michaela fell back against a wall, completely overheated now and exasperated. She couldn't leave Brit there. But then there she was, red-faced and laughing, pulling a full bottle of vodka out of each coat pocket like a six-gun. By the time they hit the stormy street, they were pulling each other along the slippery sidewalks, laughing like teenagers and feeling alive the way only the young and the new can.

# Five

ROMÉO LEDUC rifled through his top dresser drawer, look-ing for a pair of clean underwear. He couldn't remember whether he'd left some at Marie's or not. He could, of course, bring a few pairs to throw in with her laundry, but he did not want to show up like some dumb college kid on school break with his dirty clothes for *maman* to wash. He finally found an old but still serviceable set of boxer briefs and threw them in his small duffel bag along with a fresh shirt and the sweater Marie had bought him for Christmas. He didn't like it much and hadn't worn it after the holidays ended, but he suspected it would be a welcome gesture tonight. Roméo downed the dregs of his single malt as he stepped into his bathroom and peered at his reflection in the mirror over the sink. As he examined the stubble of beard, he thought about shaving—but then he'd never make it in time. He had to get ahead of the imminent snowstorm, or he wouldn't make it to Marie's at all, and his window of opportunity was closing fast. He examined his left then his right profile, and thought he saw the beginnings of a double chin. He was definitely not shaving now. Marie always told him he looked like her childhood heartthrob, Gregory

Peck, as Atticus Finch in *To Kill a Mockingbird*. Despite being the healthiest of the cops he knew—all of whom seemed to eat nothing but McDonald's and Tim Hortons—he couldn't help but notice he seemed to have aged since he turned fifty. Had he taken a *coup de vieux*? He scratched at his beard and noted how much grayer it was than just a few months ago. Marie often pointed out yet another gendered injustice of aging: male gray was distinguished and female gray was just old and over the hill. He had to admit that men certainly got the better deal when it came to—well, practically everything. Still, what was a barely noticeable thickening when he quit smoking was now definitely a paunch, despite how many sit-ups he did. His once perfect vision was perfect no longer. He'd become one of those people who peered at a book or newspaper an arm's length from his face but refused to buy glasses.

Roméo quickly ran a comb through his still mostly dark brown hair, and then checked his watch. He would be there in forty minutes if he left right now. As he passed through his small and spartan living room, he glanced at the two thick sets of files on his kitchen table. He had been looking through his new case load that morning and debated bringing them along. As Chief Inspector for Homicide in the district of St. Jerome, a bedroom community in the lower Laurentians, the good news was there hadn't been a homicide in his largely rural district for almost three months. The bad news was there hadn't been a homicide in his largely rural district for almost three months, so in the interim he had been put in charge of the Sûreté du Québec's Cold Case squad for the greater Montreal region. Roméo was tasked with tackling a backlog of unsolved murders dating back almost fifty years, focusing on cases involving women and children, especially.

Roméo had never worked cold cases before, and he couldn't help but think this was the SQ's way of telling him retirement wasn't so far off.

The other good news was that he was now head of a team of about seventeen officers, and one of them was Nicole LaFramboise, finally returning after a one-year maternity leave, and a one-year transfer to Labelle, two hours north of Montreal. Nicole was his best officer. Despite the very drunken sex they'd had one night several years earlier, they were still very good partners as detectives, and now that Nicole's baby was in daycare and she had lost that disaster of a boyfriend, things were looking up. Roméo remembered when Nicole first told him she was pregnant, and how for one terrifying moment he had thought the baby was his. But it wasn't. Nicole was so thrilled to find a good man, who was so doting and so in love with her and the baby. Or the *idea* of *a* baby. But he quickly became a liability. He flew into rages when the baby kept them up all night. Left Nicole for hours and then days at a time. She finally threw him out when the baby was only eight months old, and she discovered he had a new girlfriend. Nicole was too angry and disappointed to be heartbroken. She just wanted him gone. Now the father saw the baby one weekend a month, which seemed to be what he wanted all along. Poor Nicole. It was a constant source of amazement to Roméo how often people totally misjudged each other. Or in her case, invented an entire person who didn't actually exist. They were doomed to fail.

Roméo's thoughts wandered back to the first time he and Marie had had sex—or tried to. They had planned a romantic evening at a hotel in Old Montreal. They booked supper at l'Epicurien—a restaurant that was so upscale and soigné that it didn't even have a sign. Marie ate an enormous surf and turf-ish thing. Roméo couldn't even remember what he had—he was not such a fan of high-end anything, and as a vegan, there were few options on the menu. He just remembered Marie's beaming face, how much she enjoyed teasing the obsequious waiter, their mutual nervousness over the expectation of inti-macy—the knowledge that they were going to soon cross that romantic Rubicon. By the time they got to their very chic and tasteful room, Marie was already feeling queasy. By the time Roméo emerged from the bathroom ready to romance, Marie had thrown up all over the bed. Then she projectile vomit-ed all over the bathroom. When it was all over twenty-four hours later, he joked about the lengths women would go to *not* to have sex with him. Marie was as weak as a newborn and smelled pretty awful. But still, he could not get over how lovely she was. Roméo smiled as he thought about how they finally did the deed the next day. At first they were so nervous, they couldn't stop laughing. Then Marie just took his face in her hands and kissed him with such tenderness it was the most erotic experience he'd ever had. Roméo wondered if moving in together could ruin their relationship. In fact, he was quite nervous about it, and sometimes he felt like they should just leave things as they are. *On ne réveille pas le chat qui dort.*

Roméo picked up the files and then dropped them back on the table. He would be too tempted not to pore over them, and he and Marie's Saturday evenings together were sacred—they permitted no phone or email checking, no texting, no communication with the outside world—unless Roméo got called to an emergency. Suddenly, Roméo heard a rush of wind at his front door, which actually seemed to blow his daughter, Sophie, into his tiny foyer.

"Sophie? What're you doing here? I wasn't expecting you—"

"Papa—Can I stay with you? I am not going back to that apartment. With. Him. I am not." She gasped the words out between sobs.

Roméo watched as she dropped her coat on the floor and kicked off her boots.

"Sophie, I was just literally heading out the door—"

"In *this*? I just drove here from the city—it's starting to get bad out there." Her voice drooped in disappointment. "Oh. You're going to Marie's place."

She dropped onto Roméo's sofa and collapsed into tears again. "He's just become a different person—a real asshole. I don't know what happened!"

Roméo had warned her about moving in with him. Her mother and stepfather had not opposed it, but Roméo had. She was too young, and from what Roméo witnessed, his great passions were video games and bottomless bowls of spaghetti with meat sauce. He had often wanted to smack the boy's baseball cap off his head when he wouldn't even look up from a game long enough to say a proper hello. They were like two kids playing adults, and that rarely ended well. Even adults playing adults often didn't pull it off.

"Why didn't you go stay *chez maman*?"

"They're in Mexico, remember?"

Roméo couldn't keep up with the life of Riley his ex-wife, Elyse, had found for herself with her smug and perpetually partying husband, Guy. Sophie returned from the bathroom with a roll of toilet paper and loudly blew her nose. "I needed *you*, Papa."

"Sophie, you can stay here, but I have to leave now. Will you be okay? I think there's some pizza in the freezer. I'll be back tomorrow evening, okay?" He hated being caught between his daughter and Marie. Still, Roméo could see Sophie was suffering and couldn't bear it. He never could. But he would have to this time. He grabbed his car keys and headed for the door.

"He pushed me."

Roméo stopped in his tracks. "*Quoi?*"

"He pushed me. Up against the wall. Hard. I thought he was gonna hit me, Papa."

Her admission prompted another burst of tears. He felt like *he'd* been punched. In the heart. Roméo dropped his bag and returned the keys to the antique *Gauloise* ashtray where he kept them. He sat down next to Sophie on the sofa and held his sobbing child in his arms. He'd have to let Marie know he'd miss supper and their Saturday night together. Now why did he feel a bit relieved?

# Six

ROSIE HAD TO GET AWAY from the road. Pulling herself along by her one good hand, she managed to crawl and drag herself over the low concrete barrier and rest against the steep embankment. The snow and wind whipped around her, and at first she hadn't felt much. But now, the pain somewhere in her hip and right leg snatched her breath from her. She desperately tried to get air into her lungs, but the pain was so excruciating she could only gulp small, shallow breaths. As she dragged herself up the embankment, she felt the wind tear at her body again. She had to move a bit more—if she could get out of the wind she might survive the night until she could get help. When she turned on her stomach to crawl, her head exploded in pain. She lay on her back. No. Her side. No, her back. She had to keep breathing. Stay awake. Stay awake. Stay awake. She tried to pull her legs up in the fetal position to keep the heat in, but the pain was so intense and shocking she felt herself losing consciousness. She tried to open her eyes, but she couldn't seem to. She tried to move her legs, but now she couldn't feel them at all. She clutched at her stomach. Was he still there? She couldn't feel him. Nothing at all. And then, a warm and beautiful image came to her. The sea smell of the bay. Her grandmother's hands plucking eider ducks. A few feathers lifting away in the gentle summer breeze that kept the bugs away but wasn't too cold. Perfect. Just perfect. Her grandmother's hands. Brown. Wrinkled. Skilled. So fast. Her mother lighting the fire. Delicious smell of dripping duck fat. The summer sun strong. Her sister, Maggie, playing the piano. No, that's something else. Another day. Piano Day. The eighty-eighth day of the year, for the instrument's eighty-eight keys. She and Maggie playing "Heart and Soul." Rosie and Maggie. Maggie and Rosie. Maggie played the one-hand part, she played the two-hand. They did it real serious for the show, then after they were laughing and laughing, so pleased with themselves. People clapping. Maggie never played any-more, but she did. She could play a hundred songs. Make them up, too. Now she couldn't breathe at all. Breathe. She didn't want to die like this. Like a…like a dog. Her grand-father had to shoot them all—all his dogs. He couldn't take them in the relocation because they couldn't go in the canoe. Didn't want the whites—the RCMP to do it, like they did all the others. Had to shoot them all. Grandmother still cried and cried when she told it. Everything changed after that. She didn't want to die. Breathe. Maggie. They would get a piano, they promised each other. Play "Heart and Soul" every day.

"What happened to you?" A voice. Ecstasy of relief. A voice. A face. Not a face. Eyes and a mask. A scarf. A man. Was speaking to her, asking her if she was okay. She tried to move, but the pain was so knife-intense she retreated from it and tried to breathe again.

The voice was drowning now. Far away.

"Help me. I. Can't." Her voice now. She felt something

under her head, holding her head. Something heavy over her. It was warm. Warmer. She tried to open her mouth to breathe, but there was no air. No air.

"I will help you. Don't be scared. Help is coming. Help is on the way."

And then. There was nothing.

# Seven

*Monday morning*
*January 28, 2019*

MARIE QUICKLY CHECKED her watch. Two minutes left. Her timing was impeccable. She looked out at the forty or so faces and knew that almost every one of them was actually listening. Although she wished this was all due to her gifts as a teacher, she knew that in fact, it was the subject she was discussing. "In 1967, Roger Payne and Scott McVay recorded humpback whales singing—yes, singing—off the coast of Bermuda. Four years later, they released a record of those songs. Amazingly, it became a bestseller. More importantly, it altered the fate of the humpback whale, hopefully forever. Now. Can anyone think of why?"

A few tentative hands were slowly raised. Marie called on a very shy girl in the second row. It took a lot of courage for her to speak up in class at all, and she blushed a furious fuchsia. "Is it because they were able to talk to us?"

A few of her classmates erupted in laughter. Marie overheard one boy say, "I speak whale. Don't you?" His cronies snickered again. The second-row girl wouldn't answer another question for a long time now.

"Actually," Marie hesitated as she tried to recall her name. "Katie. You are absolutely right." Marie looked directly at the sniggering gang of four in the back. "Can any of you expand on that?" The class went silent, puzzling over the question. "The whale songs were so strangely beautiful and haunting, they completely captivated the public's imagination. Although humpbacks were the 'musicians,' this fascination and urge to understand them carried over to most whale species. Suddenly, these animals that were hunted for over four-hundred years to near extinction for such things as lamp oil, soap, corset stays—I'll explain what those are later—margarine, and even for perfume from whale poop, were seen as something we could relate to, to have compassion for, because as Richard Ellis explained—it was like they were *singing their own dirge.*" Marie checked her watch again. "Okay! That's all for today. Please read and take notes on chapter four of your course pack on whale vocalization. See you all right back here on Thursday!"

With a scraping of forty chairs, her class began to gather their things and exit the room. Almost everyone was staring at their phones or madly thumbing a text. About a half a dozen of them hovered around her desk, still bristling with questions. This was often Marie's favorite part of teaching. "Miss, what *is* a corset stay?" asked a girl named Zaynab. A boy standing beside her explained what it was. "That's horrible!" the girl gasped. Marie nodded and asked, "Which? The corset or the slaughter of whales to make them?" Another boy, Francois, wanted to know what *dirge* meant. Marie spelled it for him and then told him to look it up. He checked his phone immediately and smiled. "Okay. That makes sense now." One of the gang of four from the back of the class had surprisingly remained behind. "Miss!" Marie started to correct him—she had repeatedly reminded her students to call her Ms. Russell, Mrs. Russell, or Marie. Just not "Miss," a holdover from high school and so much less respectful and commanding so much less authority than the "Sir" used to address her male colleagues. But he seemed so enthusiastic about his question, Marie cut herself off. He wore the uniform of his crowd—a backwards baseball cap, sweatpants, and a faded hoodie with some logo Marie didn't understand. He had a little bit of dark hair over his lip, and a few more patches under his chin. No real beard yet. "Miss—whatddya mean they make perfume from like, whale poop?"

Marie laughed. "Okay, so short answer?" The boy nodded. "It's called *ambergris*, and it's a substance sperm whales make in their bellies to protect themselves from giant squid beaks that they can't digest, which might puncture their intestinal tract. So, they coat the squid beaks with this substance, and poop them out. Only about one percent of sperm whales do this, so it's very rare, and highly valued by famous perfume makers—because it fixes scent to human skin. It can be worth thousands of dollars. *An ounce.*"

The boy opened his mouth dramatically, then remarked "Holy shit!"

Marie laughed. "Exactly."

Marie glanced out the window of her classroom door and noticed several students and an annoyed-looking teacher waiting. She gathered her papers and made for the exit. As she headed down the bustling between-class halls, most of the hangers-on wished her a good day and disappeared into the crowds. Just one followed her, the one who'd written the brilliant paper. Michaela. "Professor Russell? You wrote on my paper you'd like to speak with me?"

Marie smiled. "Yes. I'd like you to present your paper to the class—you don't have to read it, but just go over the main points. It's outstanding."

Michaela didn't seem as enthusiastic as Marie had expected. "Am I the only one presenting my paper?" So that was it. Some students loved to be singled out to show off their work. Many more, especially the really smart ones, didn't like it. They'd probably been teacher's pet since kindergarten and had paid the price for it socially.

Marie shook her head. "No, there'll be one or two others. How about two classes from now? Say, next Monday?"

Looking pleased in spite of herself, Michaela agreed. "I'll do it if you promise to tell more stories about your life as a marine biologist—I'd like to hear the one about the time you got drenched in whale snot. You promised you'd tell it, but you never did." Students loved personal stories. And Marie had many tales to tell. She agreed to Michaela's conditions, but added, "Just cut me off when they get too self-indulgent and um…too personal."

Michaela nodded. "It's a deal."

Marie arrived at her office door and waited to see if Michaela would follow her in, but she checked her phone instead, and gasped. "I'm late for anthropology. I'll fail if I'm late more than twice. Thank you for the great class!" Marie watched as the diminutive young woman hastened down the hall. It was students like Michaela Cruz that made teaching such a privilege. It was a big cliché, but it was true. Marie could stand up in front of a class and discuss what she felt so

passionately about to seventeen- and eighteen-year-olds forever—or until they dragged her out of the college feet first.
This morning, Marie was feeling like she'd never retire.

Marie dropped her books and papers on her chair and
tried to stuff them into what few square inches of surface area
remained on her desk. She rolled back in her chair and took
a moment to consider the few photos she had on her wall.
Very dated ones of her kids' high school graduation—Ben's
open and sincere smile, Ruby's more guarded smirk. Another
one of her mother, Claire, and her older sister, Madeleine, in
poofy peach dresses at her middle sister Louise's wedding,
and one of Marie in a kayak on the Sea of Cortez, paddling
very close to a humpback whale. Magnus had taken that picture. The Norwegian love of her life. They had sworn to sail
the seven seas together, and they did manage four of them
before Magnus opted for number five without Marie. He got
on a boat for Madagascar and left her behind. She followed his
career obsessively at first, then on and off for years as he rose
through the ranks of whale researcher royalty, but she never
heard from him again. Sometimes, Marie could still feel the
actual physical pain of her separation from Magnus. It took
her years to recover from his betrayal, and Marie had kept
her emotional distance from all men until she'd met Daniel.
They were an unlikely couple. The closest he came to life at
sea was a canoe on a Laurentian lake. Daniel had dyslexia and
a lifelong resistance to reading. His idea of outdoor adven-
ture was his childhood camp in the Laurentians where the
counsellors unpacked your clothes for you. But Daniel had an
encyclopedic mind and endless curiosity. He was a charming
fast-talker, the opposite of laconic, Viking Magnus. He ran
his father's successful *shmata* business and was well off. He

was sexy and fun and he loved Marie, at least for the first ten years of their marriage.

"Would you like to hear the latest?" Marie's colleague, Simon, a history teacher two offices down the hall, dropped into her spare chair and sighed deeply. Marie waited for him to launch into his usual litany of complaints about his students' shocking ignorance, and he didn't disappoint. "So. I am reviewing the material for their first in-class test, a test, by the way, they would like all the questions to *beforehand*." Marie had heard this one many times before. "And then one bright light in the peanut gallery at the back of my class says, 'Sir?'" At this point Simon was imitating his lazy consonants and teenage slur. "'Sir, do we have to know who fought who in World War Two for the test?'" Marie smiled her sympathy, but only half-listened as Simon bemoaned their general illiteracy and total absence of any knowledge of history. "I mean, what happens to an ahistorical generation? To a generation of moral relativists? To a generation that is constantly told their *opinions* are most valuable and precious, regardless of the facts?" Marie watched as he kept talking. She and Simon had had a brief encounter a few years earlier when Marie was about two years divorced. They had had a lovely evening, as long as they talked about nothing but Simon himself. Then, for some inexplicable reason, Marie agreed to go to his place for a nightcap. Within minutes, he had groped at her on the sofa, and kept placing her hand on his erect penis. She told him she wasn't ready for sex with him. Then he started to cry and apologize. Marie wasn't sure which was worse.

"What happens is Trump. The rise of fascism in the United States. And Doug Ford. Demagogues the world over." Simon waited for a response, but Marie offered none. There was an awkward silence. Then he rose from the chair and sauntered back to his office, his load lightened perhaps, Marie thought. Once again, Marie felt so grateful for Roméo, even though he'd missed their Saturday night date, and he had yet to explain to her what fresh drama Sophie had concocted to ruin their night. Marie checked her watch and realized she had seventeen minutes to pick up a very necessary coffee before her next class.

Once the Motherhouse to the Gray nuns, the imposing nineteenth-century greystone buildings at the corner of Atwater and Sherbrooke streets were sold to the Quebec government in the early eighties and turned into Dawson College—or CEGEP—as they are called in Quebec. The convent's chapel was turned into a spectacular library. Few other traces of the nuns remained, but most significantly one did—the great dome—and at its apex, the Virgin Mary holding baby Jesus in her arms. For some, this overt religious symbol on a public, government building should have been removed years ago. For others, it was an important historical landmark that preserved the *patrimoine* of Quebec. Quebec was once again flirting with *laicité*—the complete separation of church and state in terms of religious symbols, including personal apparel items such as the kippah, the crucifix, and the hijab. Many Quebecois supported this in backlash reaction to the past autocracy of the Catholic church. A minority (usually including minorities) saw this as overt xenophobia, and in the case of the public servants the hijab ban applied to, cruel and petty. Within minutes, Marie had passed several students, each wearing one of the controversial religious symbols as she navigated the main staircase down to the busy atrium of the school. She refused to be pushed and jostled by students, cell phone in one hand, Starbucks coffee in the other, rushing to class. She secretly loved all that teenage hormonal energy. She loved watching the confident girls strutting down the hall, the others who thumb at their phones to avoid eye contact, or to look like they're never alone. She loved the gaggles of obstreperous boys, the sheer energy of almost ten thousand students on the move. Marie decided to cross over to the mall by the underground metro level, her preferred route in winter, as she didn't have to actually go outside, and wouldn't need her full cold weather regalia. Besides, the aftermath of the snowstorm—snowbanks three feet high and sidewalks still not fully cleared—made stepping out into the January air even less appealing. She emerged from the Dawson doors into the actual metro station and passed by the Jehovah's Witness couple flogging their version of Christianity, who still looked so hopeful that she might stop for a little proselytizing. She could already taste that café latte with an extra shot of espresso. Maybe she'd treat herself to one of those blueberry oatmeal squares that cost a fortune and about eight thousand calories.

Between the metro turnstiles and the shopping center proper, this part of Alexis Nihon mall was known for its high concentration of homeless people. Marie recognized some of them from over the years, and some were more transient, their faces changing every few months. A few of the regulars were there, their empty Starbucks or Tim Hortons coffee cups held aloft, begging for a loonie or a toonie. A couple of them were passed out inside filthy sleeping bags, their few possessions gathered around them in tired plastic bags. Sometimes one would begin to shriek aggressively at a shopper, but for the most part they were harmless, too drunk or high or sick to be a threat to anyone. Except sometimes to each other. Marie always walked quickly past what she called the gauntlet of guilt on the way to her daily coffee. She passed the first guy who wished her *"Bonne journée!"* with a cheery wave and a snaggle-toothed grin. Another regular, an old woman swaddled in layers of mismatched clothes and a floral babushka on her head, lifted her cup and smiled weakly at Marie, mumbling something in a language Marie didn't understand. She used to stop and ask how they were. She always used to drop some change into their cups and every now and then she still did. But over time, a feeling of frustrated helplessness had eroded her empathy. She wanted to ask what had happened to them that brought them to this state and this place. She wanted to ask what she could do. But she didn't. Instead, she held her purse a bit tighter and hastened past them, making just enough eye contact to remind herself that they were human, too.

Just as Marie turned past the vegan burger shop, she heard shouts and then terrible screaming. Ahead of her, surrounded by a small group of onlookers, were two uniformed cops. One held a woman by the waist, and the shrieking came from her tiny body, as she tried to kick and twist herself out of his grasp. The other cop held the arms of a second struggling woman behind her back, and she seemed to be writhing in pain, screaming something Marie couldn't make out.

*"Qu'est-ce qui se passe?* What's happening?" Marie asked an older woman with a Pharmaprix uniform on, watching the scene unfold next to her.

"What do you think? The usual. They're drunk, and got into a fight, and the cops are breaking it up. *Les ostie d'Esquimaux!*" She shook her head, gave a dismissive shrug and left. The crowd seemed to have lost interest as well, and started returning to their mall activity, one or two looking back to see if anything else might happen. The policeman finally wrestled the kicking woman to the ground very roughly, causing her to hit her head hard on the mall floor. The woman started to wail, holding her head and rocking back and forth.

"*Hey! Qu'est-ce que vous faites là?* What the hell are you doing?" Marie heard herself yelling. "You're hurting her!"

The cop who had the other woman finally subdued and quiet was speaking calmly into her shoulder walkie-talkie. She looked right through Marie like she wasn't even there. The policeman growled "*Occupés-toi tes oignons!* Mind your own business!"

Marie watched as they half-dragged the two women away, and then decided to follow them. The cops pulled them through the double doors onto Atwater Avenue, directly across from the old Montreal Forum. A couple of very rough-looking friends were waiting for them there out in the cold, their breath suspended in the frozen air, howling at the cops in protest. The injured woman patted at her head gingerly, while the other woman was pulled away by a different gang. The two police officers returned to the warmth of their squad car and watched impassively through the window. Marie hastened over to confront the police, then stopped herself. Was it because of her relationship with Roméo? Had he turned her into someone who tolerates police abuse? She checked her watch and realized she was already three minutes late for class. No chance for a coffee now. Marie ran back into the mall. She would definitely discuss this incident with Roméo as soon as possible. It was just fucking unacceptable.

# Eight

"*AH! BONJOUR, MONSIEUR ISAAC. Comment vas le Bon Samaritain ce matin?*"

A very short and very wide bakery clerk beamed at him as she handed over the bag of freshly made sandwiches. She had a very pretty face that the severe hairnet she had to wear did nothing to enhance. Isaac took the bag from her with a quick bow.

"*Très bien, merci, Madame Yvonne. Vous changez des vies aujourd'hui!* You're changing lives today!" He placed the bag in his giant backpack, careful not to crush the contents. He already had several thermoses of sweetened tea in there, and the packing had to be careful. Isaac Blum made his way out the door of the Atwater winter market, nodding to a few clerks at the specialty shops lining the long corridor. *Le Boulangerie de Babette* was the only one of them who generously offered him food for the homeless every Monday and Thursday. Of course, the bread was at least a day old, and the *charcuterie* older than that, but Isaac took what he was offered. To the people on the streets that he served, the food sometimes made all the difference. Before he stepped outside, he pulled his thick woolen tuque lower over his ears, put on his enormous mittens, and zipped his jacket up so it covered his nose. The key to surviving winter in Montreal, especially on his rounds, was excellent winter wear. As he stepped onto what seemed to be the sidewalk, he took a moment to take in the day. The sky was so perfectly and cloudlessly blue that the massive blizzard that rampaged through two days earlier seemed like a hallucination. Of course, its aftermath was everywhere—the temperature plummeting to minus 25, the still unplowed sidewalk with the furrow down the center where people struggled to walk in each other's single tracks, the glistening snowbanks, the roofs of the buildings almost sagging under the weight of the snow.

Isaac headed towards the tunnel. So far, he was relieved to see none of the usual suspects—the storm must have driven them into whatever shelter they could find. It was unusually quiet for a Monday morning, as though the storm had given everyone a day's reprieve from the quotidian. It was so quiet, the only sound apart from muted traffic was the squeaking of his boots as he walked on the snow, compacted by the frigid temperature. Isaac decided he would check the area around the tunnel, then make his way up Atwater to Cabot Square Park. Once he had distributed all the sandwiches and emptied the thermoses of tea, he would treat himself to a little McDonald's breakfast sandwich at Alexis Nihon.

Isaac had to put his hand over his eyes to protect them from the glare of the sun off the snow, so white it was almost blue. He scanned the area at the west end of the tunnel. Nothing.

That was good news. When he turned to make his way back towards the market, something got caught in his peripheral vision. When he looked again, he spotted what looked like a garbage bag and peered at it again. Probably a dead dog or coyote; he knew they frequented this area at night. But as he drew closer, he felt a visceral dread. He began to run, his breath bursting out of his lungs in white puffs hovering in the frigid air. Isaac dropped to his knees. What he'd seen was not a pile of discarded clothes. Not a dog. Not garbage. It was a human being, so small he thought she was a child at first. Then he looked closer at her face, her eyelashes frozen shut, thick white frost lining her lips, eyebrows, and nostrils. Isaac gently broke away her scarf, so frozen it was rigid, from the tiny neck. He checked for a pulse, but he knew she was dead. Isaac put his mitten back on but remained on his knees. He covered his eyes, and began to recite the *kaddish*, the ancient Jewish prayer for the dead.

Isaac took out his phone. He looked at the woman again. She lay peacefully on her side, one outstretched frozen arm under her head. One boot seemed to be missing. Why was she *here* of all places? Where had she come from? Isaac hesitated, then he took off his huge mittens and checked her coat pockets for identification. She had none on her that he could find, and no money. Maybe she carried something in her pants pockets, but he couldn't bring himself to look there. At the bottom of her deep coat pocket were what looked like a few dog biscuits, a tiny carving of some kind of deer, a creased photograph of a very pretty woman—maybe in her forties—standing beside what looked like Beaver Lake. On the back of the photograph, a name was written, with a phone number. Isaac quickly took a snapshot of both sides of the photograph with his phone and returned the picture to her pocket. Experience had taught him that the police often don't bother to investigate the deaths of the homeless, especially Indigenous ones. All people are definitely not equal in the eyes of the law. Justice was anything but blind when it came to people who weren't white. He would at least have some information himself in case he needed to use it later. Isaac touched her forehead for just a moment and felt an empty sadness. He then took his phone out once more and took several close-up photos of her face from different angles. He stood by the woman's side, closed his eyes, and lifted his chin towards the sun. It was a dazzlingly beautiful winter day. Then he picked up his heavy backpack and headed to where he knew was one of the last working payphones in the area to call 911.

# Nine

*Tuesday morning*
*January 29, 2019*

"*MAMAN, ON PEUT manger un croissant au chocolat? S'il vous plait? S'il vous plait?*" She was walking with her daughter to the local bakery, *Chez Amandine*, known for the best *patisserie* this side of the Atlantic. She held her hand very tightly, as the traffic was heavier and faster than usual. They chatted away with each other, and she felt perfectly at peace with the world. She didn't think it could get much better than this. They stopped at the red light and waited for the little white figure to tell them it was safe to cross. She felt her phone vibrate, and paused to check it, letting go of her daughter's hand just for a moment. Julie ran towards the bakery across the street directly into the oncoming cars. Danielle screamed at her to stop, but there was a sickening screech of tires, and the excruciating sound of shattering glass. It was too late. Danielle screamed and screamed, but no sound came out of her. The driver jumped from her car, and people gathered to stare, but she was paralyzed, frozen to the sidewalk. She couldn't look. She couldn't *look*. Danielle Champagne woke up soaking in sweat. Her night dress was drenched, as were her freshly laundered sheets. She looked around her bedroom, now filled with delicate early morning sunlight, and reminded herself that her daughter, Julie, was seventeen years old and very much alive. It was just another terrible dream.

Danielle took a few minutes to bring herself back to the real world, and peeling off her wet nightie, headed straight to the shower. She had a huge day ahead, and she would have to gather every bit of her energy to get through it. As the water poured over her body, she realized she was still very shaken by the collision with whatever animal was in that tunnel. She hadn't really slept much all weekend. Danielle examined her face in the enormous bathroom mirror. Those bags under her eyes wouldn't go away, no matter how much of that stupidly expensive cream she applied. Someone once suggested she try Preparation H hemorrhoid cream. It would be a lot cheaper. Although she inherited great legs from her mother, she also got her eye bags. Danielle applied even more cover-up and powder, and overall, thought in the right light she'd be okay.

She selected a salmon-colored power suit for the insanely busy day ahead. It was a bold choice, and very feminine. She wanted them to know she wasn't afraid to be a woman. That morning she had a critical meeting to discuss the expansion of her company into the northeastern United States, and then an interview for a local TV station. Then she was flying to Toronto for meetings in the afternoon and catching the red-eye home that night. It was the kind of day she lived for. Danielle headed straight for the espresso machine and started to prepare a triple. On the breakfast peninsula lay the remains of Julie's breakfast—a half-eaten bowl of granola and yogurt, and an empty coffee cup. She'd already left for school but had written her mother a note—*à bientôt, hasta luego, arrivederci, bis später, see you later, alligator!! xoxo.* Julie wanted to study linguistics at university and already spoke four languages fluently. Danielle wanted her to study at the Sorbonne or Oxford and couldn't quite believe that was even a possibility, but it was. Julie was a brilliant student, and at this point in her life, Danielle could afford it. She wanted to make everything possible for her daughter.

As she waited for her assistant, Chloé, to text her that she was waiting in the car outside, Danielle scrolled through her emails on her phone, and nibbled at a piece of dry rye toast. Her new boyfriend, Sidney, had made reservations at Joe Beef for tomorrow evening. Danielle smiled at the thought of him. He was a lovely man, made few demands, and seemed to actually love being with her. Of course, it would all go south sooner or later, probably sooner, but for now she decided to enjoy the idea of being a little bit in love, and to imagine he was a bit in love, too. Danielle answered his text and quickly flicked on the local news on her kitchen television. A polar vortex was bringing life-threatening cold to Chicago—which was now colder than Antarctica. The weather woman was somewhat hysterically announcing that it was so cold a person's corneas could actually freeze. The thought of Americans shivering in the cold made Danielle smile. Her friends from south of the border often teased her about the igloos all Canadians lived in, and how they got to work by dogsled. Then the news shifted to the trial of Bruce McArthur—who was accused of killing homeless gay men in Toronto. An awful story, that. The police kept digging up their remains, buried in people's gardens where McArthur had worked as a landscaper. Danielle switched to the local news. As usual, there was lots of coverage of the big storm, stock images of cars buried in snow and people leaning into the blizzard clutching at their coats. She turned up the volume as the Atwater Tunnel appeared on the screen. The body of an unidentified female had been discovered near the tunnel on Monday morning. Then there were images of paramedics loading a body into an ambulance. She appeared to have been a victim of a hit-and-run, and police were investigating. There were no more details. Danielle Champagne managed to get off her chair and to the kitchen sink just in time to violently throw up.

# Ten

NIA FELLOWS was sitting in the cavernous vestibule of St. John the Evangelist church, blowing on her very hot coffee in a small Styrofoam cup. She glanced around at the walls, every square inch of them covered in bulletin boards with cheery pastel-colored titles: referrals for legal aid, housing, mental health counsellors, nutrition advice. So many people trying to do good. Nia looked down at Hamlet devotedly licking himself. At least she didn't have to lick herself clean. She'd just had her first hot shower in six days, and it was glorious. She had scrubbed the grime off her feet and fingernails, washed her hair with fragrant shampoo, and even got to put a little cream on her dry, chapped hands. She had found some fresh clothes in the hand-me-down bin as well. Life that morning was pretty good. They'd managed to spend the night of the snowstorm at The Bunker, an emergency shelter for homeless youth. At twenty-one, Nia was still considered a youth, but at twenty-five, Christian wasn't, so they were lucky to have

53

been let in. She was just waiting for him to be done with his shower, and then they could head down to the housing office to check where they were on the waitlist for emergency housing. Their "problem" was that they had a dog, so none of the shelters would take them in except the Salvation Army one, but there they felt pressure to attend bible study, and that was a problem. There was a guy there, though, who sometimes took pity on them and snuck them into a utility closet. He barely said a word to them, but always greeted Hamlet with "Well, hello there, gorgeous!" and kindly offered him a few treats. But Christian was creeped out by his uniform, and so they avoided that shelter, too.

Most of the time, they were forced to wander around the city, bedding down in the metro stations until they were kicked out at one a.m., or finding a warm grate by one of the big stores downtown. Sometimes, they found a temporary squat with friends, but they kept those for the really cold nights, like last night. She smiled as she thought how delighted Christian had been to get into the mission this morning—they were often too late, and all the shower spots were long gone. Hamlet had stopped licking himself and slumped onto her feet with a big sigh. He looked like someone had played a cruel and possibly painful joke—crossed a St. Bernard with a Jack Russell terrier. Nia made an enormous yawn and tried to stretch out her legs, but Hamlet grumbled and refused to move. There was nothing to read here, so she was forced to look at the walls. There was a really old-school image of Jesus—blond-haired and blue-eyed—with one hand on the head of a small child, the other on the head of a lamb. Christian had been super-religious once. His folks bought the whole Jesus died for their sins thing. He grew up in a church where people spoke in tongues—he said his father often did this thing called *xeno-glossy*—where the possessed dude speaks a real language, but one that he doesn't actually know how to speak. Sometimes members of his church prayed in these crazy made-up languages. *Glossolalia.* Nia loved the sound of that word.

Christian decided to run away when the elders of his church kept trying to cast out the demons from his body. One of those elders seemed to think forcing Christian to give him blow jobs was the best method. It didn't work. Christian saw the devil everywhere, especially when he was off his meds. Nia herself came from a couple of atheists. To her parents, Jesus and Buddha and Mohammed were just a bunch of scam artists who figured they'd finally gotten the religion market cornered. Her mom once told her a story about the day the pope visited Montreal. Apparently, he was rolling down St. Urbain Street in his Pope-Mobile—this golf-cart thing with a bullet-proof windshield—doing that celebrity-pope wave at the throngs of people lining the street. Nia's mom just happened to be there, returning home from a walk on Mount Royal. When the pope zoomed by, a couple of women standing on either side of her just collapsed on the sidewalk, overcome with religious ecstasy. Nia's mom always told this story laughing her head off, saying she'd never seen anything like it before or since.

Nia's memory was interrupted by a cold blast from the door of the church. A guy with a long, grizzled beard came shuffling in, swaddled in an assortment of scarves, jackets, and blankets. It was impossible to tell how old he was—he could be thirty or seventy. He was politely talking to himself, and shuffled past Nia without even a glance, the stench of urine and vomit following him. At least it wasn't that Isaac guy, who always seemed to turn up at the oddest places. He was always trying to get them to talk to him, with his sandwiches and his tea. Nia heard he'd been accused of assaulting a girl at a school when he was a teacher. Others on the street loved him; they said he did all this work on his own dime. Nia had a pretty good sense about people—and that Good Samaritan guy gave her the creeps.

Christian was taking way longer than normal, and Nia was starting to get antsy. They had a lot to get done that day. He was supposed to scout out a new place for the night, and she needed to get to the housing office. Hamlet was now completely laid out across her feet, sound asleep. She leaned down to scratch behind his ears and smiled at the memory of their first encounter. It was in *Carré St. Louis*, a gorgeous Parisian-style square surrounded by Victorian houses, boasting a beautiful fountain at its center. It was one of the most upscale addresses in Montreal, and also where homeless people often hung out, especially during the hot Montreal summers. Christian was shirtless and looking very ripped. He was wading with Hamlet in the fountain, throwing a stick for him and laughing every time Hamlet brought it back. He had gorgeous blond curls that were becoming dreadlocks and not a single tattoo on that beautiful body. Nia sat on the fountain's edge and joined in the game with the dog. Hamlet immediately adored her, which impressed Christian. He was not given to trusting humans.

"My dog likes you."

"You're English?"

Christian affected a lousy British accent, "Oh, yes, milady. All the way from South Porcupine."

"Oh? I'm from *North* Porcupine! What a coincidence!"

His smile narrowed. "There is no North Porcupine. Or East or West Porcupine. Only South." His dog was now hanging in mid-air, attached only by his jaw to the stick in Christian's hand.

"I'm Nia. I'm actually from the imaginatively named town of Rockville. That's about two hours southeast of here. But I live in Montreal now."

Christian stepped out of the fountain, dragging Hamlet along behind him. He beckoned to her to join him on the park bench.

"Would you like to join me for a small repast?" He pulled out of his knapsack a lightly squished sandwich, half an *Oh Henry* chocolate bar, and a can of beer, which he popped open and sipped from a paper bag. He offered it to Nia. He had the most penetrating blue-green eyes. Nia took a small sip. She hated beer. He gestured for her to drink more, so she did. She was eighteen then, and he was twenty-two, and they'd never really been apart since.

Suddenly, there was a commotion at the door to the mission, and Christian emerged, shouting, "*I am dead to sin!*" Someone had clearly offended him. Nia grabbed Hamlet's leash and pulled them both outside. Christian could not afford to be barred from any more shelters. He could be as calm and chill as a monk, but when he was off his medication he was sometimes unpredictable and scary to others. The day was weirdly warm, definitely above zero, probably twenty-five degrees warmer than two days earlier. It was global warming, and Nia found it very scary. Christian kept reminding her that soon climate change refugees from all over the world would be moving to Canada, and more and more desperate people would be scrambling for the crumbs that were left for them. For that morning, anyway, Nia was grateful for the relative warmth. It would make the day ahead a bit easier.

"Listen, Christian." Nia handed him the leash and pulled his hat down over his ears. "I need to get to the housing office and see what's going on. I want you to get over to that squat on Berri and get us a spot. Can you do that today?"

Christian looked straight at her and nodded, but his eyes weren't properly focused. She repeated what she'd just said. Nia was loathe to let him go off alone, as he was very vulnerable when he was like this. But she was determined to get them into housing, especially since Christian wouldn't hear of placing Hamlet in a no-kill shelter until they could get on their feet and get him back. "I'll go to the food bank at the Welcome Hall, then I'll meet you at the squat." Christian nodded, held her tightly for a few moments, and then began the trudge along the snowy sidewalk, as Hamlet followed behind.

Nia watched them disappear around a corner, heading in the right direction, then made her way to the nearest bus stop. She planned to nick a few pairs of warm socks for Christian from The Bay. Three of his toes still had not fully recovered from the frostbite he'd suffered in the November cold snap. Nia jumped on the #80 bus through the side exit door. An old lady gave her the stink eye, but Nia stared her down. This was going to be a good day. She could feel it. What she didn't know was someone had been watching them and following them all morning.

# Eleven

"WELL, FOR STARTERS, he plays with his penis all day long. I mean, is that normal?" Nicole LaFramboise looked Roméo directly in the eye, as though only a man could understand or comment on such a thing. He responded with a shrug. "I only had a girl—I don't know. And if you're asking with regard to my personal experience? No comment."

Roméo and Nicole were drinking coffee in his precinct office in St. Jerome. As usual, all eyes on the other side of the window were trying not to stare, but certainly most were speculating about their conversation. It was a slow day at the precinct, and they were acutely aware of the past relationship of the two people in that room and were hoping for some drama that morning. Nicole was getting Roméo caught up on the latest atrocities her two-year-old had committed. "Last week, he somehow managed to get a pair of scissors, and cut off the tails from half his stuffed animals. And he loves them, I know he does. Am I raising *un maudit* psychopath?"

Roméo smiled. "All two-year-olds are basically psychopaths."

"And yesterday? I walked into the living room, and there was a very large, smelly poop on the sofa. His diaper was on the floor. When I asked him what happened, he said his *toutou*, a big brown monkey, did it." Roméo had to raise an eyebrow at that one. "I mean, I only left him in the living room with his toys for like, three minutes!" Roméo offered Nicole a second coffee from his brand-new espresso machine, a gift from Marie. It had changed his life. Nicole waved her hand at the offer. "I'm trying to keep it to two a day. I'll be needing one later just to stay awake until five o'clock. I go to bed when the baby does, at like, seven p.m. It's doing wonders for my social life, let me tell you." Nicole laid her forehead on Roméo's desk, and pretended to snore.

"I have to say, Nicole, that anyone who raises a child is a hero. Especially someone who raises one alone." Roméo could see the tears starting to gather in Nicole's eyes. He made himself busy with the coffee, so he didn't have to witness it. She couldn't stand crying in front of anyone.

Nicole switched to a more familiar tone, "*Dis-moi.* How the hell do people have *two* kids? I mean, I think I'd end up bringing back human sacrifice."

Roméo spooned a bit of sugar into his cup. "Does the father help out at all? Does he still see the baby on some weekends?"

Nicole grimaced. "When he's around. He missed last weekend because he's off skiing with the new *guidoune* in…in Zermatt? I don't even know where that is."

"It's in Switzerland. And I guarantee you that you're getting the better deal here. It's hard to see it sometimes, but he is the one missing what really matters."

Nicole reached out to take Roméo's hand, and then

thought better of it. Instead she fiddled with her pen. "I know that. I do. *Merci*, Roméo."

Roméo caught the eye of one of the new uniformed officers who was openly observing them. He pushed himself away from the desk and stood up. "So. *Au travail*. Let's get to work."

Nicole pulled the two huge files from her black briefcase. "*Oui*, boss." She opened the first one and turned it around so Roméo could read it properly. "I've flagged two cases—I mean, if that meets with your approval."

He nodded. "Yes, I had a look at these. I agree."

Nicole started to go over the first one, "A ten-year-old boy, Dieudonné Masoud, disappeared on his way home from school in St. Eustache eighteen years ago. His body was found three months later in a field next to an abandoned farmhouse."

Roméo looked at his photo, one obviously taken at school. The boy's eyes shone brightly, and a broad grin animated his chubby face. *Dieudonné*. A gift from God. He wondered how people survive losing a child. They don't really. They just stay alive.

Nicole continued, "Many different eye-witnesses gave conflicting testimony as to who he was last seen with, and the parents never gave up on finding out what happened to him." Roméo leafed through the file quickly. Their appeals for help, and their repeated offers of a reward for information were heartbreaking.

The other case involved a seventeen-year-old girl, Chantal Lalonde-Fukushima, who vanished from a party in Laval, north of Montreal, in 1997. Her body washed up on the shores of the St. Lawrence weeks later. She had been raped. The cause of death was drowning, but her body was so battered by the rapids she had come through that it was impossible to determine anything else conclusively. There were many witnesses who came forward, but all their testimony had led nowhere.

"The girl's mother has contacted our Cold Case squad already. She's demanding that we open the case again." Nicole handed Roméo a photo of the girl. It appeared to be some kind of modeling head shot. She was unusually beautiful and photogenic.

"Is the father alive?"

"Yes, but they are now divorced. Since…." Nicole checked a paper. "Since 'ninety-nine. He seems to have accepted what happened and moved on. She has called several times since yesterday."

Roméo nodded. "Let's assign the Masoud case to Robert and his team. You and I will take the girl's case. Let's get started right away. We'll re-interview the last people who saw her alive at that party. Interview the mother again. And the father. We'll start there. Get Isabelle to go over the medical examiner's report. On both cases." Roméo glanced out his office window to the room full of cops. He nodded towards the one who had been watching them so intently. "Take *chose*—what's his name—with you. He seems really keen and could get out of the office for a—"

Roméo was interrupted by the insistent buzz of his desk phone. He held a finger up to Nicole to excuse himself and answered it. She took the opportunity to stretch her legs a bit and check out his office. Besides the expensive new coffee machine, and a framed photograph of Marie holding—she had to admit—a gorgeous baby, nothing much had changed in Roméo's office. Every surface was covered in files and papers, but neatly arranged. Organized clutter. Nicole knew that Roméo had received several citations and awards for exceptional service over the years, and not one was displayed anywhere. They were probably buried in a drawer or sitting somewhere in that awful apartment of his. Roméo returned the phone to its receiver.

"That was the SPVM. Precinct twelve. Downtown."

Nicole raised an eyebrow. "The *Montreal* police? And? What do *they* want?" There was no love lost between the Montreal force and the Sûreté du Québec. Suspicion and loathing would more accurately describe it.

"An unidentified woman's body was found Monday morning in the Atwater Tunnel. A suspected hit-and-run. A piece of paper was found in her pocket, with…my name and number on it." Roméo stood up and started patting his pockets for keys, his phone, and phantom cigarettes. "They want me to come in to answer a few questions. Looks like I'm going to Montreal."

Nicole scraped her chair away from the desk. "As in now?"

Roméo nodded. "Yes. I think I will go now. And will you hold down the fort here until I get back, Detective Sergeant LaFramboise?"

"Yes, Chief Inspector Leduc." She wagged a finger at Roméo. "You're riding right into the mouth of the enemy. *Attention à toi, anh?* Just watch your back."

# Twelve

JEAN LUC DAVID sipped at his second espresso of the morning and looked out over the frigid St. Lawrence river moving relentlessly downstream to the Atlantic, under the new Samuel de Champlain bridge to his right, and the Jacques Cartier to his left. Off in the perfectly blue winter sky, he could just make out the mountains of the Eastern Townships, and beyond those, the Green Mountains of Vermont. He used to live on the western slope of *Mont Royal*, the extinct volcano with the giant cross atop it that was the dominant landmark of Montreal, and from which the city took its name. True blue *Montrealais* just called it *The Mountain* or *La Montagne* even though it is really a big hill. He loved its gorgeous park, the slope by Beaver Lake where people could ski or skate in winter, or just lie and laze and smoke pot in the summer. It was all landscape designed by Frederick Law Olmstead himself, including the city cemetery, on the mountain's northern slope, which was also an arboretum and a haven for an extraordinary number of birds and animals. But he had to admit that he loved the river more, so he had bought this entire building on a cobbled, seventeenth-century street in *Vieux Montreal* ten years earlier. As he watched the St. Lawrence from his penthouse home office, he sometimes liked to imagine what those early European explorers thought when they first arrived in the sixteenth century—before PCB's, raw sewage, and tanker oil had contaminated the river. The intoxication of the sheer abundance before them. The exhilaration and terror of what might await them on shore. A country waiting to be owned. The freedom to invent themselves anew. He was himself descended from Jean-Honoré Desjardins, the Marquis of Limoges, who came over in 1664 with a shipload of *Filles du Roi*—French women whom Louis XIV paid to cross the ocean and marry the settlers of New France. Jean Luc had read somewhere that more than nine percent of the genetic heritage of Quebecois derives directly from these "Daughters of the King" who arrived here 356 years ago. Close to four million Quebecois over fifteen generations were descendants of these women.

Although the story of *les Filles du Roi* had been told in many permutations, he'd still love to do a series, the *definitive* TV series about that time. He would tell it better now—from the points of view of the women who married a total stranger, and who often bore at least ten children, and from the Indigenous people who'd just been "discovered" after living here for millennia. His version would be bolder, more complex. A bit controversial. He'd swing big, as Aaron Sorkin, his idol, always advised writers to do. Jean Luc observed as a massive container ship moved slowly downriver through the huge chunks of pack ice. In 1627, Cardinal Richelieu granted the newly formed Company of 100 Associates all the land between the Arctic Circle to the north, Florida to the south, Lake Superior in the west, and the Atlantic Ocean in the east. *Imaginez vous.* Sometimes, he felt like the river belonged to him, that all this was his domain, his *seigneurie*—but his was not given to him by the Sun King's cardinal. No, Jean Luc had busted his ass for every single acquisition in his growing empire. And he was willing to work harder for even more.

Gennifer Moran watched her boss as she waited to interrupt his reverie at just the right time. He was sitting in the beaten up armchair from his very first apartment that he kept for both sentimental and superstitious reasons. Watching the river sometimes gave him his most creative moments, so she never disturbed him before the second espresso was done. But Gennifer had two urgent issues on her agenda, and the morning was slipping away. "J.L.? It's seven forty-five."

He gestured for her to join him without taking his eyes off the river. She was already in her chair and clicking away at her laptop by the time he turned around, crossed his hands and leaned his elbows on the desk. That meant he was ready. She began.

"We need to finalize some details for Margeaux's birthday bash. The restaurant will close immediately after lunch service and will be at your disposal for the next twenty-four hours. Here's the finalized menu. Is there anything you'd like to change? Speak now or forever hold your peace." She turned the computer so he could read it. Jean Luc peered at the screen and frowned.

"*Escargots?* Margeaux doesn't do shellfish. Change it."

Gennifer hesitated. "Escargots aren't exactly *shellfish*. I've had them at *Toqué*. They are prepared exquisitely. Better than sex."

"Change it."

Gennifer smiled at the thought of Margeaux's tastes,

which definitely ran towards the more proletarian. She'd probably be happiest with a *poutine* appetizer followed by a few all-dressed *hot dogs stimés*. But she was turning forty, and so Jean Luc was pulling out all the gastronomical stops. Gennifer was also very appreciative of the many lucrative kickbacks that she got in her arrangements from the chosen ones who catered Jean Luc's many parties. He was a sucker for *le grand geste*, so it was easy to urge him on to even greater ostentation.

"Okay. Item two: Suzanne will be able to be here in time for the surprise, as her flight gets in from Paris at five in the afternoon. Monique is not able to attend, as she's at an ashram in New Mexico, and she's not allowed to speak for another twenty-one days."

Jean Luc rubbed his forehead like Marlon Brando in *The Godfather*. "*Merde*. Margeaux would really want her here. They go way back—to kindergarten together."

Gennifer hesitated before the next one. "And. Her friend Cyndy? She's five months pregnant and forty years old, so her doctor is not letting her fly. She won't be coming." Gennifer braced herself for his reaction.

"Are you *kidding* me? Women are such precious flowers now they can't get on a plane anymore?" He thought of *les Filles du Roi*, having fifteen kids by the time they were forty. "Fuck. Fuck Fuck. That is so going to disappoint her."

Gennifer was pretty certain Margeaux would be way more dismayed by the fact that her girlfriend was pregnant at forty, than her not attending her party. Margeaux had been pressuring, actually begging Jean Luc to have a baby with her, and her biological window of opportunity was closing fast. Jean Luc had three grown kids, and Gennifer knew he had no intention of ever having another one if he could help it. Not even for Margeaux, whom he loved, in his fashion. Jean Luc got up from his chair and began to pace. Gennifer needed to distract him. They were looking to cast a new role in their hit series, a kind of Canadian version of *Gilmore Girls* meets *Girls*. It was wildly popular with the under-forty female demographic—and was translated into about twenty languages. They wanted a fresh face, someone really out of the box. Preferably brown, Black, or Asian.

"Item three: The casting cocktail party this weekend. We've invited about a hundred and twenty-five people—the usual suspects from the casting agencies. The usual local actors are being rounded up, as well as a few freshly minted ones from the theater schools." Jean Luc was always on the lookout for that diamond in the rough.

"Can you make sure that some of the girls who attended last week's party are invited? There were a few I met who might fit the bill."

Gennifer made a quick note. "Done." She couldn't resist. "Anyone particular in mind?"

Her question was interrupted by the buzzing of Jean Luc's cell phone. He checked the caller ID and gestured at her to leave him alone. Surprised, she grabbed her laptop and stepped out, closing the door softly behind her. She of course pressed her ear to his door to listen, but she couldn't make anything out. It sounded serious.

A few minutes later, Jean Luc opened his door with such force that if Gennifer had not just retreated from her eavesdropping she would have fallen face first into his lap. Instead, he wrapped his arms around her thin shoulders and squeezed the breath out of her.

"That was Pierre Boucher. The decision came in a few days early. They've dropped the lawsuit. All of it. Every charge. It's *OVER!*" He yelled the last words at such volume that Gennifer had to block her ears. Then he grabbed her again and kissed her hard on each cheek with a comical smacking sound. "Where do you want to go? I'm feeling on top of the world, and I'm offering you a trip—anywhere in the world you want to go. Name it!" Jean Luc stared at her with those laser blue eyes of his, lit up with relief and joy. "I offer you the world!"

Gennifer extricated herself from his arms. "Let's get the birthday party over with, cast the next girl, and trust me, I am going somewhere really far and stupidly expensive." But Jean Luc had already turned away from her and was on his phone, excitedly sharing the good news.

# Thirteen

THE DETECTIVE ROSE from behind his desk and shook Roméo's hand a bit too firmly.

"*Bienvenue à Montréal*, Chief Inspector."

Roméo nodded silently and sat down in the chair opposite Detective Louis Cauchon who just sat and took him in for a moment, perhaps trying to place Roméo's name. He was very well known to most in the police forces as the cop who caught William Fyfe, the serial rapist and murderer.

"Well, if it isn't the maple syrup man." Cauchon declared with a sardonic smirk.

Roméo's most recent high-profile arrest was the "Maple Gang," who broke into a maple syrup warehouse and stole millions of dollars worth of Quebec's sweetest export. Their crime trespassed into Roméo's territory when they murdered one of the two guards on duty that night. His network of informants, cultivated over his many years of police work, finally led him to the killers' hideout. Because of the somewhat comical nature of the crime, it went viral, and Roméo had become an internet star: SEXY SQ COP IN SYRUP STAKEOUT! It was all very embarrassing and, given that he had almost lost one of his officers in that raid, infuriating as well.

Roméo waited for the requisite offer of coffee from Detective Cauchon but none came, so he studied the man for a moment. He was a burly man—*costaud*—as they say in French, his barrel chest straining the seams of his suit jacket. He had fingers the size of sausages, a wedding ring embedded in one of them. He'd obviously been in the sun recently (Mexico? Cuba?)—a deep mahogany tan camouflaged the acne pockmarks on his cheeks and neck. He had a full head of cropped hair that crested into what they used to call a *brush cut* in Roméo's day—a classic military style. Roméo looked straight into his gray eyes, but they revealed absolutely nothing. Cauchon blinked first. He pulled a blue file from his drawer and removed several photographs from it. He pushed one in front of Roméo. "Do you know this woman?"

Roméo took a few moments to examine the image. "No. I have never seen her before."

Cauchon leaned back into his chair and folded his hands behind his head. "Then why would she have your name and phone number in her pocket?"

"I have no idea."

Cauchon smiled. "Is she one of your girls who got away?" Cauchon was referring to the systematic abuse and sexual assault of Indigenous women by Sûreté du Québec officers in Val-d'Or. Women who were taken into custody by the SQ were particularly targeted. It had scandalized the country.

Roméo ignored the question and responded with his own. "How are you enjoying your new police chief?"

The Montreal police force had been in such crisis a couple of years earlier, over scandals like spying on journalists, punishing whistle blowers, and rampant corruption, that the government appointed the former head of the Sûreté du Québec to replace the suspended and disgraced Montreal chief of police. The Greens of the SQ had infiltrated the Blues of the SPVM, and the long rivalry between the two forces had seriously ramped up. Cauchon rose to his feet. "We may need to talk to you again. Hopefully not."

Roméo didn't move. "Why did you wait four days to contact me?" He picked up the photo. "This was taken on Monday. I am clearly a person of interest in your inquiry."

Cauchon shrugged, "She was found frozen on the side of the road, with enough booze in her blood to pickle her. Do you know how often we see these? I didn't even want to bother you, but we have to ID her." He returned the photo to the file.

"I'd like to see the body."

Cauchon snorted. "I don't think so. She was very cold, but I mean, not cold enough for your new job."

So, he knew about the Cold Case squad. "I want to see the body now. I want to see the preliminary police report, and the medical examiner's report."

Cauchon laughed. "And I want to retire at fifty and move to Tahiti."

Roméo stood up and placed his huge hands on the desk. "*Écoute, mon ami.* Your new chief and I go way back. I strongly suggest that if you want to even have a job at fifty, you alert the medical examiner that I will be arriving shortly." Cauchon blinked again. And then he picked up the phone and made a call.

The autopsy report put her at about twenty-five years old, but Roméo was shocked by how tiny she was, like a child. He examined her face carefully and was certain he had never seen her before. They had yet to identify her, as no one has filed a missing person's report, and she had no ID on her whatsoever. There was considerable trauma to the body. The medical examiner believed she was probably hit by a car travelling about forty to fifty kilometers an hour. She had a fractured right femur, several broken ribs, a ruptured spleen, and many deep contusions. How could someone have done this and just left her there? If he were a religious man, Roméo would like a special circle of hell reserved for hit-and-run drivers. The medical examiner was gone for the day, so Roméo was being "supervised" by a morgue technician who looked to be about fifteen years old. He was working at his computer, but Roméo had glanced at it and clearly saw him on his Instagram account. He flipped through the report again. The cause of death was listed as a combination of exposure and traumatic force.

But as Roméo looked more closely at the details of the autopsy and the body, there were signs that she might have died of some kind of traumatic asphyxiation. This suggested she did not die from being hit by the car, but something or someone had suffocated her in a way that was consistent with something Roméo remembered from police academy. Two nineteenth-century "entrepreneurs," Burke and Hare, had a little business excavating graveyard bodies to sell to medical schools. Eventually, they decided preying upon live alcoholics would make their job a lot easier. Burke would sit on the victim's chest and use one hand to cover the victim's nose and mouth and the other to close the victim's jaws, resulting in traumatic asphyxia. This way they acquired a body without the digging. This kind of homicidal smothering was actually still called "Burking." The medical examiner's cause of death was uncertain, but foul play wasn't mentioned anywhere, and Roméo was shocked that it wasn't in the report. There was no way given the state the body was in that homicide by asphyxiation could absolutely be ruled out. Could they be so negligent as to omit this possibility entirely? Or was it more a question of criminal indifference? Glancing at the technician to make sure he was completely absorbed in social media, Roméo took out his phone, and snapped a photo of the critical page of the report. The boy didn't even look up. Then Roméo cleared his throat to get his attention.

"Could I see what effects were with the body, please?"

The boy looked up at Roméo but was clearly struggling to pull his eyes away the screen. "Are you allowed to see those?"

Roméo smiled. "Yes, son, I am."

The boy handed him the clear plastic effects bag. Roméo spilled the contents out on the table, and there it was. His name and cell phone number were written on the back of a 3-by 5-inch photograph. Roméo peered at it closely. A woman, probably in her forties or fifties, her arms outstretched and palms open, as though announcing her possession of this landscape—which looked a lot like Beaver Lake. The photo was not perfectly focused, and a bit creased, but Roméo knew it was her. Was it possible? It was clearly a picture of Hélène Cousineau. *Hélène de Troie* as they all called her, as she was so unusually, ethereally beautiful, and the object of almost every boy's desire in Outremont High where Roméo, Hélène, and her younger brother, Jean-Michel, a.k.a. "Ti-Coune" attended. Hélène, who had run away from a violent home, and then several abusive foster families. Hélène, who lived in a Hells Angels bunker with Ti-Coune when they were teenagers, and whom no one messed with. She had headed out west before she was eighteen and had been living out there for years, thousands of miles from Montreal. Roméo found out she went missing in 2016. But the trail had gone cold. He examined the photo again. There was no mistaking that expression. And the place. The chalet next to Beaver Lake where people went for hot chocolate after skating, or for snacks in the summer, was clear and recognizable. A well-known tourist destination, and beloved by Montrealers as well. Roméo took a photo of the picture with his phone. But when was this taken? And by whom? How did this dead woman know Hélène Cousineau? Was Hélène still alive?

# Fourteen

THE YELLOW LILIES caressed the canoe as it slid silently through the water, dappled with light where the sun penetrated the trees in full summer leaf. The breeze was so warm and gentle it was like Mother Nature herself was conspiring to create a perfect moment. Just for them. He took in the lovely shape of her head and neck, her black hair pulled up in a careless ponytail, the rise and fall of her shoulders as she paddled, stopping to point out the frogs and the enormous heron stalking them. He loved everything about the way she moved though the world. Just as he reached out to touch her, to show her the kingfisher that was warning them away, she dropped her paddle in the water and turned around to face him. But it wasn't her. It was someone else. The Man. He was pointing and laughing at him, shrieking, "You're up shit creek without a paddle, my boy!" When he looked at his hands his paddle was gone, too, and his hands were bleeding. He tried to staunch the blood and plunged them into the water. The whole lake began to turn red. When he pulled them out again, his hands were gone. And she was, too. He had no hands, and no paddle in a lake of blood. As he slowly returned to this world, it took him a few moments to remember he was in his bathtub and had fallen asleep again. The water was freezing now, and his fingers had gone wrinkled and pruny. His heart was beating faster than he liked—it always happened when he dreamed of her. But this was a variation on the nightmare he'd had now for years and years. It always began so beautifully and ended so horribly.

He checked his phone on the bathtub edge—he was already late. He hefted his bulk out of the bath, and reached for a towel to rub himself dry, taking meticulous care with every inch of his body. He had told her everything. Well, almost everything. Some things could not be fully revealed. He had promised her he'd care for her, never let her want for anything. He told her the things he had never told anyone else. All the social workers, all the therapists, all the do-gooders who wanted him to talktalktalktalktalktalktalktalk. She was the only one who really listened because she *knew what it was like*. And now she was gone.

As he straightened the epaulettes and insignia on his uniform, he smiled with self-satisfaction. No reasonable person could think he was not a good-looking man. He had a good face. A strong chin. Clean teeth. Clear eyes. Excellent posture. As he slid the wedding ring on, he glanced at her picture on his wall. He kissed the tips of his fingers and transferred it to the photograph. As he stepped out into the tepid light of mid-afternoon in a Montreal January, he felt a surge of resolve. She would understand why he was doing it. Why it was so very important.

# Fifteen

*Thursday evening*

MARIE STEPPED OFF the #138 bus several blocks before her stop. It was a crisply cold but windless evening, and Marie wanted to walk a bit before she disappeared into her house for the night. Marie loved to walk. At her absolute lowest moments, when her marriage had failed and she was looking at raising two teenagers alone, even when she felt so low you could scrape her off the floor with a spatula, she still forced herself to go for a long walk. As long as she kept moving, she could face anything.

Marie walked west along Côte St. Antoine and smiled at the memory of this same walk in the summer—the sibilance of the swaying maple trees that lined the street, the gardens at almost every house in glorious bloom, the hiss of the sprinklers keeping them that way, the seductive smell of barbecue, the call of children playing outside even after supper, and the sharp whistle of the cardinals. She glanced in the houses as she passed, and could see people preparing supper, kids at their homework, televisions flickering in living rooms. Marie had always liked to look at the interior of every house—it fascinated her to think of all the dreams and struggles and tragedies and triumphs the people lived in just these few blocks. Daniel, her ex-husband, used to tell her she was just nosy and weird, but looking into strangers' lives for just a few moments comforted Marie with the knowledge that they were all in this thing together somehow. The road started to descend, and she could see her park—Girouard Park—coming up on her left. The trees formed a kind of ethereal black web against the lights along the pathway, and the sky was just turning from royal blue to cobalt. Because it was suppertime and a school night, the park was entirely deserted. Or almost. On the hockey rink skated one lone man in concentric circles in its warm yellow lights. Marie thought he looked so self-contained, so beautiful in his solitude. It was an iconic image of Montreal on a winter night. She remembered with a smile one of her first dates with Roméo, when they'd gone skating at Beaver Lake. Despite being a born and bred Montrealer, Marie never did take to skating. She pushed herself along the ice on stiff wooden legs, and realized too late that she didn't really know how to stop. Roméo, on the other hand, skated around her effortlessly, like he was meant to glide through life with two thin blades on his feet. She still remembered the exhilaration she felt when he placed his arm around her waist and pulled her gently alongside him, matching his sure stroke to her hesitant one. She thought that was perhaps the very moment she fell in love with him.

Marie was startled by two huskies that suddenly turned the corner onto Côte St. Antoine and rushed towards her, dragging their owner who was running to keep up. They reminded her of a book she loved as a kid—in it were pictures of husky sled dogs pulling Inuit children to school up in the Arctic. The idea had thrilled her. For months, she kept asking her parents if she could get her own *dogs of winter*, as she called them, just like the Inuit kids. But no, they just had a crabby old tabby cat who took a nasty swipe at Marie every chance he got. Marie recognized the two huskies from a house one street over from hers. They were such magnificent animals. Quiet, obedient, gorgeous, and completely out of their element in the city. She watched them continue to prance along the sidewalk and disappear into the park. Hopefully they would soon be unleashed and allowed to run free.

The doors of the day care suddenly opened and a frazzled mother pulled her toddler down the stairs behind her, beeping the alarm off on her oversized SUV parked in front. Marie felt bad for the kids who were stuck in *garderie* this late. She felt bad for the parents, too, who had to leave them there often from seven in the morning until six at night. In the depths of a Montreal winter, that meant they never saw their kids in daylight except on the weekends. Marie continued past the grandiose façade of St. Augustine's church, and instinctively looked up to where two peregrine falcons had started nesting a few years earlier. She often heard them before she could see them, and then it was only a quick shadow—they were the fastest birds in the world and would plummet from the bell tower of the church to hunt. The park, which had once been full of pigeons was now almost pigeon-free. But peregrines ate songbirds, too. Between the falcons, and the roaming cats of the neighborhood and climate change, she feared for the future of the little passerines that sang against the silence of the winter.

She turned up her street to her apartment on the second

floor of a rather eccentric duplex and saw she'd left the light on in her bedroom. It now emitted a very inviting, orangey-red glow, and for a moment she just wanted to get into bed and read her book. This time of year, Marie often didn't see her neighbors for weeks on end, sometimes months. Winter could be lonely and many Montrealers fell prey to depression. But just when it seems no one can take another snowstorm, or another dark, frigid day, spring (which lasts about two weeks) finally arrives. Pasty-faced people emerge from their houses, the kids are a few inches taller, and everyone once again talks of who had the worst flu, how hard the winter was, and of course, their plans for the summer.

As Marie left the sidewalk for the little path to her door, she noticed with gratitude that her next-door neighbors, a lovely young couple with three very boisterous kids, had shoveled her walkway, and scattered salt to melt the ice. Marie realized with a small shock that's because they see her as *old. Older. A senior* now.

Marie dropped her house key on the little table by the door and rifled through her mail. She would normally start preparing supper, but she and Roméo had a dinner date at Pasta Giacomo, her local Italian restaurant. Marie was already anticipating her glass of Chianti and the antipasti followed by either the osso bucco or risotto. Roméo would eat the vegan ali olio with spelt pasta, a dish the waiter served with some disdain. Every Christmas season Pasta Giacomo recreated an entire Italian village in their window, with the crèche and Jesus at its center. There were miniature donkeys pulling cartloads of grapes, shepherds carrying their lambs up to pasture, goats eating the weeds off rooftops. There were sausage makers, cobblers, and tailors. When her kids were young, they loved pointing out and naming each occupation and activity. There was also a mother with a child over her knee perpetually spanking the child. Her kids were especially fascinated by that one. It was a village they'd never see in their actual lives, but was enchanting for them, of course. Their village was the local *dépanneur* owned by very friendly Syrian refugees, a vaping store, tattoo parlor, too many banks, a vet's office, a musty but excellent used bookstore, a perpetually closed ice cream parlor, and a local café where the breakfast was overpriced but too convenient to stick to the promise never to go again.

Marie slipped out of her heavy winter boots and padded over to the television. She couldn't help herself. She flicked on CNN, or "Trump TV," as Roméo called it. It was like a car wreck, and Marie couldn't stop watching. Like so many women her age, she was gutted and heartbroken that a brilliant, capable woman had lost to such an overt and brazen kleptocrat. The bigger, more devastating fear though, was that if Trump could be President of the United States, then literally *anything* could happen *anywhere*. Over the last three years, Marie has joked that she suffered from PTTSD—Post-Trump-Traumatic Stress Disorder, but it was actually true. There he was now, surrounded by a crowd of red hats with the Make America Great Again logo, cheering him on. It reminded Marie of what they used to call Grand Prix Wrestling, now called the WWF. His fans—what pundits call his base—know it's all fake, but *it doesn't matter.* They cheer for him anyway. That was the scary part, in this Trumpian world. Up is down. Lies are facts. Truth is fake news. It was tribal. Primitive. It was us against them, and *them* are different and therefore scary, and so we want to *crush* them. Do a flying kick jump on their brown and black heads. Marie couldn't keep from watching some nights. It was epic. It was Greek. What would it take, finally, to cause the fall of the tyrant?

Her speculation was interrupted by the beep of her phone. It was Ben, sending a video of her grandson, Noah. He was only two years old, but they already had him on skates. There he was, walking around a rink very gingerly, padded well with a thick snowsuit and helmet. *Future Dima Golikov!* was the caption. Marie answered with a double heart emoji. She would have them over for supper sometime next week, and just hold that delicious boy for hours. Marie then noticed she had another text—from Ruby: *got the internship !!! will be the new baby legal aid person for the Native Women's Network— thrilled! tell u more later xoxo.* Marie answered that one with a dancing dog sticker. She actually hated texting but had finally succumbed to its power. It was that or not communicate much with her kids, and she would always choose the former. Ruby's text reminded her to discuss the awful incident with the cops she witnessed outside Dawson with Roméo. Marie checked the time. She was starving. She debated preparing herself a little pre-supper snack, but then her phone actually rang. It was Roméo. "Hi. How was your day?"

Marie felt immediately wary. "Back-to-back classes, one great and one not. Are you at the restaurant already?"

There was a slight pause. "No. I'm actually downtown at the coroner's office."

"What? Why?"

"Long story. I'll tell you about it later."

"So you'll be late then. I'll just start drinking without you—"

"I'm not going to make it for supper. *Je suis désolé*, Marie. There's something I have to do." He waited. Marie was silent.

"I'll be over later, okay?" Marie was silent. He paused again, and then hung up. At least he knew better than to sign off with a cloying *love you.*

Marie felt disproportionately disappointed. Angry, in fact. She had been looking forward to this all week, especially since Roméo had missed their Saturday date night. Maybe he still wasn't ready. Maybe she and Roméo needed to take a step backwards, not forwards. She decided to get into her pajamas, order herself a big, meat-covered pizza, and watch the next few episodes of *Nasty Women*, that great series on Netflix that every woman she knew was raving about. Marie decided to forgo the wine and go directly to the single malt whiskey.

# Sixteen

ROMÉO RETURNED THE KEY to his pocket and closed the door quietly behind him. He knew there was nobody home, but he called out their names anyway. He was answered only by the hum of the refrigerator and a muffled ambulance siren from the street. The apartment was very small, but surprisingly tidy and clean. Maybe because there wasn't much in it except a giant screen and what looked like video game controllers before it on a coffee table, as though they were waiting to come to life. A bookshelf with few books and a couple of cacti, an old sofa he recognized from his home with Elyse, a tiny galley kitchen with an empty fruit bowl on the counter. He didn't go into the bedroom—that he did not want to see. When he heard the key in the door Roméo took a seat on the one listing armchair and waited. The boy didn't see him at first, and nearly leapt out of his boots when he did.

"*Tabernac! Tu m'as fait peur, ostie!* You scared the shit out of me!" He removed his jacket and threw it on the sofa. "How did you get in here?"

"Sit down."

The boy didn't move. "Does Sophie know you're here?"

Roméo crossed his long legs, placed his clasped hands on his lap, and then calmly asked, "Why did you push my daughter up against a wall?"

The boy started to swear at Roméo again, but cut himself off. "Is *that* what she told you?"

Roméo studied the boy's narrow face, the sparse, scruffy beard, the lank hair tied into a man bun. This guy made her last boyfriend, the Anglo guy Trevor, look like a winner.

"She pushed me first. Really hard. And then she just started attacking me, slapping me and punching me. So, I pushed her back."

Sophie was always what they called "headstrong." As a little girl, she pretty much did what she wanted. If she was thwarted, she could pull a pretty frightening tantrum. Roméo and Elyse saw a therapist and tried to understand how to deal with her, how to "actively listen," but Sophie often proved too much for them. It always seemed to Roméo that she would create these great big dramas—with her girlfriends or her mother, and then seem to enjoy watching them play out. But this was different. Completely different.

"You pushed her against the wall, and she hit her head."

The boy was still standing his ground. "I've never done that before, I swear." He swallowed hard. "She just provoked me until I couldn't take it anymore."

Roméo slowly got to his feet. The man towered over the boy. "In my experience, *mon grand*, by the time a woman first reports abuse, it's happened many times before."

The boy shook his head. "Not this time. Ask your daughter. Ask Sophie!" He ducked past Roméo and headed to the kitchen. In an effort to regain some control, he cracked open a bottle of beer and took a sip. "I love her. I do. *Mais, elle est folle, okay?* She's crazy sometimes."

Roméo walked over to the kitchen where the boy stood drinking his beer. He got very close to him without making any contact. "I have strongly recommended to Sophie that she not return here. But if she does, and you are again 'provoked' into touching her with any intention to hurt her, believe me, *mon p'tit gars*, you will live to regret it."

Roméo pulled on his coat. "This is your first and last warning."

The Cock and Bull pub was very appropriately named, Roméo thought. As he took a seat at the bar, he made sure to position himself so he could see what was coming. It had been a fixture on Ste. Catherine street near the Forum for at least forty years, as Roméo used to come here as an underage teenager to drink, strut, and play pool. The place hadn't changed much. Same empty-eyed drunks clutching their sweating drinks. Same loquacious barflies talking up some bull. A couple of heavily tattooed women with peroxide-blond braids and tans so deep they looked like worn leather stared intently into twin VLT machines. Roméo wondered if they were twins as well. They both wore matching hot pants and high heels even though it was fifteen below zero outside. The hockey game was on a giant TV on one wall. Three younger guys in backwards ball caps were staring at it, mouths slightly open, clutching beers. The *Canadiens* were losing. Again. Even with that amazing Russian player, they were struggling to make the playoffs. The guy couldn't do everything by himself.

Roméo ordered a beer and discreetly checked out the bartender as she poured it for him. Her hair was a two-tone mix of steel gray and bright auburn, and it almost matched her painted orange eyebrows, arched in what seemed like permanent surprise. Roméo thought that was particularly ironic as he imagined there wasn't much that surprised this woman anymore. Sparkly gold eye shadow blossomed from her eyes outlined in thick black liner—she vaguely resembled Elizabeth Taylor as Cleopatra entering Rome in triumph. She had an enormous tattoo of a red and black snake coiling itself around her right arm from her shoulder to her wrist. Its head and fangs appeared poised to strike from her forearm. Once she served him his pint, she moved to the other end of her bar and started to check her stock. Roméo knew that she knew he was a cop. He would give it another minute or two.

"*Madame?*" he gestured her over to him. "My name is Roméo Leduc—"

She cut him off. "You're not Montreal police."

"No, I'm Sûreté du Québec. Detective Chief Inspector." He quickly flashed his badge.

She would have raised an eyebrow if she could. "SQ?"

Roméo shifted in his chair and pulled out his phone from his coat pocket. "I'd like to know if you recognize this woman?"

The bartender peered at the image and then looked away. "What the hell happened to her?"

Roméo slid the phone closer on the bar. "She froze to death. We are trying to identify her to let her family know."

She frowned for a moment, then ducked under the bar. When she came back up she was wearing eyeglasses, which in one gesture seemed to turn her into a kindly grandmother. She held the phone closer.

"*Pauvre petite.*" She returned the photo to Roméo. "I don't know her. But it's hard to tell them apart. *Chuis pas raciste, moé.* I'm not racist. It's just that they all have black hair and brown eyes, and when I see them…Let's just say they're not at their best."

"You seen anyone in the bar lately, any of these guys—been especially aggressive? Likes to prey on women? Especially Indigenous women?"

This time her eyebrows did actually lift. "You *are* kidding, right?"

Roméo didn't respond.

"There's always these slimy guys—almost always white—who just know how to get to them, you know? There's one—I mean, I know he's some kind of pimp. And the cops know about him, too. But no one does anything. Why didn't they take him out years ago? I mean, what is *wrong* with you guys?"

A customer had joined them at the bar and was obviously trying to listen in.

The bartender removed her glasses, delivered a beer to him, and reminded him to mind his own business. Roméo scrolled through his phone to the photo of Hélène taken from the dead woman's pocket.

"Do you know this woman? Her name is Hélène Cousineau."

Once again, she took the phone and peered more closely. "*Oui.* I seen her. Maybe. three…No, maybe six months ago? It was like August, September maybe? She used to come in here once, maybe twice a week."

"Are you sure? This woman?"

"I'm pretty sure."

"Did you ever see her with the woman in the other photo?"

"No. Like I said, I never seen that one. But this one," she tapped the photo with a very long, red index nail. "Not a big drinker, but she was a really good tipper. Which means she probably worked at a bar, too."

Roméo pulled two twenties from his wallet and left them on the bar. "Listen. If you see her again, can you please let me know right away?" He placed his card by her hand.

"Can I give you a call even if I don't see her again?"

Roméo smiled and took the last sip of beer. "*Merci, Madame.*" He put on his coat, turned up the collar and headed towards the door. It was time to call Ti-Coune Cousineau.

# Seventeen

*Thursday night*

"HERE YOU GO, BOY. Wait! Let me get it all out—there you go. You're such a good, good boy." Christian squatted by Hamlet as he emptied the last tiny bit of kibble into the dog's bowl. Hamlet swallowed the food in a less than a minute, but he didn't beg for more. He knew from experience that that was all there was. For now. Christian gently scratched the dog's head and crawled back into his thermal sleeping bag. Hamlet curled himself up tightly beside him and the two settled in for the night in the recessed side door of St. Edmund's church, directly across the street from Westmount Square, where the very cheapest of their condos went for two and a half million bucks. But St. Edmund's days were numbered. Once a home to a thriving community, it was about to go the way so many churches had in Quebec—it had been recently deconsecrated, sold to developers, and would be transformed into more condos. Christian pulled his sleeping bag over the top of his head and tried to stay warm. He concentrated on his breathing. *In through the nose, out through the mouth. Stay in the present. Stay in the present. What I am feeling is scary. But it is not dangerous. Look at something specific. Concrete.* He stroked Hamlet again. He was here, with his dog. He would be okay. He would be *okay*. Although he had finally taken his medication as promised, he was struggling to control the panic that was rising up in him and ready to implode. Where was Nia? Where was Nia? Where was Nia? He hadn't seen her since yesterday morning, when she went off to the housing office, and he was supposed to get a spot at the squat on Berri Street. He did manage to secure a place for them, but Nia never showed up. He had spent all that day looking for her. He and Hamlet went to all their usual haunts—the Sherbrooke metro, then the Berri/UQAM station, and finally Christian had headed west along Ste. Catherine street towards Cabot Square and Alexis Nihon. They didn't tend to wander over that far west too often, but it was really his last hope. No Nia. He had spent the day panhandling at the Atwater metro, and made $18.50—not bad at all. A regular at that spot had agreed to watch Hamlet so Christian could run to the IGA to buy a few bananas, a jar of crunchy peanut butter, and a loaf of bread. That combination was Nia's favorite, and he was looking forward to surprising her.

He had forgotten to get more dog food and felt furious with himself. "I'm sorry, Buddy. We'll find Nia tomorrow and get you a good bone. She knows all the best places for that." At the sound of Nia's name, the dog opened his eyes and became more alert. He watched Christian for a few seconds, and then resumed his position, his nose buried deep in his tail. Christian covered him in the flannel blanket Nia had found on the street—some mom must have dropped it off a baby stroller. It was covered in cartoony flowers, birds, and butterflies. Hamlet began to snore quietly. He was exhausted. Christian stared up at the Dawson College dome, glimmering in the evening light. He could just make out the statue of Mary, holding her baby, Jesus. He kept breathing. In through the nose, out through the mouth. Christian tried to think of the things that made him feel happy and peaceful. Hamlet. He was right here. Nia. Nia's not here, though. What happened to Nia? What if Nia had an accident? What if Nia was *dead*? Stay in the present. Happy. Peaceful.

He thought of St. Léon's, a beautiful church a few blocks from where he was right now, where he and Nia sometimes hung out in the afternoons because there was never anyone there. They loved to watch the sun playing with the colors of the stained glass windows. They were so rich, so heartbreakingly beautiful. But there was Adam and Eve—Eve raising her arm and covering her eyes in shame. For eating from the tree of knowledge? *Why* was that a bad thing? Why were they driven out of the garden? Why was sex shameful? Why were people punished for it? Why did *anyone* care about who had sex with who and *why*? Nia always told him not to get so worked up about it, and just appreciate the skill of the illustration, the passion of the colors.

A blast of frigid air suddenly came rocketing around the corridor from Atwater and de Maisonneuve. Christian tucked further into the doorway to protect himself and Hamlet from the wind. That sandwich guy who showed him this spot was right. What was his name? Ishmael? No. Isaac. Abraham's legitimate son. The sacrifice that God, in the end, did not demand. He just wanted proof that a father would murder his son for Him. This *was* a great place to bunk in for the night. If only Nia were here with him and Hamlet. Something must have happened. No. She was okay. Nia knew how to take care of herself. She was okay. *Breathe in through the nose and out through the mouth.* Christian was very grateful for the couple of Ativans the sandwich guy gave him—*gave* him—to calm him down and help him sleep. He thought he'd take one and keep the other for later, in case. But in the end, he'd swallowed both. They were already kicking in. Satisfied that Hamlet was warm enough and feeling like he had to close his eyes and rest, Christian fell into a profound sleep.

As he expected, the dog, Hamlet, woke up as soon as he approached. It got immediately to its feet and growled softly. It was afraid. In his pocket was the treat, which he removed and pulled from its plastic wrap. It took a bit of quiet coaxing, but the dog finally, tentatively pulled the food from his hand and swallowed it whole. He spoke softly, tenderly to it the entire time, until it, too began to succumb. Poor thing. Although they had fashioned a dog coat for it, it was mostly in tatters, and the dog had patches of mange that must be agonizing. After a few minutes, he crawled over to the sleeping man, but it wasn't easy to get close. His layers of clothes reeked of the street, and no matter how many showers he took, that couldn't be washed off. He looked around quickly to make sure no one was out for a very late walk with their dog, or some random student leaving the college after a night of cramming. He turned the man gently on his back, trying not to inhale too deeply, and straddled his chest.

"I will help you. Don't be scared. Help is coming. Help is on the way." It didn't take very long. Within four and a half minutes of his first approach, it was all over.

# Eighteen

*Friday night*
*February 1, 2019*

MICHAELA CRUZ EMERGED from the metro station, pulled her hood over her head carefully so as not to wreck her hair, and began to trudge up the hill towards the Place d'Armes square. The neo-Gothic façade of *l'église* Notre Dame rose before her, illuminated garishly against the evening sky. She was trying, rather unsuccessfully, not to be too excited to be attending the Diamond in the Rough party at Jean Luc David's house. Although she had abandoned her family's Catholic faith many years earlier, she still crossed herself quickly before the church's towers and said a little prayer for this evening to be everything she was hoping for. Michaela's mother had watched her get ready for the party, but she did not tell her parents where she was really going. They were Italian over-protective and would not approve. She was their only child, and they lived intensely and vicariously through her achievements. Her mother reminded her a crop top was not appropriate for the winter weather and that she had too

much makeup on. Michaela ignored her. She worked weekends at her parents' bakery, and they were constantly bringing
Italian boys to the store to meet her who still sported faux
hawks and soccer jerseys. Her parents had gotten married as
teenagers, and they fretted about Michaela's love life—she'd
never had a boyfriend and didn't really want one just yet. She
had much more important plans.

Michaela left her coat and boots with a different greeter
from last time—a young woman who barely looked at her as
she handed them over. Then she made her way directly to the
bar, where no cocktails were being poured, but there was wine
and beer she could help herself to, and a giant cheese plate with
some fruit gracefully displayed. This was not a star-studded
party like the last one, and everyone looked to be under thirty.
This time, though, no one was dancing. The guests were hud-
dled in small groups talking quietly, with an occasional burst
of forced laughter, but Michaela could tell they were not really
listening to each other. They were glancing around the room
furtively, perhaps wondering if and when something would
happen. Michaela suddenly wished Brittany was there with
her. She didn't know anyone here, and it felt too weird to just
insert herself into a conversation. But Brittany hadn't been
invited.

After what seemed like an endless amount of time devoted to small talk with a gaggle of young women who had all
just graduated from a prestigious theatre school and starred
in plays Michaela had never heard of, she noticed the energy
in the room shift. Jean Luc David appeared, looking very
casual but distinguished in a salmon-colored shirt, perfectly
tailored blue jeans, and an expression of avuncular amusement. He slowly worked the room, greeting each circle of

wannabees. Every one of them broke into wide, perfect smiles as he bestowed his momentary attention on them. His presence was electric. Michaela found it a bit nauseating. He had not even looked at her yet.

She felt a hand gently touch her shoulder. She turned to meet the striking green eyes of a woman who looked to be in her late thirties. She had a generous mouth outlined in bright burgundy lipstick, and a delicate golden nose ring. She tucked a swath of her jet black hair behind one ear, and held out her other hand.

"Hi! I'm Gennifer Moran, Mr. David's personal assistant. You're Michaela Cruz, right?"

Her voice was quite deep and pleasant. It made her sound older than she appeared to be. Michaela nodded and let her hand be shaken.

"Mr. David asked me to contact you to attend the party this evening—I tried to reach your agent first, but—"

"I...I don't have an agent. Yet." Michaela stammered.

"Well, that's not a problem—Oh! You don't even know what I'm talking about, do you?"

Michaela could feel dozens of eyes watching, trying hard to hear this conversation.

"I knew as soon as I saw you that you were the one."

Michaela was mortified to feel herself blushing. "The one what?"

"We are looking to cast a new 'girl,'" Gennifer Moran gestured in inverted commas, "even though at eighteen years old, she's really a woman."

Michaela felt her heart pounding.

"We think you might be her." Gennifer scrolled through her phone's files. "I see you did a lot of acting in high school, but not much after. That's okay. We're looking for fresh. Raw. No one who's been around the track a hundred times by the time they're twenty-one years old."

Michaela found her voice and offered, "I am mostly a writer now. I've written two screenplays—I won best screenplay award two years in a row at my college, and I'm waiting to hear if I get early acceptance at Concordia film school."

Gennifer Moran held up her hand to quiet her. "I'm sure you're very talented. But for now, Mr. David would like to discuss *this* possibility with you. It's not a big role right now, but it's not an SOC, either—"

"What's an SOC?"

Gennifer laughed. Michaela could see the bones of her shoulders sticking out from her clingy black dress. "It means Silent On Camera. No lines." She checked her phone again. "I'll be back for you in a few minutes. Have another glass of wine. Eat!"

Michaela watched as the woman strode away in impossibly high heels that she made possible. She moved to the bar, poured a glass of wine, and immediately texted Brittany.

"*omg !!!!! might get a role on NW !!! meeting JLD. how much do you think they pay?*"

She surveyed the room to see where the women she'd been chatting with had gone and noticed that at least half of the guests had already left. A few crestfallen-looking ones slumped on sofas, and the rest seemed to be heading for their coats. Michaela wondered when Gennifer Moran was coming back, and just then, she did.

"Come with me."

Michaela followed her down a flight of stairs, past what she remembered as the kitchen, and then to the same

Hollywood walk of fame corridor. The assistant opened a door, and ushered Michaela into the huge office she had only glimpsed before. It had wall-to-wall windows overlooking the city. An enormous shelf lined with books, the trophy table with all the Emmys, and a stunning Persian carpet dominated the room. Jean Luc David was seated in an old-looking armchair, facing out the window towards the river.

"*Merci*, Gennifer." He swiveled around and addressed Michaela. "Gennifer has a few things to take care of with the others. Can she leave us alone for a few minutes?"

Michaela smiled cautiously. "Of course."

"Please sit down."

Michaela had the choice between an uncomfortable-looking chrome and plastic chair, or a sleek, low-slung sofa. She opted for the chair. There was a longish silence while he just looked at her.

"As my assistant mentioned, we are looking to cast a new character—for next season—and you're pretty much perfect. Our girl is seventeen, the daughter of Middle Eastern refugees who is caught between the two cultures of her old and new home—"

"I'm mostly Italian and a bit Portuguese, Mr. David. Not Middle—"

"You read as exotic. Spirited but vulnerable. Very intelligent but naïve. That's who we're looking for."

Michaela smiled awkwardly. "Um. Okay. If that's what you're seeing. Thank you."

"Can you stand up, please?"

"Um. Okay. Do you—how do you want me to stand? This feels weird."

He tilted his head at an angle. "Could you let your hair down, please?"

Michaela reached up and slowly pulled the clip from her hair. She had just washed it, so it tumbled full and shiny onto her shoulders.

"Lovely! Now, this might seem like a strange request, but would you just go into the washroom over there and remove the makeup from your face. We just need to know how you read unadorned. Unenhanced. It's very critical to this character." He turned away from her and back towards the river view. She hesitated, and then got up from her hard chair and headed towards the bathroom. She locked the door behind her and stared at herself in the huge mirror. She pulled out her phone and saw that she had a text from Brittany.

"*a shit-ton of $$ !! am at home call me xoxo*"

Michaela began to wash the makeup off her face. When she felt that she looked as "unenhanced" as she could, she unlocked the door and pulled it open. Jean Luc David was standing in the threshold. He had removed his glasses, making him look much older somehow. Michaela could see the crow's feet around his eyes, which were no longer bemused. He surveyed her face. Her entire body, from her hair to her breasts to her legs and back again. Then he stepped into the bathroom and ran his hands through her hair until he had it firmly entwined in his fingers. Suddenly, she understood what she was really doing there.

# Nineteen

IT HAD BEEN A GLORIOUS DAY. Marie had gone for a long and arduous cross-country ski on the network of trails that started right out of her back door. It was perfect weather for it—about fifteen degrees below zero, not even a sigh of wind, and a cloudless, sunny sky. She had climbed the mountain that rose up directly behind her house and descended into a little valley, then up again to a spectacular lookout that offered a view of Mont Tremblant in the distance and the hills that gave way to its summit. On the way there she had almost impaled with her ski pole a spruce grouse who was buried in the snow and startled it into frantic flight. Marie loved looking at the tracks of the animals who also made their way up and down her trails. The dead-straight line of red foxes, the wide band of a beaver tail, the giant back feet of the snowshoe hare in frenetic patterns, and the deeper but delicate step of the deer. Once, Marie had practically ploughed into a couple of moose who were clumsily getting to their feet from the crib they'd made in the deep snow. For a few moments they both just stared at each other, their breath suspended in the frozen air, and then Marie turned around and skied off as fast as her legs and arms could take her.

Marie's quota of student papers was marked for the day, and she was now lounging guilt-free on the sofa in front of the fireplace in her little house in the woods with Roméo who was opening a second bottle of wine. The vegan meal she'd made for him had been a success; Marie was feeling very pleased that it actually had tasted like something. Roméo filled their glasses again and listened to Marie attentively as she got him caught up on all the local news in her little town of Ste. Lucie des Laurentides.

"You remember that Michelle Lachance, Louis' wife, died last week?" Louis Lachance was the local *homme à tout faire* who'd worked in many of the homes in Ste. Lucie for over sixty-five years and had been married for sixty-four. He was also the person who had found the body of Marie's neighbor, Anna Newman, in the case that brought Marie and Roméo together. They both suspected that despite being a devoted husband, Louis had been just a little bit in love with Anna Newman.

"Mr. Lachance's daughter is insisting he move into a nursing home and he is *devastated*. Apparently, he is refusing to leave his house or give up his tools. He wants to keep working. But his daughter is also stubborn. The house is on the market and they're selling all his stuff. I think she's sending him to *Louiseville* of all places, where he knows no one. But his daughter lives there."

Roméo frowned. "I guess it's easier for her to dump him in a home—"

Marie cut him off. "Is that what you think I did with my mother?"

Roméo took her hand and kissed it very gently. "Of course not. You had no choice. But from what I remember of Mr. Lachance, he *is* very old, but he is also very lucid and capable."

Roméo didn't believe in retirement if the person was still competent and wanted the work. He saw what happened to old people when they didn't feel needed anymore. It was an often hasty decline towards isolation, depression, and death. He wished Louis several more years of whatever work he wanted to do.

"Madame Lachance's funeral is next week—the very last before they deconsecrate our little church," said Marie. The white clapboard Ste. Lucie church stood at the crossroads of the little town. They hadn't had a resident priest in years, and the congregation was down to about thirty people.

"Another one bites the dust. The church, I mean. Good riddance."

Roméo frowned. "I don't know why, but I find it a bit sad. No more Italians parading through town with the blind Santa Lucia, no more Christmas crèche, no more midnight mass with that terrible choir—"

"And no more priests assaulting children."

"Let's not discuss that, shall we? Maybe not tonight?"

Roméo extricated himself from Marie and got up to put two more logs on the fire. Barney and Dog, passed out in front of it, were unappreciative of how carefully Roméo stepped around them. *Let sleeping dogs lie*, Roméo thought.

"We are invited to Joel and Shelly's for brunch tomorrow, remember? It's a Groundhog Day party. A day late."

Roméo squatted on his haunches and poked around at the logs.

"I don't believe I've ever been to one of those. Is it an Anglo thing?"

"February second is the exact half-way point of winter in the north—Joel and Shelly are old hippies—they celebrate that."

"Will there be a groundhog present?"

Marie laughed. "Are you kidding? All the groundhogs are still hibernating up here. Except us."

"Who knew life could be so busy in little Ste. Lucie?" Roméo mused.

Marie rearranged her feet on his lap as he returned to the sofa and got deeper under the blanket.

"And…we are babysitting for Ben and Maya three weekends from now. They have a wedding in Toronto, no kids invited. I can't wait to get a whole weekend with that little boy." Marie was often overwhelmed by the powerful, animal love she felt for her grandson.

"Can you be up here with us?"

Roméo hesitated. "I think so, yes."

Everyone kept telling Marie how lucky she was to have Roméo in her life. No one ever said to him how lucky he was to have her. Was it because she was ten years older and fortunate that anyone, let alone a man who looked like Roméo, even looked at her? She knew perhaps that things should be left the way they were—they were good companions who had occasional great sex, but Marie wanted more. She wanted to share her life completely again, but she sometimes worried that Roméo felt too pulled into her orbit, that he didn't have his own life anymore. Maybe that was why he resisted the move into her house. In the early days of their relationship, Marie thought, they would have torn each other's clothes off by now and done it in front of the fire. Now the sex was still passionate but less frequent and certainly no clothes were ever in danger of ripping. Marie took a big gulp of her wine, and decided to remind Roméo that they were supposed to make The Decision that weekend.

"I guess we are not going to discuss the elephant in the room tonight, are we?"

He took a deep breath. "There are a couple of things going on I need to deal with."

Roméo hadn't told her that he'd rented an Airbnb flat in Montreal, just for a few weeks. For him and Sophie. In fact, he hadn't told her anything about Sophie's crisis, and amazingly, Marie hadn't asked.

"I told you about that hit-and-run case—"

"Oh, that poor woman. It's so—awful! Did they find who killed her?"

"So, I told you they found my cell number in her pocket, and—"

"But you didn't know her at all, right?"

Roméo made the face he did when Marie wouldn't let him finish his sentence. She got quiet.

"No. I don't know her at all. But my phone number was written on the back of a photograph found on her body—"

"What?"

"And…I am pretty sure the person in the photo is Hélène Cousineau—"

"Who?" Marie interrupted. "Oh. Sorry. I'm just a faster talker than you."

"Hélène Cousineau is Ti-Coune's sister."

"Ti-Coune is that friend you went to high school with, right? Who lives near here?"

"Well, he's not a *friend*, exactly. Just someone I've known a very long time."

Roméo paused, waiting for the interruption that didn't happen.

"Hélène pretty much fell off the radar three years ago—she went missing out west. Ti-Coune asked me to look into her disappearance then, but I never turned up anything, so this…this is a big deal, because the photo is fairly recent, I'd say."

"Do you think she's living in Montreal?"

"I'm hoping there's a possibility that she's alive, for starters. I'm going to talk with Ti-Coune about all this more tomorrow. They were very close as children."

Marie emptied the last of the wine into their glasses.

"So you think this young…woman—knew Hélène? This Inuit woman? Did they find who ran her over?"

Roméo hesitated. "No."

"Are they even bothering to look?"

"I would hope so."

Marie withdrew her foot from Roméo's hand and sat up. "I meant to tell you this at supper on Thursday, but then you didn't show up…."

Roméo nodded for her to go on, and Marie described the police abuse she had witnessed against the two Inuit women at the mall.

"I mean, the police were completely out of line. It's not the first time I've seen them practically beat up the homeless. And then this awful woman called them *Eskimos*, for God's sake. When was the last time you heard that word?"

Roméo grimaced and shook his head.

"Montreal cops are so fucking racist."

Roméo thought of Detective Cauchon and how shocked he'd been by his attitude towards the dead woman. Still, he hated when Marie painted everyone with the same brush. It was too simple.

"Marie, sometimes I have seen such kindness from those cops. They have to deal with some very difficult people every day—"

Marie began to protest.

"—and every single day they have to deal with the same problems, the same mental health and addiction issues. And most people get to walk right past them. It's not so black and white. It's much more complicated—"

"That's what people say when they know they're wrong. It's *complicated*. Imagine if Ruby was homeless, or, or... Sophie? Imagine some cop grabbing *your* daughter like that. It's a disgrace, Roméo. I mean, they're treated like animals. And that poor girl who was hit by the car—and just *left* like that."

He went to embrace Marie. "I agree."

Marie squirmed away from his arms. "Something ought to be *done*."

"It is a huge, systemic problem, Marie—"

"And we're the system, so *we* are part of it."

Roméo briefly closed his eyes. He just didn't want to get *into* anything tonight.

"If she were a young white woman from a 'good home' the cops would be all over this. You know that's true, Roméo. You have to investigate this—"

"Marie, I have no jurisdiction in Montreal—I have no influence on this case—"

"Can't you work with the Montreal police?"

"I'm not sure 'working with' is accurate. I would more aptly describe it as 'working around.' Or 'in spite of.'"

"You have to—you *have* to…find the fucker who killed that woman, Roméo. Who just…left her there like she was worth…nothing."

Roméo fell back deeper into the sofa and exhaled.

"I guess I could leave Nicole LaFramboise in charge of the cold cases for a few days. I could look a little closer at this hit-and-run—and how she was connected to Hélène."

A large log suddenly split and fell, startling both dogs awake.

Neither Roméo nor Marie got up to fix it. Marie took his free hand in hers and squeezed it.

"Thank you for this."

They both stared into the dying fire and finished the last of their wine.

# Twenty

SHE DIDN'T EVEN SEE HIM COMING. That fat-fuck security guard had her by the arm and was already on his stupid radio before she even realized what was happening. That's why she hadn't made it to the Berri Street squat, and now Nia Fellows was getting frantic.

She had spent the last two days trying to find Christian, but he was nowhere. Nowhere that they had ever spent the night together. Nia had gone to the squat on Berri first, and one guy told her Christian had spent Wednesday night there, as Nia had instructed him to. After that, the guy said Christian and the dog had just left. No one had asked where he was headed. Nia then continued her search and walked west along rue Roy to avenue des Pins and then Milton Street, to the shiny new shelter that almost everyone hated.

The nice but very young and overwhelmed intake worker there checked the register; Christian had never signed in there. Of course not. Dogs weren't allowed, and Christian would never leave Hamlet tied up outside anywhere. There was that Salvation Army closet guy who loved Hamlet, but he was only there on Tuesdays. Nia then went to The Bunker down in the Gay Village, but there too, he hadn't been spotted. When they saw the look on her face, a few of the kids tried to be helpful and speculated as to his whereabouts, but Nia had already been to most of their suggestions. He had to be somewhere that she knew—a man cannot disappear into thin air, especially with a dog that never left his side. Nia then decided to go downtown.

She ducked into the Mr. Steer on Ste. Catherine street— one of the waitresses used to live on the street, too, and she was always kind to Nia. She ordered a coffee and tried to think. Throngs of shoppers swaddled in their winter gear hustled along outside, making those last-minute runs before the shops closed at six. The manager with his stupid green vest and clip-on tie was watching her a little too closely, and she knew he'd be asking her to move on soon. Loser. She closed her eyes and tried to breathe the way Christian had taught her. Think. Think. *Think.*

When she didn't show up at the squat as planned, maybe he panicked. By why didn't he stay put and wait for her? *Because you were gone for almost two days, idiot.* She sipped at the dregs of her coffee and went over the sequence of events that had caused this particular clusterfuck. When Nia had left Christian outside St. Michael's mission on Wednesday, she had hopped the bus and headed downtown. It was almost noon by then, and she knew everyone at the housing office would be on lunch break, so she went to The Bay's basement market, and nicked a couple of apples along with a bag of walnuts and chocolate-covered blueberries.

She noticed the security guard was watching her, so she hightailed it over to McGill metro where she panhandled for about two hours. She amused herself by watching all the cheap, ditzy girls on their way to *university*—some wearing those lame, bright red McGill hoodies with their program labeled on them—Law! Medicine! Basket-Weaving! They never dropped so much as a quarter in her hat. The guys weren't much better, either. Every now and then one of them would flirt with her and tell her she was too cute to be a beggar. The best were old ladies—well, not old, but middle-aged, she guessed. They at least carried change. She could see them struggling with their consciences—her sign helped them along. *Anything helps— even a smile—but we prefer $$!*

On her way to the housing office, she decided to get Christian some new socks—his were finished because he had lost his shoes on one very difficult afternoon and had walked around in his socks all day. Nia would not let him get frostbite again. She ducked into the huge department store, Simon's, on Ste. Catherine street and headed up the escalator to the sock section, right next to the linens, where she meandered for a few minutes. She liked to just go and touch the brand new duvets and sheets. When she and Christian got their own apartment, she'd try to find some of this stuff secondhand. Or maybe when she got a job, she could finally afford to buy it new.

A saleswoman in a tight skirt and an even tighter face moved closer to her, and asked, "*Je peux vous aider?*"

Nia just shook her head, said a bright "*Non, merci!*" and wandered back to the sock section. She knew better than to draw attention to herself. She had to move fast and get out of there, so she stuck three pairs of heavy men's socks down her pants and was already down the escalator and heading to the main exit when she felt the hand on her arm. Security. The next thing she knew he'd called the manager, and the same bitch who'd spotted her upstairs came down, barely able to move in that skirt. She demanded that Nia remove whatever she'd stuffed down her pants. And shirt. Nia refused.

Two cops arrived in minutes, and her heart sank as she recognized one of them. He knew Nia from an older shoplifting incident—and he'd ticketed her and Christian several times for indigence. When you couldn't pay the tickets, which was always, you just spent a night or two in *detention*. That was a euphemism for getting locked in a room by yourself while horny cops said filthy shit to you and made you feel like no shower would ever wash it off. Sometimes the women cops were bad, too. She should've kept her cool. But when Creepy McCreeperson put his hand on her in that store, she'd lost her shit. It had been her problem her whole life—she just couldn't keep her mouth shut when it really mattered.

By the time they released her with a fine and a warning that one more arrest would put her in a whole new category of offense, it was Friday afternoon. She hadn't seen Christian and Hamlet in almost forty-eight hours.

After two coffee refills deeply resented by the manager, Nia stepped out of Mr. Steer and onto Ste. Catherine. It was frigging cold. The sun rarely penetrated the high-rise buildings that lined the street, and now it had been down for a few hours. Nia pulled her jacket tighter and flipped her hood up. Which way should she go? She suddenly recalled a story she heard once. Somewhere in the South Pacific was an island called Yap—Nia loved the name. Certain Yap sailors can navigate from the South Pacific all the way to Japan in a canoe, just by tasting the water. *Tasting* the water. Nia wondered if she could just taste the snow and follow Christian and Hamlet's trail to wherever they had wandered.

Although they didn't usually hang out in Cabot Square, Nia remembered Christian liked the scene there and particularly the shelter Alexis Nihon mall offered—especially in the winter. She decided to walk the twenty or so blocks, tucking her hands into her jacket, chilled raw in the frigid air. Someone had nicked her mittens at this place in the Plateau where they had couch surfed for a few nights. Nia glanced in every doorway and checked every single pile of bedding on her way west. No Christian and Hamlet. She felt a panicky dread begin to overwhelm her, and she stopped to control her breathing again. Christian and Hamlet were what made her matter. If she lost them, she could imagine no future at all.

Cabot Square was pretty deserted for a Saturday night. A couple of cops were sitting in a squad car drinking coffee and keeping an eye out. Nia instinctively gave them a wide berth. She headed towards a few of the street regulars who were hanging around the Atwater metro station doors, sucking on cigarettes and huddling in the warmer air. Two women were in some kind of drunken tussle, while a toothless man pointed at them and laughed uncontrollably. Nia went up to the metro lurkers.

"Hey. I'm looking for a friend of mine. His name's Christian. Tall. Skinny. He has a dog with him. He was maybe looking for a place around here?" Nia pulled out a photograph of Christian and Hamlet he'd given her, taken about three years earlier, and passed it around.

"You seen him? He's with our dog. This dog."

Nia lit a cigarette and offered her pack to the group. They each eagerly grabbed a smoke, all but one tucking it away for later. The picture was passed around but each one shook his head in turn and mumbled various versions of "no." One guy who'd refused the cigarette offer but had watched the scene unfold from his perch on a bench asked to see the photo again. He examined it carefully and then shook his head as well. "Sorry. I didn't see him."

For one moment, Nia felt certain she'd heard that voice before, and was about to ask him if they knew each other, but he was already tucked back into the warmth of his coat, the hood pulled low over his forehead. Nia carefully returned the photo to her pocket and headed back out into the cold. A very light and gentle snow had started to fall, like the kind they create for movies that require a charming winter scene. Nia was just starting to cross the street to go into Alexis Nihon when she felt a strong hand on her shoulder. She turned around, thinking it was the guy who'd asked to see the picture again. Had he recognized Christian after all? But it wasn't. It was the man with the tea. The Good Samaritan. He was a bit out of breath.

"Hey. Nia, isn't it? You need a place to stay tonight?"

Nia shrugged his hand off her and kept walking. "No. I'm good. Just heading to a place I got lined up right now." Then she stopped and turned back to him.

"I'm, um…wondering if you saw my friend around here at all? Christian? I'm usually with him? With the big funny-looking dog?"

Isaac Blum looked at her intently. "Yeah, I saw him here…maybe two nights ago? Not a tea drinker, though, your friend." Nia smiled in spite of herself. "He was hanging out with this guy—I've seen him a few times around here. Then I saw them head off west on de Maisonneuve."

"Together?"

Isaac nodded. "Yeah. I got the impression they had a destination."

Nia tried to figure out where they had in mind. There was Dawson College, but it was always crawling with cops. Isaac Blum squinted off in that direction as though he could see them and exhaled loudly. "There is a church over there. It's been closed for a few months now, but there's a pretty protected spot by the side door—by the alley. You want me to show you?"

Nia walked in silence alongside the Good Samaritan past the old Forum, past Dawson College's main door, and continued two blocks further. The snow was less gentle now, and the few people who were still out hurried by them. As they approached the church, Nia began to feel a terrible sense of dread, and she tried in vain to breathe slowly through the hammering of her heart. Isaac Blum pointed ahead.

"Just along the alley there—there's a kind of recess in the side door. I've seen people there. And if he's not here, we can check St. Léon. There's a shed-type building by the rectory that not too many people know about."

Nia stopped walking and turned to him. "I've got this now, thanks. Thanks for your help."

She waved off the Good Samaritan and watched him go back the way they had come. She made sure of it. At first, Nia couldn't even see the place he was talking about, but as she drew closer, she saw the recessed area by the side door, and in it, she could just make out what looked like the hump of a person in a sleeping bag. Nia started to run, skidding and sliding in the wet, fresh snow. She fell to her knees besides the sleeping bag that she recognized as Christian's, and pulled it away. At first she thought he was just sleeping, and she practically fell on him in relief. But his body was hard, unresponsive. He was frozen. His eyes were half-open, like he was squinting to see something in the distance, and Nia tore away at his layers and layers of clothes to listen for his heart, but she knew. He was dead. Christian was dead. Nia tried to hold him in her arms, but he was so rigid she was terrified he would break into pieces. Rocking back and forth hugging herself, Nia howled and howled in her grief. It was only after a few minutes when she thought she might die herself, that she realized Hamlet wasn't there. He would never have left Christian alone. Never.

# Twenty-One

*Sunday afternoon*
*February 3, 2019*

JEAN-MICHEL COUSINEAU, also known as *Ti-Coune* as long as anyone could remember, was hustling to get everything done before Roméo Leduc came to pick him up. He had cleaned up his tiny kitchen and thrown out whatever was making his fridge stink. His bed was made, and the sheets he had tacked up over the windows of his little bungalow outside Val David were lowered. He turned off the hot water and turned down the heat to ten degrees—enough to keep the pipes from freezing and his plants alive, but not enough to pay the thieves at Hydro-Québec any more than they had already stolen from him. He had also watered all his plants—a veritable indoor garden of herbs, tomatoes, and a few perennials he took in from outside.

In the old days, he would've had nothing but pot plants, but now, Ti-Coune Cousineau, former professional low-life, had turned himself around after the severe beating he took at the hands of his former colleagues, the Hells Angels. He had been clean for seventeen months, two weeks and five days—no booze and no drugs. Just cigarettes. He took one final look around his house to see if he'd forgotten anything. Then he dropped into his old La-Z-Boy chair and started to roll a smoke. Pitoune, his aging but still feisty Chihuahua, and the only one of his three dogs to survive the vicious attack almost two years earlier, jumped into his lap and stared at him anxiously. She knew something was up. He stroked the top of her head and explained what was happening very gently.

"I have to leave you with Manon for a few days." Manon was Ti-Coune's sort of girlfriend who ran a small dog kennel in her home and did landscaping work with Ti-Coune during the six months a year when it was possible. "You'll like it there. I know you will. You'll get to run around with all the other dogs and play. But play nice! You're not as big as you think you are, and someone might play too rough and hurt you." He held her tiny head firmly in his hands. "Am I the only one who knows what a sweet girl you are, really?" He released her and she immediately curled up in his lap. But she didn't fall asleep. She was too wary to do that.

Ti-Coune reached into his jacket pocket and removed the photo that he always carried with him. It was of him and Hélène when they were kids, taken at the Granby zoo—the only photo he had from their entire childhood. They were scowling at the camera because they couldn't afford any cotton candy, and he remembered an elephant tethered by a huge chain rocking back and forth behind them. Then he picked up the flier Roméo Leduc had given him two years earlier—the one of Hélène identified as a missing person in British Columbia. He folded it carefully into a tight square and placed that in his pocket as well. Was it possible she was still alive? And living in Montreal? Why didn't she come to find him? She knew where he was—Ti-Coune had been living in Val David for years—she had even visited him here twelve years ago. He had no family except Hélène and Pitoune. He would go to Montreal and do everything he could to see her again.

Suddenly, Pitoune scrabbled to her feet and hurtled herself towards the front door, snarling and baring her teeth. Ti-Coune heard two short honks. That would be Roméo. He slipped on his jacket, pulled on a tuque and folded his gloves into his pockets. He picked up a small nylon shoulder bag, attached a leash to Pitoune and tucked her under his free arm. Before he turned off all the lights, he took one last look around. For some reason, he kissed the tips of his fingers and touched them to the frame of his front door before he stepped out into the damp February cold. It wasn't much, but this was the only real home Ti-Coune Cousineau had ever had.

# Twenty-Two

HE WOKE UP WITH A START and blinked his eyes repeatedly against the blinding sunshine that was streaming into his bedroom. What *time* was it? He checked his phone, which lay on the floor beside him and was shocked to see it was 10:43 a.m. He had somehow slept for almost ten hours. He hadn't done that in years and years. For once, his sleep had been dreamless, or at least he'd had no dreams or nightmares he could remember, and that was a blessing. Especially not to dream of her.

Today was Sunday, and he loved Sundays because he didn't have to do anything at all. He had no obligations, no work, no places to go and people to see. He slowly and methodically woke up his body; he rolled onto his knees first. Then he stretched out his back and arms in a downward dog, and then up into a cobra. He then asked for permission to stand up and moved into the mountain. He liked to stand in that position for at least three minutes, while he contemplated the inspiring words that he had framed on his wall.

*You are not obligated to complete the work, but neither are you free to abandon it.*

He stepped off his mat and headed towards the bath-room, where he relieved himself. He picked up the filthy clothes he'd left on the bathroom floor, and reminded himself to put them in the incinerator later. After he'd scrubbed his hands, face, and genitals, he headed to the kitchen to see what if anything was in the fridge for breakfast. He paused on his way there before the second of his inspirational quotes.

*If I am only for myself, who am I?*

He put the kettle on for his tea and went to his front door for the morning paper. He looked forward to reading it, hoping perhaps to see any more news about the girl, or even about the boy. As he returned with the paper in hand, he stopped before a very special arrangement on the wall of his small, sparse living room. In perfectly symmetrical order, a collar and attached leash was hanging on a peg, each one exactly four inches apart. The empty peg he had screwed into the wall on Thursday morning now wore a new collar. They didn't need them anymore. Over this display he had framed and mounted the most important words to him of all.

*Stone walls do not a prison make, nor iron bars a cage.*

# Twenty-Three

*Sunday night*

"MIKA? SWEETHEART? Are you coming down for supper? This is the third time I called you. Michaela?!"

She lay in the fading evening light on her bed and remained in the fetal position, hugging her stuffed bear pillow tightly to her.

"I'm doing my homework. I'll come down later."

"WHAT?" She could hear her mother's voice coming up the stairs.

"I. Am. Doing. My. HOMEWORK! I have a huge essay to finish. Just DON'T DISTURB ME!"

Her mother's voice was suddenly right outside her door. "Your *nonna* is here. And she made those cannolis you love."

"Nonna is here every Sunday."

Her mother's voice changed from cajoling to chilly. *"Scendi giù adesso se no ti faccio vedere io!"*

"Okay! I've got to finish this. I'll be down in a bit."

She could hear her mother hesitate at her door, and then retreat back down the stairs. It must have taken every iota of willpower for her not to open the bedroom door and glance in. Michaela had forbidden her from doing this when she turned sixteen, and her mother mostly respected that rule.

Michaela forced herself out of her bed, and collapsed in her chair before her vanity, a rather rococo piece of a bedroom set that her parents had bought her on her thirteenth birthday. She looked at herself in the gilded mirror. She looked normal. But when she tried to run her hands very gingerly through her thick hair her head was so painfully tender she couldn't do it. He had grabbed a fistful of her hair so violently to force her head down that now clumps of long strands of it came away in her fingers. Michaela could still hear him unzipping his fly as he held her head with one hand until both his hands were free. Then he forced her mouth open by pulling on her lip and squeezing her cheek until the pain forced it open, like a man fitting a bit into a horse. He pushed himself so far inside her mouth she thought she would die from choking. When he was finished in her mouth, he pulled her panties down and shoved his fingers in her as far as he could. She felt such intense burning she was afraid she would pass out, but then she suddenly felt the strangest sensation—like she was floating up above her body and watching the whole event from a corner of the room. She stayed there until he began to swear at her, because his fingers were bleeding. She thought he must have cut himself on her somehow. He withdrew his hand and dropped her onto that beautiful carpet she had so admired. He said he was sorry, that he didn't realize she was a virgin. She had vomited then, but for some reason made sure to do it into the tub, not on that carpet. Then he told her to clean herself up and left the room. She couldn't remember how she got home.

Michaela watched her face in her mirror and felt a sob rising in her that terrified her. If she started crying now, she might never stop.

Her phone buzzed again, and Michaela glanced at the messages—there were about a dozen from Brittany—the last one just read *WTF WHERE R U?* Then she picked up her phone and as best she could, snapped pictures of the small bald patch starting to reveal itself on the side of her head. She got up from her chair and gently pulled her pajama bottoms down. There were bruises on her labia and down her thighs. She took pictures of those, too. Then she retrieved her bloody panties from the very back of her drawer and forced herself to take a photo. Her phone rang in her hand. It was Brittany.

"Mika? What the fuck? Where are you? What happened? How was the party? Mika?"

Michaela couldn't make any words form yet. She just kept breathing.

"Mika? Michaela. What is it?"

Michaela returned to her bed and lay on her side. In a very small voice she said, "I should have gone to the hospital, and now it's too late."

"What? Why? What happened? Fuck, Mika, you're scaring me. I'm coming over—"

"NO! Don't come here! I don't want my parents to think there's anything weird going on—"

Brittany's voice went very quiet. "Michaela? Can you tell me what happened?"

Michaela began to tell her friend what had happened to her at Jean Luc David's party. Of course, she didn't tell her everything. That was much too shameful. She would never tell *anyone* everything. After Michaela finished, there was a long silence. Brittany just kept saying how sorry she was it happened. Over and over again.

"Do you want me to come over?"

"NO. I don't want to see anyone. I want to be left alone."

"Mika? He didn't put his penis in you, right? Like there was no…penetration, right? So at least you can't be pregnant. No STDs, either."

There was another long pause. "So it's all good, right, Brit?"

"Oh my God, Mika, I didn't mean it that way."

"I should have gone to the police. Now it's too late." Michaela started to cry, but quietly so her parents wouldn't hear.

"It's not too late, Mika," Brittany assured her, "But I'm not sure you want to do that. I mean, what proof will they find? It's he said–she said—his word against yours, and guess who they'll believe? That's what everyone says. And even if they believe you, you'll have to go to court and tell everything that happened again and again."

"But if I do nothing, he'll do it again. To someone else—"

"They might ask why you went off with him alone—"

"I WASN'T alone—his assistant was there."

Brittany's voice was soft again. "But then she left, and you were alone with him. I am just saying that they often blame the victim for…putting herself in a…situation."

"That was before Me Too. It's different now. But it doesn't matter because I have no real evidence." She didn't say it to Brittany because she couldn't. Mika had brushed her teeth so hard she made her gums bleed. She had swallowed most of a giant bottle of Listerine.

"Jean Luc David is a major player in the industry—"

"DON'T say his name!"

Brittany hesitated. "Devil Man is a major player. You've got something on him now. I would use it. He promised you a part, right? Make sure you get it."

Suddenly Mika wanted desperately to be off the phone.

"I have to go."

"Mika. I'll come over. I can be there in half an hour. You need me!"

"No, Brit. I really don't." Michaela ended the call. A few seconds later, Brittany was calling back. Michaela turned off her phone. She slowly got up from her bed, slid her legs over the side, and pulled off her pajama bottoms. Then she grabbed a pair of baggy work-out pants, slipped on a well-worn oversized T-shirt, and went to her vanity to wipe her face and add a little cover up. She opened her bedroom door to the laughing and arguing sounds of her family downstairs.

# Twenty-Four

*Monday morning*
*February 4, 2019*

DANIELLE WAS TRYING TO FOCUS on the words coming out of the very bright and well-painted lips of the young woman sitting across from her, who was wearing a shocking amount of TV makeup. She was so utterly cheerful and earnest that Danielle felt like giggling. What did she just say? Danielle hadn't slept much the night before, and when she didn't get her six hours in, she couldn't be fully functional, no matter how many espressos she poured down her throat. She had spent all weekend obsessively checking all the Montreal newspapers, French and English, looking for any information about the woman in the tunnel. It had been just over a week, and there was nothing. Nothing more about her. Like she had never existed. Had she hallucinated the whole report she'd seen in the first place? She'd had another nightmare so awful and terrifying that she was scared to fall asleep and experience anything like it again. She obsessively worried about CCTV cameras—like the ones she'd seen on British murder mysteries—where they can easily track the criminal on any street *anywhere* it seemed. She poured over the *Ville de Montréal* website and discovered that there was a camera at the exit of the tunnel, but at least a block away. Could they track her car coming out? Could they see her license plate? Was she on camera driving *into* the tunnel? Could they check her computer and see her search history looking for the fucking cameras? Every time her phone rang or buzzed she was terrified the police were calling. Did she kill that woman? She killed that woman. She *killed that woman*—

"Danielle Champagne, not only are you a lifestyle guru, a fashionista, and an entrepreneur who empowers women to be fearless and pursue their dreams, but you are also embarking on yet *another* project." The interviewer's tone changed completely. Now it was somber and sincere. She leaned in. "Tell us about this new, very important organization you have created," she checked her notes, "called *Ça Suffit*?"

Danielle offered her a tight smile, uncrossed her legs and leaned closer. "As you know, *Ça Suffit* means *That's Enough.*" And that is what our organization is saying—we have seen too many women fall victim to domestic, to conjugal violence, and it has to stop. The statistics are horrifying. Did you know that a woman or girl was killed every two-and-a-half days in Canada last year?" Danielle's voice softened. "I have an eighteen-year-old daughter—my only child. Did you know that for women between eighteen and twenty-five, the leading cause of death is conjugal violence? Did you know that conjugal femicide is not treated as seriously by the authorities, because women killed by male partners are still seen as *property*? They call it the 'intimacy discount.' Can you imagine?" Danielle noticed the producer tapping his watch at the interviewer. Time was up. "Women are still most at risk with men they are intimate with or who they should be able to trust."

The interviewer had to shift emotional gears quickly. "One last question, Danielle Champagne. How on earth do you *do* it all?" Danielle had answered this question so many times she was on verbal automatic pilot. "Good sex, good sleep, good coffee," she paused for effect, "and although I am a woman, great big gonads." The interviewer laughed a little too long and enthusiastically, and then kissed Danielle on both cheeks to thank her. Within seconds, she was on to her next guest.

Danielle decided to take a few minutes to check her emails in the lounge they provided for visitors, and sat down on a bright orange plastic chair. A young man already in the room—a later guest she presumed—was thumbing so madly on his phone he didn't even look up when she came in.

Maybe someone else had hit the woman. Hers wasn't the only car in the tunnel that night. There must have been dozens. Hundreds. But Danielle thought about the damage to her Lexus that she'd had fixed. Like a criminal, she went to a shop in St. Eustache far from her home, and the guy fixed it right then and there on the spot. She had paid him in cash. He folded the bills into his pocket without saying anything. But what was she expecting him to say? Did you just hit someone with this car and leave her there to die? Danielle wondered if he could identify her later. A ping from her phone pulled her out of her speculation, and she quickly tapped out a response to her assistant, Chloé. She had to focus on her work now.

At first she thought she'd turn herself in. Go to the police and tell them exactly what happened. There was a blizzard.

She didn't see her. She came out of nowhere. She thought it was a dog. Too scared to stop. It was wrong not to stop, she knew that, but she just couldn't. It was an honest, a *human* mistake. But if she turned herself in, the press would go wild. Her reputation would be destroyed. So would her business and everything else she had. Because in the end, the product Danielle Champagne was selling so successfully in Canada and all over the world, was herself. What possible good would her confession do? It would not change anything. Except Julie's life would be destroyed, her dream of the Sorbonne or Oxford shattered. Not to mention the hundreds—and soon, thousands—of people working for Danielle whose jobs would be on the line. Her confession would only destroy. It would not bring anyone back. It would not be just. It would not be *right*.

Danielle returned her phone to her purse and gathered her coat and gloves. As she headed for the door towards the elevators, she glanced up at one of the several large screens which were mounted on one wall of the lounge. At the bottom of the screen the caption read: *Victim of Hit-and-Run Identified*. On the screen was an out of focus picture of a young woman in a white parka, standing on a huge rock by a lake, smiling broadly at the photographer. She looked to be Indian. Or maybe Inuit. *Twenty-six-year-old Rosie Nukilik.* Danielle felt like someone had sucker punched her hard in the stomach. Now she had a name.

# Twenty-Five

ROMÉO WAS GRATEFUL TO BE ALONE in his car and heading to Station 12 downtown. He was listening to the fantastically eclectic classical music station *la première chaîne*, which was always restorative. Sometimes Roméo felt that if he had another few lives to live, he would certainly have been a concert violinist in one of them. Of course, he'd never taken music lessons. His father forced him into playing hockey, like all Quebecois boys did. When it was clear that Roméo had a special talent for it in spite of himself, his father made sure that dream wouldn't come true. After Roméo's coach explained he had won a life-changing hockey scholarship, Roméo's father turned it down. Roméo supposed that was his way of reminding him of the total control he had over his life—the perverse, arbitrary power. He had dangled that treat in front of Roméo then snatched it away, like a naughty child with a hungry dog. Imagine if he'd asked his parents for *violin* lessons. His father would have laughed in his face and then smacked him right across the room.

Roméo turned up the volume on the sublime Brahms concerto. How was it possible that these extraordinary sounds could just materialize in someone's head? How did a person express that kind of heartache and yearning by vibrating strings on a box of wood? They say that the violin is the instrument that sounds most like the human voice, but Roméo needed to hear no human voice for at least a few more minutes before his work day really began. He had driven Ti-Coune Cousineau into Montreal from Val David yesterday afternoon, and Ti-Coune had not stopped talking the entire way in. He had been clean and sober for eighteen months now, and he was like a convert to a new religion. He kept talking about the evils of his old life and his devotion to no more soul-sickening booze and dope in his new life. Roméo wondered if he himself had been this insufferable when he quit smoking two years ago. The difference was that Roméo didn't want to proselytize against smoking—he still craved a cigarette at least once a week, and still woke up inhaling the phantom aroma of cigarettes on his pillow. He did notice though that Ti-Coune's resistance to bodily desecration stopped at cigarettes. He must have rolled and consumed half a dozen on the way in to Montreal, blowing the clouds of smoke out of his window, opened just a crack against the cold air.

Still, Roméo was impressed that he had kicked a few habits that pursue and eventually kill so many people, and given Ti-Coune's abusive background, it was a minor miracle. Roméo had also heard through the village grapevine that Ti-Coune was becoming a highly sought-after landscaper, which could be a lucrative business with the rich Anglos who had either no time or inclination to do the yard work around their "country" houses. Roméo, who had a deep and abiding appreciation of irony, marveled at how a man who had been so unnurtured, a man who had been refused almost every opportunity to grow his entire life, had a real gift for growing things. The one thing they did not discuss much, was the one thing—or person—who had brought this unlikely pair together in the first place. The search for Hélène Cousineau.

Roméo had dropped Ti-Coune off outside a three-story brownstone that was clearly down on its luck. A crooked *Chambres à Louer* sign hung from its second floor window. It was two blocks away from Cabot Square where many of the Inuit homeless population of Montreal hung out, so Ti-Coune would be right in the thick of things, Roméo thought. If Roméo's spotty memory of grade 8 history served him well, explorer John Cabot, a.k.a. Giovanni Caboto, made a claim to the land in Canada for English King Henry VII, mistaking it for Asia, during his 1497 voyage. He was the first of many who thought he'd found China. There was even a bedroom community a few short miles from downtown Montreal named *Lachine*.

Roméo had dropped off Ti-Coune after they had agreed to check in with each other over the next few days and share whatever they had learned about Hélène's whereabouts, and anything they might find out about the hit-and-run case. Then he went to pick up a few necessary supplies and groceries, and headed to the two-bedroom flat he had rented for a few weeks for himself and Sophie. He was hoping that if he could get her away from the situation she would realize she had to be rid of that idiot boyfriend forever. But when he got to the flat she was on the phone with said idiot and ended the call with a furtive kiss when Roméo arrived. He felt such sadness and frustration with his daughter that *he* felt like throttling her. He had tried to talk to her about it, tried to use all the skills he had learned in domestic violence sensitivity training—but Roméo knew it was more nuanced and complex than he could understand. What was it about Sophie? He had tried to be a good father. He had been as present in her life as he could. He knew she always came to him if she was in real distress. She had been given everything she wanted—her wealthy stepfather had made certain of that. But still, her sense of self-worth was diminished enough that she didn't feel she deserved to be loved by someone who didn't scare her. Who didn't hurt her.

Roméo suddenly needed to talk to Marie. Why hadn't he told her about Sophie? Was he trying to protect her from Marie's—what? Disapproval? Judgment? Or from Marie jumping right into the fray with both feet and alienating Sophie further? He hated that he and Marie had argued on Saturday night—he always felt *unbalanced* after an argument with her. He had to put it right or he would feel incomplete until he saw her again. He knew he had to make a decision about their life together, but just now he felt he could not—he had too many plates spinning in the air and he didn't want any one of them to break. The call to Marie went right to her voice mail. Roméo checked the time—she must be in class. Did she occupy too large a place in his life? Roméo was not the hopeless romantic like his namesake. He had always been guarded with his feelings, always protected his heart, even with his wife, Elyse. Maybe that's why he found her in his bed with her high-school sweetheart.

With Marie, he had let himself go so much further than he ever had—but it seemed like it was never enough for her. Did she want *all* of him? That's what it sometimes felt like. But Roméo knew that wasn't a fair depiction of Marie, either. Now who was being the drama queen? Roméo quickly compartmentalized his personal life and packed it away as he pulled up to Station 12 on Stanton Street. He squeezed into a spot alongside a couple of squad cars and put his Sûreté du Québec sticker on the windshield. Hopefully that wouldn't inspire any of the cops inside to smash it.

Roméo made his way directly to Detective Cauchon's office. He appeared to be wearing the same suit and the same smug expression as the first time Roméo saw him. He sank his bulk into his chair, which sighed under the weight of him. He dropped a blue folder on his desk and opened it up.

"Her name is Rosie Nuk...Nuk-ilik. She is twenty-six years old and from," he hesitated over the word, "Salluit. Actually, that's an easy one to pronounce compared to the other names up there."

Roméo looked at the photograph of the young woman. "And who finally identified her?"

Cauchon leaned back in his chair and swallowed the last of his Tim Hortons coffee.

"A case worker—Annie Qin. Qinn. Uak—from the Le Foyer shelter. She's known her for about a year now." Roméo jotted down the information.

"I don't think there's a whole lot more you're gonna find on this one. We checked the CCTV cameras in the area—"

"And?" Roméo tried to move him along a bit faster.

"And...a hundred and sixteen cars went through that tunnel in a twelve-hour period coinciding with estimated time of death. That's nothing, of course compared to the traffic there would normally be in that area. When the biggest storm in the last five years isn't happening. However. We couldn't get any plates because the snow on the cameras either obliterated a clear view, and/or snow covered the plates."

Roméo said a quiet "*Merde.*"

"That's right, *mon ami*. Now, if you want to look up the…" Cauchon brought up a file on his laptop. "Fourteen Hondas, thirty-seven Toyotas, twelve Volvos, three Lexuses, one Tesla, etcetera…, etcetera…who went through that tunnel in those twelve hours—be my guest. We do have one officer on that right now." He nodded in the direction of someone across the room.

"I had a chance to read the medical examiner's report very carefully. It was clear to me that this could very well be a homicide. She was asphyxiated. Probably after the collision—"

Cauchon cut him off. "The report was inconclusive. There was no recommendation for the coroner to proceed further. We would like to know who hit her, though, and we are pursuing it."

Roméo leaned onto the desk. "So you are telling me, that despite significant evidence suggesting homicide, you will not investigate it further?"

Detective Cauchon looked at Roméo evenly. "No. I am telling you we are pursuing a hit-and-run."

"If this young woman was white and not marginal, you'd be on this like a bloodhound."

Cauchon smiled. "I find that a very offensive statement, Chief Inspector Leduc. We have all had our aboriginal sensitivity training."

"Looks like it didn't take."

"And despite your having no jurisdiction here, and your *marginal* connection to the case, I will show you the courtesy of introducing you to Officer Pouliot. He is investigating the hit-and-run." Cauchon stood up and buttoned his jacket over his substantial *bédaine.*

"Thank you for coming in. We're always happy to help the Sûreté."

Roméo couldn't very well stay behind in Cauchon's office so he had no choice but to follow him to the tiny and very tidy desk of a young uniformed officer. Roméo pulled up a chair. He could feel the eyes of every cop in that room watching. And every ear listening. Roméo explained who he was and his interest in the case. In a lowered voice he also added that he was almost certain this was a homicide. Officer Pouliot looked up from his computer sharply. He said nothing, but his eyes were clear. Roméo got the message. "Let's step out to the canteen, shall we? I need some more bad coffee."

Officer Pouliot, who insisted Roméo call him Steve, was very slight and very short—almost the size of a jockey. That cannot have been easy for him in police academy, or on the job either, Roméo thought. Neither one of them got a coffee.

"I know that you are on the Rosie Nukilik hit-and-run case. I think there is substantial evidence of deliberate traumatic asphyxiation. I think someone sat on her and choked the life out of her."

Steve Pouliot raised both eyebrows but said nothing.

"There doesn't seem to be much interest in this possibility, but I intend to look into it further, so anything you can share with me would be very appreciated." Roméo removed his card and placed it on the canteen table. Pouliot played with it in his hand as though he was not sure he'd pocket it. He leaned towards Roméo and spoke quietly.

"Two other women—*both* twenty-six years old and *both*

Inuit have died under suspicious circumstances in the last four months. Vickee Quissak and Shannon Amittuk. Vickee was deemed accidental, and Shannon a suicide." His voice lowered even more. "You did *not* hear this from me. Shannon was found in circumstances that would suggest foul play, but there was no further investigation."

Roméo looked him straight in the eye. "And why didn't you insist there be an investigation?" Pouliot smiled tightly and shook his head.

"Let's just say there's not much *motivation* around here to look into these deaths."

"Was the suspicious death—Shannon…Amittuk possibly committed by the same person? Was she asphyxiated?"

"I would have to say no. The MO is different. I have their files. I can get them to you. But if anyone ever asks, I know *nothing* about this. It's been hard enough."

Officer Pouliot got up from the table, all five feet of him, and headed towards the door without looking back. Roméo felt outraged, especially after what the Viens Commission exposed about treatment of First Nations and Inuit women at the hands of the police in Quebec. It seemed like nothing at all had changed. But he was out of his jurisdiction, and Rosie Nukilik was not a cold case, so Roméo's hands were officially tied. He could only ask himself what the hell was going on here. He promised himself he'd find out.

# Twenty-Six

LUCKILY, MARIE HAD her go-to fun fact lecture ready to rock today, because everything else she had carefully planned for her class that morning had gone awry. So, she got to share some of the many stories about humpback whales that had led her to devote much of her life to their study. "Humpbacks are known for singing loud, complex 'songs' and the sounds they make are the most varied in the animal kingdom, ranging from high-pitched squeals and whistles to deep, rumbling gurgles." Marie played a few minutes of song for the class. "Someone once described it as the sound of a violin crossed with a Wookiee." There was a burst of laughter across the room. "Only the males actually sing. We're not certain why yet, but we think they do it to attract females or to challenge other males—to let them know it's their territory. Amazingly, each population of humpbacks communicates in its own dialect, and sings its own whale song. A humpback's song can be heard as far as thirty kilometers away." Marie paused for effect. "But a Blue whale, the largest mammal that ever lived—and the length of three school buses end to end—can be heard *across the Atlantic ocean*—by other Blue whales, of course. Humpbacks are known to repeat the same song over and over again for hours. One was recorded singing for twenty-two hours straight. Imagine trying that yourselves." Marie's class chuckled again.

"And without vocal cords, don't forget." Marie paused and then asked, "Who has something to add?"

A dozen hands shot up. "Whale lungs are the size of small cars."

"Humpback whale migration can be twelve thousand miles long—from Samoa to the Antarctic."

Marie let the students share a few more facts, and then she checked her watch. Five minutes left. "Are there any questions so far?"

One student's hand shot up. "How long do whales live?"

Marie looked out at the class of young, earnest faces. "Can anyone answer that?"

If Michaela Cruz had been there, she would've offered an encyclopedic response. But one girl with carrot red hair and a prominent nose ring said, "It depends. Do you mean in captivity or in the wild?"

The boy looked puzzled. "I don't know. In the wild, I guess." The girl went on to explain quite concisely that captive whales die younger, but of course whales in the wild are vulnerable to predators, disease, boat strikes, and entanglement in nets. A budding teacher herself, Marie thought. But now she was starting to lecture the class, and that was Marie's job.

"Our time is almost up, so I'll leave you with this mind-blowing fact about how long whales can live." She began to collect her papers, glasses, and phone. "A few months ago, the tip of a two-hundred-year-old harpoon was found in a bowhead whale in the Canadian Arctic. *Two hundred years old.* Which of course means the whale was at least that old."

One student raised his hand. "How did the whale die?"

Marie responded in a matter-of-fact tone. "She was killed in the hunt up in Nunavut."

The same student's mouth opened incredulously. "Like, recently?? People are still killing them? How are they allowed to do that?"

"The Inuit are still allowed to hunt."

The class reacted indignantly. "That's disgusting."

Marie shushed them with a hand. "It was the first bowhead whale killed in eight years. It will feed hundreds of people in that area."

Marie glanced out the classroom door. The next class was impatiently waiting to be allowed in. "As we've talked about for three weeks now, the Indigenous whale hunt cannot be compared to the wholesale slaughter and near eradication of whales by...well, by people like me. And by me, I mean white people of European ancestry. So *I* can't get too self-righteous about the Inuit hunting them." The class broke out in little circles of discussion, which almost salvaged the morning for Marie. A few stragglers hung on to chat at her desk, but with the next class coming in, she made a quick exit and escaped to her office.

Marie sat at her desk fuming. She had been so excited to get to class, as Michaela's presentation was that morning, and she had prepared a class activity that should've been very successful, based on the content of Michaela's paper. Marie checked her work emails again, but Michaela had left her no messages, no apology for not bothering to show up that morning. She had asked of few of her classmates if they'd seen her, but they claimed to have no idea where she was. Marie knew it was possible that an emergency had come up. But she had experienced this kind of bullshit behavior way too many times. Almost as though he had picked up Marie's disappointment on his teacher radar, Simon came sidling into her office. He bit into an apple and between chews pronounced "Well, seventy-eight percent of my class failed their first test. I guess that makes me a pretty bad teacher."

Marie smiled ruefully at her colleague. "The worst." She could've let it go there, but she wanted to get her own complaining in. "If it makes you feel any better, I got stood up *again* by a student I really like and whose work is terrific. She just didn't show. No message, no nothing."

Simon dropped the apple core in Marie's wastebasket. "Did her grandmother die?" Teachers often joked about their students having at least four grandparents and several emergency spares considering how many suddenly took sick and died in the course of the year.

Marie shook her head. "I'm just really pissed."

Simon started in on a litany of his recent disappointments when Cassandra, another of their colleagues from down the hall, stuck her head in Marie's door.

"Hey. Did you guys hear? They found a body at that closed down church two blocks from here. I was walking past it on Saturday—there was like a huge crime scene or something going on—yellow tape, people in hazmat suits. It was like fricken CSI."

"Wow. Do they know what happened?" Simon asked.

"I haven't seen anything on the news yet," Marie offered.

"It was a man. A young man, I heard. Probably homeless. It's so sad."

"Very sad." Simon added.

They waited for Marie's response. Marie didn't feel she had anything more to add to the conversation. Disappointed, her two colleagues left her office and kept chatting as they walked down the hall. Marie picked up her phone and checked the breaking Montreal news. There was nothing she could find about the body near the college. But then a face appeared on her screen that she recognized. She immediately tapped in his number. He answered on the fourth ring.

"Marie? Is everything okay?" Marie rarely called him during the day.

"Oh my God, Roméo. I just saw her picture on the news!"

"Who?"

"The girl who was hit by the car—Rosie Nuk-ilik? They just showed her on the news—"

"Yes, they've finally identified her."

"I know her from Alexis Nihon—I used to see her at the McDonald's sometimes. And, and *around*. I mean, I don't *know* her, I never talked to her, but I recognized her white parka—it has this very distinctive, beautiful embroidery on it. It's why I noticed her, maybe." Marie stopped and thought about what she'd just said. "It's just fucking *awful*." Marie heard a beeping on Roméo's phone.

"I have another call I have to take. We'll talk later, okay? I'd like you to tell me everything you can remember about this woman." Roméo cut her off. She stared dumbly at her phone for a few seconds, and then up at the photos narrating highlights of her life on her office wall. She realized that she really knew nothing about Rosie Nukilik that would be helpful at all.

# Twenty-Seven

*Tuesday night*
*February 5, 2019*

JEAN LUC DAVID lifted a glass of Veuve Clicquot and turned to each of his distinguished guests. *"Nastrovnya! L'Chaim! Santé!* Cheers! Did I miss one?" They all raised their glasses in confirmation and almost in unison swallowed the champagne. Dima Golikov downed his in one gulp. His girlfriend barely touched the glass to her lips, as she knew one of them had to stay sober. Cheryl Wiseman, the showrunner for *Nasty Women*, somehow inhaled the bubbles and snorted champagne through her nose. Her wife hustled Cheryl away to the bathroom to clean up the spray she'd showered herself with. Jean Luc sipped from his glass after first making meaningful eye contact with Margeaux, who was a stickler for such protocol. Then he took a moment to appreciate his surroundings. Gennifer has secured them a private room at Touché, one of the most exclusive and difficult restaurants in the city to get a reservation. Seated across from him was his American producer and his wife. Next to them was Mylène, who was on the cusp of mega fame as Quebec's latest homegrown pop diva, and who went by her first name only. Jean Luc had scored a major coup when she'd agreed to perform the theme song for their new season. He wondered if she could act, too. Maybe she could be the lead in his *Filles du Roi* series. Although the people who frequented Touché were used to seeing *vedettes*, he couldn't help but notice the patrons at other tables staring— even for the blasé elite, this collection of stars was unusual and impressive. Jean Luc took Margeaux's hand and kissed it very tenderly. Sometimes, it felt like life couldn't get much better. Suddenly three waiters appeared with several platters of *fruits de mer, charcuterie,* and of course for Cheryl and her wife, a plate of *végétalien* food. Jean Luc could not understand how anyone would willfully choose to eat that vegan sawdust, but he made sure it was available at all times to Cheryl. He knew that without her, his show was dead in the water. She and her wife returned to the table and made no attempt to hide their disgust at the plate of meat before them. Jean Luc was about to offer another exuberant toast when he noticed Gennifer standing discreetly with the *maître d'* near the entrance to the room. She tapped her right index finger to her temple, their code for: direct communication is required immediately. He excused himself and made his way towards her. She turned on her heel, headed back to the main part of the restaurant, and waited for him in a corner of the service bar.

"*Qu'est-ce que tu fais ici?* What are you doing here?" Jean Luc took Gennifer by the elbow and led her further down the bar, away from any possible eavesdropping.

"I'm sorry to interrupt, but I texted you a bunch of times and you didn't answer—"

"I'm trying to focus on my *guests*, who if you've noticed are very key people to *our* future success, so I have not been checking my phone every five minutes. What is it that's so important?" He removed his glasses and rubbed his eyes. Gennifer thought how very old and tired he looked sometimes.

"That girl—the one who you invited to um...read for, you know, a very small role for next season."

"Yes. What? What about her?" Jean Luc glanced quickly around the room, then returned his attention to Gennifer.

"Michaela Cruz. Her name is Michaela Cruz."

"Yes. I remember her. So?"

"Her friend—someone named Brittany—She messaged me and...." Gennifer took a deep breath and continued. "She said that you sexually assaulted her friend at the Diamond in the Rough party. And, she demanded I tell you that they will go to the police if *we* do not agree to meet with her tomorrow."

Jean Luc did not respond at first, and then in an almost stage whisper, he answered. "What the hell are you saying? What is she talking about? You were there. She looked at a contract. I explained what we were looking for. She excused herself to go to the bathroom, I went back to the party. I guess she left. That's it, that's all."

Gennifer looked down the bar for a moment and focused on the animated conversation between the bartender and a patron. "Um. J.L? I wasn't there the whole time. You were alone with her."

"No, Gennifer, you were there the whole time." Jean Luc David almost smiled. "You know, it is the little bitches like her who get away with this shit. Who knows what they imagine in their fucked up little heads? I cannot be responsible for that."

"She said you forced her friend to perform oral sex on you."

Jean Luc slammed his hand on the bar, hard. "Have you seen my wife? Do you think I need some stupid little girl with stars in her eyes to suck my cock?"

There was a long pause. Gennifer kept her gaze even with his, and then she had to look away. "I guess she wants some money. Or that contract signed immediately. Or a more... prominent part in the show?"

"It's disgusting what depths certain people will sink to. I have always been a target."

"Women...misunderstand your charm. And your power, Jean Luc—"

"Exactly!"

Gennifer touched his hand ever so briefly. "So. What do you want to do?"

Jean Luc smiled and kissed her hand with the lightest touch of his lips. "I want you to deal with it. The way you always do."

He turned away from her and without hesitation returned to his guests.

# Twenty-Eight

NIA FELLOWS SAT ON one of the reliable but weary-looking armchairs in The Bunker. A solicitous social worker had just brought her a cup of steaming tea and now sat across from her looking very concerned. Nia was exhausted beyond whatever exhausted was. She kept feeling Christian's frozen body in her arms. How he felt like he might break into a hundred pieces. How that beautiful man she loved so much was completely absent from that horror by the church. She couldn't remember how long she sat there with him, but she finally realized she had to go and get help. She ran to Alexis Nihon mall and begged for someone to call 911. But no one would. They took one look at filthy and terrified Nia and practically ran the other way. Finally, one man stopped and offered her his phone. After that, everything seemed to happen so fast and so slowly, like one of those surreal movies where you're not sure what's real or what's a dream.

Therese, the social worker leaned closer. "Nia? What did the police say? Will there be an investigation?"

Nia answered in a flat monotone, as though any expression in her voice was too exhausting. "They took me to the station. Asked me a lot of questions." Nia stopped to take a breath. "They made me feel like I did it." Nia looked down at her feet. "And I did. I knew he wasn't in good shape that day. But I really wanted to get to the housing office, and Christian would slow me down. I should never have left him alone. Never!" On this last word, Nia's voice finally broke. Therese took the teacup from Nia's red, chapped hands and tried to hold her, but Nia felt repulsed by that much contact and tucked herself tighter in the chair. A few of the kids had gathered on the periphery and were listening intently to Nia's story.

"One of the cops was actually very kind—now that Christian is dead." Nia's voice had returned to that deadly monotone.

"Did they say they suspect foul play? Did someone hurt him?"

"I don't know. Their questions were weird. They kept asking me if anyone would want to harm Christian." Nia finally made eye contact. "Who would want to hurt him?"

Therese, stroked Nia's hands very gently. "No one. Christian was very special."

"That man—the Good Samaritan? He...told me—that night—that some guy was hanging out with Christian and took him to that...place by the church. I'd like to know who that guy was."

"Did you tell that to the police?"

"Yes, I did. But. I have no…description. It was weird, though. I stopped outside the metro station—at Atwater. I asked some people there if they'd seen Christian and Hamlet. Gave them my last smokes. And. One of them…seemed like, familiar to me. Like I knew him from someplace else. Where he was somebody else. More his voice than anything. I just feel like I knew that voice." Nia looked off into the distance. "And, like, what was the Good Samaritan doing there—"

"Isaac, you mean?"

"Yeah. There's something wrong with him. I just feel like, like he was almost following me. Like he *knew*."

Therese took the empty cup from Nia's clasped hands and placed it on the floor.

"Isaac is…I think Isaac is pretty harmless. But I can see how his…devotion might strike you as a bit creepy."

"They just took Christian away like…that. Like he was nothing. Like he was a bag of garbage. I didn't even get to see him again—and I have to. I have to let his family know, don't I? His family doesn't know. But he ran away from them—he hated them. But he loved them, too, I know it. Oh my God, someone has to tell his mother."

"I would think the police have notified his family, Nia. You know they will probably ask you back to ask a few more questions." Therese pulled a card from her pocket. "This guy… Detective Pouliot came by here and left me his card."

"The police aren't gonna do anything." She hesitated and then added, "I don't want to talk to the cops again. I have so many tickets I haven't paid—they'll arrest me again. I know they will. I owe like a thousand dollars!"

Therese tried to comfort her. "Nia? I can talk to the police for you." She hesitated before asking the next question.

"Would you like to call someone? Is there any…family or… someone that you'd like to call?"

Nia thought of her family. There were only the three of them. Her mom, Janey, who Nia remembers teaching her to read by the time she was three. Nia's first book was *Hazel's Amazing Mother*, about a mother who defends her daughter against bullies. Nia loved the book because she had an even more amazing mother—who knew how to keep beehives, raise chickens, and do a perfect swan dive into the little pond behind their house. Nia worshipped her. Her father, Gavin, had built their little house on a few acres of weedy land outside of Lennoxville, a busy university town two hours southeast of Montreal. He did odd jobs around the town, but mostly worked at home. An avid birdwatcher, Gavin could entice the chickadees and jays and even crows to come to him and eat out of his hand. He taught Nia how to save a bird when it hit a window and knocked itself out. He would hold it in his two hands, and jiggle it around, all the while asking, "What's your name, little bird? Come on, tell me your phone number. Wake up!" Nia couldn't remember a single bird who didn't come back to life in her father's hands and fly off frantically back into the trees when he released them. It wasn't until Nia was eleven years old that she found out what her parents actually did for a living.

"I have no family to call."

Her mother was in a halfway house in St. Jerome, after serving three years in a detention center in Laval. Nia hadn't seen her in almost four years. Her father was arrested after a high-speed chase with three Sûreté du Québec cars, which lasted, amazingly, for seventy-three kilometers down the Eastern Townships highway. They got him with several kilos of heroin in the trunk of his old Volvo. That night, Nia waited with her mother in their beautiful little house for her father to call. He never did. Two days later, Nia's mother was arrested. That was when she discovered that her gentle, funny, and eccentric parents were almost single-handedly responsible for the epidemic of heroin amongst the local college crowd.

"I have to find Hamlet. Do you think he's dead?"

"I don't know, Nia. I think it's possible he's still alive. I'm just not sure what more you can do to find him."

After Christian's death, Nia had had an explosion of energy fueled by adrenaline and shock. She had called the Montreal SPCA so many times they started blocking her calls. She had also called every shelter she could Google, but not one of them had Hamlet. She had roamed every block in the area where they found Christian, but no Hamlet. She asked everyone she knew on the street if they'd seen him or heard anything about him. She insisted the people at several shelters and missions put Hamlet on their websites and Facebook pages. Then she had literally collapsed at The Bunker. She was haunted by what might have happened to him. Was he run over by a car? Was he in a ditch somewhere, dumped by someone who couldn't care less? Did someone take him to hurt him? Torture him? These images played over and over in her head until Nia felt like she would implode with worry and grief. But that morning, as the bright light of another sunny winter day dappled the floor of the lounge at The Bunker, she closed her eyes. As Therese covered her in a fleecy kids' blanket covered in smiley faces that someone had donated, Nia Fellows finally fell into a deep and dreamless sleep.

# Twenty-Nine

*Wednesday afternoon*

TI-COUNE COUSINEAU SUNK HIS TEETH into the doughy sesame seed bagel that was still warm from the wood oven at Fairmount Bagel. They had been baking their bagels exactly the same way for almost 100 years. Each one was cut from a batch of dough, hand pulled and rolled, dropped in a water-and-honey infusion, and then rolled in any one of several savory toppings. Then they lined them up on a long wooden board and baked them in a wood-burning oven that was perfectly calibrated to produce a bagel crispy on the outside, and soft on the inside. Some people liked them best with lox, cream cheese, and a bit of onion. But Ti-Coune loved them like this, unadorned and eaten straight from the paper bag they came in. He remembered reading in an Anglo newspaper that there were heated debates about New York versus Montreal bagels—but everybody knew that Montreal's were the best. The rivalry between Fairmount Bagel and St.Viateur Bagel barely two blocks away, however, was one that the *Montréalais* would never allow to end. He walked west along

Fairmount, his boots crunching in the hard packed snow of the sidewalk. By the time he hit Park Avenue and crossed over into Outremont, he had started his second bagel—this time a poppy seed, his second favorite—and he realized his feet were somehow taking him to the place he hadn't been to in more than twenty-five years. Everything was different now, and somehow nothing was. There were fewer Greek restaurants now, as they had moved out of the area to Park Extension about fifteen blocks north. There were many more cafés and some swankier shops—the kind Ti-Coune would never have dreamed of going to as a kid, and would be too intimidated to even think of stepping into now. But as he approached his old street, the same orthodox Jewish guys whose ancestors arrived 100 years ago were still hustling from one place to another, wearing those the big furry hats covered in plastic to protect them from the winter. Girls who barely looked old enough to be mothers were still pushing their kids in strollers, three or four more kids hanging off of them.

He took one final bite and crumpled the empty bag into his pocket. The bagel was the taste of his childhood—or one taste of his childhood, anyway. The other was Kraft dinner. The dirty feet smell of that orange powder cheese mixed in with the noodles, and his mother made it with water, not milk, and almost no margarine. Cigarettes blended with his mother's *Charlie* perfume. Hélène's patchouli oil. And infusing it all, the ammonia smell of cat pee. And suddenly, there it was. The building where Ti-Coune grew up. Or down. It was much nicer, now. The façade had been sandblasted and the red brick almost sparkled in the winter sun. The black wrought-iron balconies looked freshly painted, and all the windows looked quite new. There were no sheets in the windows, but proper curtains and blinds. Even their shitty basement apartment had a brand new red door and an address with a number he could actually see. For a few brief seconds, Ti-Coune thought he might knock on the door and ask to see the place. But what would that do? Probably some rich kids lived there now, and the place would be all fixed up with Ikea furniture or something.

Instead, he lit a cigarette from the packet of rollies he kept in his jacket and took deep drags off it as that day came back to him. He was coming home from school, and he walked right into Hélène and his mother going at it again. He remembered blocking his ears and running to the room he and his sister shared, but the screaming was so loud he came back out to see Hélène get backhanded right across the kitchen. She hit her head so hard on the corner of the table, a cut above her eye opened and was bleeding terribly. His mother just stared at her, trying to catch her breath, and then started warning Hélène to stay away from her man or she'd kill her the next time. Then his mother grabbed her coat and took off out the door, first grabbing her smokes and this green vinyl purse that he and Hélène had saved up several months to buy her from the little jobs they did in the neighborhood.

Ti-Coune helped his sister to the bathroom and tried to clean her cut as best he could. She obviously needed stitches—but she shook him off her and went to start packing her things. It wasn't the first time she'd been hit; in fact, this time was pretty tame compared to others, but Hélène had had enough. Ti-Coune kept insisting their mother would come home and suck up to her like she usually did—either with fresh bagels, or a new candy Pez, or the promise of going to a movie. When she wasn't drinking she could be very nice—especially to Ti-Coune. Hélène was really the object of her hatred and resentment. Maybe because Hélène had interrupted the party life their mother still wanted and thought she deserved.

He lit a second cigarette off the first one and closed his eyes for a few seconds. In all the years they'd lived there, he had not once stood up for Hélène. He was ten years old the first time she ran away—old enough to help her—but he was too scared. He did nothing. The next thing he knew Hélène was gone and he was left to take care of his mother alone.

Ti-Coune abruptly turned away from the building and started back east towards Park Avenue. He could hop on the #80 bus and head south. Then he would start heading west go to the place where everybody used to know his fucking name, like that show *les anglais* liked so much on TV. If Hélène was alive and here in Montreal, then he would find her. He would find her and ask her how she could walk out on her little brother. He would find her and ask for her forgiveness.

# Thirty

MARIE TRIED NOT TO BREATHE or make any sound that could possibly wake him up as she tiptoed backwards out of the room. She slowly dimmed the light to darkness and cringed as she heard the floor groan under her. She paused and waited a few seconds. She took another step and then another and quietly clicked the door shut behind her. Finally. Marie had played the same disappearing animal game with that boy for one solid hour. Then she had read him the same book ten times. Each time she finished it he would look at her with those brown eyes that made her feel like weeping for love, clap his hands, and say *"Encore?"* Then she tried to feed him the supper Ben and Maya had left for him, which became an epic journey of soaring hope and crushing defeat. By the time she wrapped his squirmy, sweetly soapy smelling body into a towel, he had soaked the bathroom walls, the floor mat, and Marie herself. She got him into his pajamas, the gender-neutral yellow ones with the red penguins on them—penguins weren't red and that annoyed her—and lay him into his crib with a heartbreakingly hopeful, "*Bonne nuit, mon amour.*"

She was *positive* he was sound asleep until the first time she headed for his door, and she heard a little voice say "*Encore?*" Hence the eleventh reading of *The Very Hungry Caterpillar* and the whole routine all over again. Marie quietly checked that the baby monitor was on and made a brief prayer to the sleeping baby gods that he would stay that way for the next ten hours. That way Marie and Roméo could have a little time together, and Noah's mom and dad might get some relief from their sleep deprivation.

Marie tiptoed down the hallway to Ben and Maya's kitchen and immediately went to the fridge. There was a tiny bit of Pinot Grigio left in a bottle squeezed into the back. She popped the cork and smelled it. Marie didn't like white wine, but this would have to do. She poured herself a glass and returned to the living room where the flotsam and jetsam of her playdate with Noah lay strewn on the floor. She took a gulp of the wine, and then settled on the floor to pick everything up. She knew she was supposed to get Noah to help her before he went to bed—they had a little clean-up song that he sang in his garbled baby language—but this time she forgot. Noah. She knew the name meant "he who seeks safe landing," but Noah was also a famous biblical drunk. As far as traditional Old Testament names, Marie liked Isaac. Or Ethan. Or Ben, of course. But Noah? Marie considered her empty wine glass and headed to the kitchen for a bit more. Just one more small glass. As she emptied the remains of the bottle into it, her phone buzzed with a new text message. It was Ruby. A meeting she had in the neighborhood was canceled at the last minute, and she was just around the corner.

Marie's beautiful, complicated daughter was going to pop by for a quick visit.

There was a little squeak and shriek and they both immediately stared at the screen. Noah had moved from his side and now was sleeping on his stomach, his bum up in the air. Then he was quiet again. They both watched for a few seconds.

"Noah TV can be pretty riveting."

Marie turned away from the baby monitor screen and laughed. "I'm sorry, Ruby. But sometimes I could just watch him for hours. Isn't he the most delicious thing you've ever seen?"

"Yes, Mother. He most certainly is." Ruby had brought a six-pack of beer and cracked one open. She took a pretty healthy swig from the bottle.

"But, wow. He is an *active* child. I mean, I save that kid's life every two minutes. Like tonight? I turned my back on him—I swear for maybe one minute while I ran to the kitchen for something. He was just playing with his little train set and singing sweetly to himself. The next thing I know, he was climbing, I mean he was *scaling* that bookcase. He was almost to the top when I pulled him off it, and he *howled* at me in protest. He is *exactly* like Ben. A bloody perpetual motion machine."

"And you wouldn't have him any other way, would you Mum?"

Marie sunk lower into the sofa and crossed her long legs up on the coffee table.

"I am *exhausted*. Flattened. How did I ever do this? I

mean day in, day out—not like kamikaze *grandmaman* I am now. I forgot what eighteen months old is like. They're complete maniacs."

"And you want me to have one of those?" Ruby asked.

"Absolutely."

"Do you think a boyfriend might be a good first step, though? Or should I go directly to the sperm bank?"

Ruby hadn't dated anyone seriously in two years, since she dumped the perfect guy. At least Marie thought he was. Ruby felt differently. But that was the heartbreak of being a parent—they actually do have to live their own lives and learn from their own mistakes—as much as Marie wanted to take them by the shoulders and shake them into seeing what was obvious to everyone else.

Marie leaned forward and took a handful of Ruby's thick auburn hair. She began to weave it into one long braid down her daughter's back. "So. Have you met any—"

Ruby wriggled out of her mother's grasp and moved to the other end of the sofa.

"Don't even think about going there, Mother. I'm not discussing that subject tonight."

Marie had promised herself she wouldn't raise the issue of Ruby's dating again, and she'd barely made it past the ten-minute mark. But now that she'd opened the window a crack, she decided to go for it. "Surely there are some…nice, smart, worthy guys at school?"

"Please don't call me Shirley." It was an old joke from an old movie, and they both pulled a face at each other. Ruby got up to fetch another beer from the fridge. Then she plumped down on the floor beside Noah's toy box and started to play with a tractor. "They're all such wannabee lawyers."

Marie snorted. "Well. You are in law school. Maybe they can't help themselves."

Ruby shook her head at her mother. "You know what I mean. You can *smell* the burning ambition on most of them. It's nauseating."

Marie opened her mouth to respond, but Ruby continued. "And now I am changing the subject." Ruby's expression shifted to faux cheerful enthusiasm. "Hey, Mom! Did you hear?"

"No, Ruby. I didn't. What?"

"Annique got a role in *Nasty Women*, that new Netflix series."

Annique was one of Ruby's oldest friends. They had also been rivals since grade one, competing for every starring role through elementary and high school. Except Ruby had decided to give up acting for law school, and Annique had persevered.

"Are you kidding me?? Good for her!!" Marie was gobsmacked. "I love that show. Who's she gonna be?"

"She can't say anything yet, so don't you. It's still a secret. But she's cast as some new girl. New storyline. Everything. She got the one good local part."

Marie lifted her glass. "Well, here's to Annique. That's wonderful."

Ruby tried hard to smile. "Yeah. It's great." Ruby pulled a truck out of the toy box and held it up. "What is going on here? I thought they were raising him gender neutral? I don't see any dolls here."

Suddenly there was a little shriek from the baby monitor. Marie looked at Noah TV in alarm. He had flipped back to his side. "See? He *wants* a doll."

"Ruby, I was just remembering tonight what a lovely baby you were. When you were about…maybe three years old. You used to entertain yourself for hours by making up elaborate stories with all your animal figurines. I mean, you'd have them all gathered around you, and you'd narrate these amazing tales. I came into the living room one afternoon when you were completely in the thick of one of these epics, and I asked you if you'd like a glass of milk and a cookie. You looked up at me and said, 'Yes, please' in your sweet way. On my way back to the kitchen I heard you whisper to all your animal friends. 'That was my mother.'"

Ruby smiled and nodded her head. "I've only heard that one about a thousand times."

Marie was taken aback by the tears gathering in her eyes. "If I could, my love, I would do it all over again—exactly the way it was. With all the terror and joy and heartbreak and exhaustion. I wouldn't change one moment of it."

"Really? How about the time I crawled into your bed and puked all over you and Dad didn't even wake up?"

Marie felt that ex-husband chill come over her. Daniel was legendary for sleeping through anything. People found it hilarious, but for Marie it meant she was the one who woke up for the fevers, the flus, the night terrors, and the good old-fashioned broken hearts. She was like so many women of her generation; she did so much of the emotional labor with their kids and the day-to-day heavy lifting that it became normalized.

"Ruby! I forgot to ask you—how is the internship going?"

"It's going. I mean, they're all very busy, so I don't think they feel like babysitting an intern, you know, so I'm trying to get out of their way and learn as much as I can. All I can really do for them is offer legal advice with the major caveat that I am not in fact a lawyer yet."

"Do you find that hard?"

"I mean, I'm trying to understand what they're up against. It's kind of unimaginable. The women are mostly Inuit—from Nunavik—the territory that makes up about one-third of Quebec—at the very top? Like waaay north. They come down here for medical care, or work or school, or…to look for a better life. And then they end up in a world they don't know. I found out this week that the shelter many of the Inuit have been going to was closed down and moved to the other side of town—so now they have no place to go. I mean, how many times do these people have to be traumatized until we're satisfied? Did you know that about *forty percent* of all homeless in Montreal are Inuit? I mean, isn't that just unbelievable? Their life expectancy is fifteen years less than the national average. I mean, what *is* that? I'm also very aware that I am not one of them. I just feel like there but for the grace of winning the birth lottery, you know?"

Marie nodded in agreement. Then she recounted to Ruby what she witnessed in the mall when the two cops roughed up the homeless women.

"Did you report them?"

Marie shook her head.

"Maybe you should talk to *your* cop about it."

"I did. The problem is they're not *his* cops."

"Well, that just sucks." Ruby glanced at her phone to check the time. "Shit. I got to go. I'm meeting someone at seven a.m. to prepare for this mock trial."

Marie was startled by her phone actually ringing and checked the caller. "Speak of the devil."

Ruby could guess from her mother's tone of voice that she wasn't pleased. The conversation was brief. She turned back to Ruby but didn't look her in the eye.

"He's busy again. He's only going to make it to my place later tonight." Marie took a deep breath. "He's interviewing someone for this new case he's on. Or not really, because it's not his case. Anyway. Last time he cancelled, Sophie was having some kind of crisis—"

"So what's new?"

"He missed our Saturday date. I was pretty pissed off—"

"What happened to her? Or rather, what did she do this time?"

"Now, now, Ruby. Let's be kind."

"Well, Mom. I *am* trying."

"Roméo just said, when your kid's drowning, you don't watch them drown. You throw them a life preserver."

Marie didn't add that Roméo had said it in that beautiful baritone voice of his, and if swooning were still an option, she'd have swooned. Ruby gathered her coat and started lacing up her winter boots. "Deep. Pun intended."

Marie walked Ruby to the front door. "Maybe he's got a girlfriend."

Ruby burst out laughing. "Are you kidding? That man is so crazy about you."

"He has an odd way of showing it."

"Well, he doesn't do everything you tell him to do. I like that independence in him."

"Ruby, I am not a control freak!"

Ruby opened the door. A blast of icy air filled the entrance. She kissed her mother's cheek, and made her way down the street, laughing even louder all the way. Marie closed the door against the invasion of cold, and returned to the living room. On Noah TV was a completely awake, screaming baby.

# Thirty-One

"WHAT TOOK YOU SO LONG to come and talk to us?" the woman asked, her hostility barely concealed. "I mean, it's been almost two weeks since Rosie died. Have you caught the bastard who ran her over yet?"

Officer Steve Pouliot shifted uncomfortably in his chair and began to put together an answer. "Well, Madame..." he hesitated, checking the paper in front of him to try to pronounce her name correctly, "Qinn-ua-yuak. We are doing our best to look into this situation in a timely—"

"Right. Sure. You guys are always 'doing your best.'" Annie Qinnuayuak, who looked to be in her fifties but who had the energy and focus of someone half that age, turned her full contempt on Roméo. "And what are *you* doing here?" I didn't know the Sûreté du Québec investigated cases in Montreal."

Steve Pouliot cleared his throat ineffectively. His voice cracked like a pubescent boy's. "Chief Inspector Leduc is here as an observer. He has a...." Pouliot searched for the word while Roméo quietly offered, "I am invited to be an observer of this interview out of courtesy from the SPVM and Officer Pouliot."

Annie Qinnuayuak raised both eyebrows, nodded her head and uncharacteristically said nothing. Roméo took a few moments to take in the room while Pouliot checked the spelling of everyone's name and looked through his notebook for his prepared questions. It was a very large and very white room. There was a row of white cubicle boxes with computers in each one. There was no one sitting before them now, as it was after five and the shelter was closed. On another white wall was written *We Remember* over several dozen framed photographs of people Roméo assumed were clients of the shelter who had died. There were several long, plastic folding tables, a bunch of white chairs, and an old-fashioned TV set with a few open boxes of DVDs before it. In a far corner was an old upright piano, but there was no sheet music to be seen. All in all, the room felt quite sterile, and it could have done with a bit of color. But Roméo imagined that the people who frequented the shelter probably brought it to vivid life. A bedraggled looking man was slowly and pensively mopping the floor behind them in deliberate, concentric circles. Another man was in a back room with the door open, staring intently at a computer. Neither seemed very interested in two cops chatting with the director of the shelter. Roméo knew the police were called here frequently.

Steve Pouliot cleared his throat properly this time and asked the first question.

"How did you know Rosie Nukilik?"

"Rosie started coming here about seven months ago. I suppose you know she was from Salluit? In Nunavik?" Pouliot nodded. "Rosie came down to Montreal with her sister, Maggie, who was diagnosed with tuberculosis. You *do* know that the Inuit in Quebec are in the middle of a public health crisis?"

Officer Pouliot nodded again. "Um…Yes, we are aware of that."

Roméo turned to his fellow policeman, and then asked, "If I may?" Roméo then turned to Annie Qinnuayuak. "Imagine that we know very little about the people who come down here from the North. So, whatever you can tell us about their…situation would be very appreciated. Please continue."

Annie hesitated for a moment, assessing Roméo's sincerity. "Okay. Here's my basic beginner's lecture on Inuit people —the very short and simplified version. As you know, those are very remote communities in northern Quebec, on Ungava Bay. Often, a lack of doctors and basic services up there forces thousands of Nunavik Inuit a year to fly south to get medical treatment in the city. As I said, Rosie came down to Montreal with her sister, Maggie, who was suffering from tuberculosis. Inadequate housing and health services in the North means rates of tuberculosis are over *two hundred and fifty times* the national average. And that's just the tip of the iceberg, so to speak." Steve Pouliot was taking notes as fast as he could. Annie Qinnuayuak continued. "After decades of—well, some would say—government programs intended to destroy our traditional way of life, there were devastating consequences. You know, many of our people remember the dog slaughters of the nineteen-sixties, when the sled dog population dropped from twenty thousand to just a few *hundred* dogs. They depended upon the dogs for hunting, transportation, and companionship: they were necessary to their survival. Many Inuit believe the dogs were deliberately killed by the RCMP as part of a government policy to force them off their land and make them 'civilized.' The government claims the RCMP had to destroy some dogs because they were sick, starving, and dangerous."

Annie paused and looked at Roméo and Steve to check if they were still listening.

"Although there were fewer residential schools for the Inuit than First Nations people, there are still many who are survivors of abuse in the schools, or are the children and grand-children of survivors." Roméo had read about the residential schools—how Indigenous children from across Canada were torn from their families and forced into church-run schools where they were forbidden to speak their mother tongue. Many were sexually and physically abused. It is believed that six thousand children across Canada died in these schools—and that was only the number that was officially reported. The last school finally closed in 1996. *1996*, Roméo thought.

"A lot of that colonial violence was internalized," Annie Qinnuayuak explained. "So you get rampant alcoholism, drug abuse, sexual abuse, domestic violence: they're all symptoms of that pain."

Officer Pouliot looked up from his notes. "We found a fairly high level of blood alcohol in Rosie's body. Did she abuse alcohol?"

The director of the shelter hesitated a moment and then added, "I just wanted you to know the emotional and his-torical baggage many Inuit carry with them—even the ones who come south for positive reasons, like to get an education or to escape abusive situations. It is hard to talk about Rosie without understanding that." She looked at Roméo briefly and then returned her gaze to Steve Pouliot. "Yes, she did abuse alcohol, but to my knowledge, that only started when her sister died in hospital here. The sister caught a secondary infection that they couldn't treat. Rosie started to fall apart after that. She adored her sister. I was told that Rosie wanted to go home, but like so many Inuit who come here, people like Rosie find themselves in vulnerable situations in a big city so different from home. They fall in with the wrong people. Experiment with drugs. Like I said, they are the least violent people I know—all that violence they've had inflicted on them if anything, they turn on themselves."

Steve Pouliot raised a finger. "So, Madame Qinn-Quinn-uayuak—"

"Call me Annie."

"So, Annie. Rosie was a regular here?"

Annie glanced around the spacious room. "Well, I wouldn't say she was a regular, and in fact, we hadn't seen her at all for maybe…three weeks before we heard she was killed. But she certainly used to come here—sometimes to use the laundry facilities, sometimes to see the nurse, sometimes for a hot meal. We serve a hundred and fifty meals every day."

Steve Pouliot nodded in approval. "That is very impressive."

Annie's dark brown eyes lasered at him. "I wish we didn't have to."

"Did Rosie have friends that you know of? Were there particular people she hung out with?"

"I'd have to say no. Not really. As far as I know, Rosie was a bit of a loner. I don't think she ever thought she'd stay south for long—most don't. And some go back home pretty undamaged. But many, like Rosie, come for a visit and end up staying for months. Years. They live in terrible conditions, often on the street. They can't seem to escape."

Roméo noticed the man in the back room had gathered his things and turned off the light. He stood in the doorway, probably wondering if he should join the interview. Annie

Qinnuayuak suddenly gestured toward the piano in the corner of the room.

"Rosie used to come here and play that shitty old piano—and you know what? She made some pretty great music come out of it. I don't know where she learned to play like that. From what I know, Rosie was really starting to turn her life around."

Steve Pouliot then started to ask, "Madame Quin—wak—"

"Just call me Annie," she snapped impatiently.

"Do you know anyone who would want to harm Rosie?"

"Why do you ask? What do you suspect happened to Rosie? They said it was a hit-and-run." She leaned in closer to the two policemen and stared them down. "Or not?"

Roméo checked in by eye contact with Steve Pouliot first. Then he looked evenly at Annie Qinnuayuak. "There is some evidence of foul play involved in the death of Rosie Nukilik. In addition to the trauma from the car."

Annie covered her mouth and gasped. "Oh, sweet Jesus."

Roméo continued. "So, do you know anyone who would harm Rosie?"

Annie recovered quickly. "Who would want to harm an Indigenous woman trying to survive on the street? You're kidding, right? This year alone in Montreal we lost eighteen women to the streets. And across the country? Four thousand murdered and missing in the last thirty years. And those are just the ones that were actually reported. The real numbers are much higher than that."

Roméo shook his head. "It is a disgrace. I do hope that situation is rectified as we understand more about—"

Annie cut him off. "These women are prey for every kind of weirdo, drug dealer, low-life scum. And they're afraid to go to the cops, because calling nine-one-one is like rolling the dice. They might get ticketed for loitering, arrested on some minor infraction. Or," and Annie looked pointedly at Roméo "assaulted by the very police officer you go to for help."

The man who had been hovering in the doorframe now came forward. He briefly put a hand on Annie's shoulder. "Annie? It's six-fifteen. If you don't leave now, you'll be late."

Annie nodded and scraped her chair back. "I have a meeting with the city council in fifteen minutes. They want to stop us from opening a satellite shelter—you know, all those rich NIMBYs—Not In My Backyard crusaders. People are a real fucking delight, you know?"

She stood up and started to put on her coat. The man looked at Roméo and Steve Pouliot, and in a surprisingly high voice for such a big man said, "Maybe you should talk to Isaac Blum."

"Who is Isaac Blum?" Roméo asked.

"They call him the Good Samaritan. He works solo, but he seems to know many of our clients," Annie responded. "Just another white guy trying to save us." She looked up at the man and smiled. "No offense, Peter."

Steve Pouliot wrote down the information. Roméo stood up and shook Annie's hand. She walked the two policemen to the door.

"You know, we Inuit are amazingly resilient people who've lived in one of the world's harshest environments for thousands of years. And women like Rosie? Despite everything, they are so fucking strong. They have survived stuff that, believe me, neither you nor I could. People see them only as victims—but many are trying to turn their lives around, go back to their traditions, to the power that being an Inuit woman gave them. I know Rosie had started beading again.

And she took a few yoga classes to manage her stress. If that bastard hadn't killed her, I think Rosie was one of the ones who would've made it."

Officer Pouliot and Roméo stood up and gathered their papers. Annie Qinnuayuak jangled a set of keys and looked back at the man as she waited for them to join her at the door. "Do you mind locking up?"

The man was already back at his computer and gave her a silent thumbs up response. Roméo gave Annie his card. "Please contact me personally if there is anything else you can think of that might be helpful." Officer Pouliot did likewise.

Annie suddenly stopped the two policemen as they stepped through the door and turned to head down the street. "Hey. You know what we say around here?" She glanced back to the man at the computer as if for confirmation. "How do Indigenous people get attention from the media or the cops? We call it the four Ds."

"And what are those?" Roméo inquired.

She answered like she'd said these words many times before. "Drunk. Drumming. Dancing. Or Dead."

# Thirty-Two

THE ENTIRE ROOM EXPLODED in cheers. Dimitri Golikov had just scored his third goal of the night—a hat trick. The Flying Russian then did a few steps of his signature Cossack dance on the ice in celebration. Ti-Coune Cousineau had to admit the guy was amazing, despite the theatrics. Ti-Coune had only ever gone to a hockey game once, when he was twelve years old. One of the bikers from the bunker where he and Hélène had lived for almost two years after they finally escaped from their mother, had taken him. They went to the legendary Montreal Forum—three blocks from where Ti-Coune sat at this moment—and experienced some of the greatest hockey in history. It was 1979 and *les Canadiens* were Stanley Cup champions. Ti-Coune remembered the elation of watching Guy Lafleur *"Le Démon Blond"* floating down the ice, his hands impossibly light and accurate with the puck. He was the first player in the NHL to score 50 goals and 100 points in six straight seasons. He remembered Yvan Cournoyer, the aging captain, a shadow of what he once was but still capable of surprisingly good hockey. No one wore helmets or face guards, so you could still actually see the players' battle scars

and gaping holes in their mouths where their teeth had once
been. Those were the days of real hockey. He hadn't been to
a game since then. Decent tickets cost hundreds of dollars
and could run to the thousands. No, hockey games were for
rich people or star-struck kids who were thrilled to sit in the
nosebleed section and not even see the puck. The biker had
bought him a hot dog *stimé* and a giant Pepsi. Then the man
took Ti-Coune back to the room he shared with his sister,
Hélène, at the bikers' "office" on rue Mont Royal. At least he
and Hélène could say they had an actual address—which kept
them out of the clutches of Child Protection Services for a
while. The worst was to be homeless. He was still grateful for
what that Hells Angel guy did for him and his sister.

Ti-Coune ordered a Coke and as the bartender resentful-
ly fetched it, went over his day. He had roamed the downtown
area looking for Hélène or anyone who knew her in all the
usual scuzzy bars and hangouts. He still knew many places
from his days in the business, so to speak, and recognized
some of the low-lifes who still frequented them. Looking for
his sister was like walking back into the fucking black hole
of hell. He had shown her photograph to every bartender,
waiter, and willing—and relatively sober—customer in at
least a fifteen-block range around Cabot Square, Shaughnessy
Village, and Little Burgundy. No one had seen her, no one
recognized her. He was beginning to think that Roméo had
made the whole thing up.

Ti-Coune stirred the ice cubes around with the swizzle
stick and took a sip of the Coke. He realized he hated the city
now. He was disgusted by the stench of it, the constant pollu-
tion of noise and light that you could never turn off. Of course,
when he lived in Montreal he couldn't imagine why *anyone*

would choose to live in the country. But now, he realized he had a pretty good life there. He felt his phone buzz his leg. It was a text from his friend, Manon, with an attached photo of his dog, Pitoune lying on Manon's bed, her head resting on Manon's pillow. The message read *elle est très comfortable... mais tu lui manques!* Ti-Coune felt tears pooling in his eyes. What the hell was wrong with him? He wrote back *dis lui que je l'aime*. Manon then asked if he loved her, too. Ti-Coune put the phone back in his pocket. He missed his dog very much. He wasn't sure about the woman taking care of her though.

He briefly glanced around the bar. It was the second period intermission of the game, and that *ostie d'anglais* who wore the stupid jackets was doing the recap. The guy hated French Canadians and had for years. Ti-Coune could not understand why he was still allowed to be on television. Plus, he was at least a hundred years old. The bartender gave him the stink eye. No one wanted some loser nursing a Coke at his bar. Ti-Coune didn't give a flying fuck. He'd watch the rest of the game, and then head back to his room.

"*Excusez moi?*"

A skinny girl who looked to be about sixteen years old touched Ti-Coune's elbow. He barely glanced at her and shook his head. "*Non, merci.*"

"I'm not *selling* anything. But can I show you something?"

Ti-Coune leaned back on his stool and almost smiled. Her accent was so thick that she was obviously an Anglo, so he tried his English out. "Maybe. Okay. Nothing *dangereux* there, *anh*?"

When Ti-Coune looked directly at her, suddenly he couldn't breathe. Even in the dim bar light, her eyes were a luminous blue. Her straight black hair was parted down the middle and framed her high cheekbones and narrow heart shaped face. She was Hélène. Circa 1980. Right around the time Hélène ran away from the shit show of her life in Montreal and hitchhiked out west. She smiled. It was clear she hadn't seen a dentist in a while, if ever. But still. It was a smile that could break your heart. The girl took a piece of paper out of her jacket. A photograph, actually. Of a man with his arms around a very large and bizarre looking dog. "This is my... friend. And our dog. His name is Hamlet."

"Like the guy in...in...Shakespeare?" he stammered.

"Yeah. You know, the guy who goes after the guy who killed his father?"

Ti-Coune tried to concentrate on the words she was saying.

"Turns out it was his mother. And his uncle."

He took a breath. "I, I, um...don't read that book."

The girl showed him the photo again. "Have you seen this dog anywhere around here? I know it's a crazy long shot, but he's lost, and I have to find him."

She looked directly at Ti-Coune. He had to turn away. He was looking into the eyes of a ghost. "No. I never seen him."

She pocketed the photo. "If you see him, or you hear *anyone* talking about a dog that sounds like him, could you please let me know?"

She tapped on the bar as though to thank the bartender for his time, and turned away. Ti-Coune touched her arm and felt her slightly recoil. "How you lost your dog?"

He offered to buy the girl a beer, and after a moment's hesitation, she accepted. Then she told him the story of her boyfriend, whom she found frozen to death beside a church where he was camping out, waiting for her. Ti-Coune was shocked that this girl lived on the streets. She described how the police treated her like someone who barely knew Christian, when in fact, she was the only real family he had. She didn't cry. But she was devastated by what happened. She told Ti-Coune that she often felt like she wanted to die. She was staying alive to find her dog.

"I'm trying to find my sister." He pulled out the photo of Hélène and waited for the girl's reaction. She didn't seem to see any resemblance. "Do you know her?"

She shook her head. "No. Sorry. I've never seen her."

Ti-Coune explained that her picture was found in the pocket of a woman who'd been hit by a car. He didn't know what the connection between them was.

"That's disgusting. What kind of person would do that?" They both took a sip of their drinks, tacitly acknowledging that there was no real answer to that question. The girl downed the rest of her beer, slipped off her stool, and extended her hand.

"Thanks. I have to go. I hope you find your sister."

Ti-Coune helped her get into her coat. "Where do you live—?" He cut the question off. "I mean, how do I find you if I hear something about your dog?"

She smiled and shrugged. "Just leave me a message here. The bartender will hang onto it." She turned to go. "Oh. By the way. My name is Nia. With an 'N.' Like Nancy. What's yours?"

"Jean-Michel. Jean-Michel Cousineau."

And then, just like that, the ghost left the bar.

When Ti-Coune sat back on his stool, the game had resumed. But now there was a fresh Coke in front of him. He nodded his surprised thanks to the bartender, who pointed to a guy sitting at the end of his bar. He was very overweight and very sweaty, although the room was not at all warm. Blasts of cold air kept blowing in every time someone opened the door. The man pulled his bulk off his stool and approached Ti-Coune.

"Ti-Coune Cousineau!!! *Ça s' peut tu??* Can it be?? What the fuck are you doing back here?" He was breathing heavily and stared intently at Ti-Coune. The top of his head was completely hairless, but a tonsure of long, greasy, gray hair encircled his bald pate.

Ti-Coune had no idea who this guy was.

"*C'est moi!*" he thumped his chest. "*Tu m'connais pas?*" The face Ti-Coune once knew was so encased in fat he hadn't recognized him. It was Guy, the bouncer at Cleopatra's, a strip club Ti-Coune used to frequent.

"Nice haircut you got there."

The man patted the top of his head and belly laughed. "You changed a bit yourself, *mon ami*." He lifted a glass of whiskey and toasted Ti-Coune. "To old friends."

Ti-Coune took a gulp of his Coke. Except it wasn't Coke. It was mostly rum with a splash of Coke. He grimaced and set it back on the bar. The man leaned into his ear.

"Hey man, I see you like them young. I got a very sweet little piece for you. Very young. Very clean."

Ti-Coune muttered, "Real men don't buy girls." His old friend almost spat out his whiskey he was laughing so hard and smacked Ti-Coune on the back.

"Shit, *mon ami*. How long has it been? Ten years? I heard you were up in the boonies there. Still working for the same people?"

Ti-Coune was trying very hard not to have another swallow of that drink. But *saint tiboir* it felt good. It felt warm. It felt *right*. "No. I have my own business now."

The man whistled in appreciation. "So what are you in the big city for?"

But Ti-Coune wasn't listening. *Don't do it. Don't do it. Walk away. Walk away. Now.*

Ti-Coune finished his drink in three gulps. "Looking for a friend." He ordered another rum and Coke. A double.

"Hope it wasn't that guy they found two blocks from here last week—frozen like a popsicle. Outside a fucking church. A giant blue popsicle." He laughed again at his own simile. "But I heard somebody killed him. Sat on him and choked him to death."

"What the fuck you talking about?"

"It's just a rumor—you know how it is. People start talking, the next thing you know there's a gang of zombies killing and eating homeless people." He seemed to really appreciate that one and laughed even louder.

The hockey game was long over, and the bar had mostly emptied out by the time Ti-Coune tried to stand up and realized he was too hammered to walk. His old friend leaned drunkenly into his ear. "You know, a few of your old buddies might not be too happy to see you. If you need a little extra...A little extra protection. You let me know, okay?" He tried to wink at

Ti-Coune but he was too drunk and the wink was a lopsided grimace.

Ti-Coune waved him off and staggered out the door and into the street. He tried to pull a cigarette from his pack of Drum but ended up dropping half of them in the snow. Then he toppled over into a snowbank. A few minutes later, he forced his frozen hand to dig out his phone and punched in a number.

Roméo Leduc was just driving home to Marie's place when he got the call. After the interview with Annie Qinnuayuak, he had gone to the flat. Sophie was pretty depressed and threatening to go back to her boyfriend, so Roméo made her a good hot supper and then made sure she was ensconced before that addictive Netflix series. Then he pored over the autopsy report on Rosie Nukilik again. Forensic evidence can be very ambiguous, but he felt this was not. She had been smothered. He also looked at the autopsies of the two women Steve Pouliot had flagged. There was definitely something not adding up there. The second woman, Shannon Amittuk, had clearly died in circumstances that did not point to suicide. Roméo was disgusted at the sloppy, uninterested investigation. His car phone rang.

"Hey! *C'est...mo—i.*" Ti-Coune was having trouble getting his words out.

Roméo listened for more, but there was a long pause. Then Ti-Coune continued, but he was barely coherent.

"I...s-s-saw. Hélène. Tonight."

"What? You found her?"

"Well. Not *Hélène*. But a ghost. A beautiful ghost. Hey, her boyfriend, he died in a church. Someone sat on him and killed him."

"What did you say?"

"She'ssss looking for Hamlet. Hamlet. Is Gone." Ti-Coune started to cry. "She loves her dog. And she lost her dog."

"Ti-Coune, where are you?"

He managed to tell Roméo that he was outside the Cock and Bull, and he was just going to have a little nap. Roméo turned the car around and headed east towards downtown.

After pulling him out of a filthy snowbank, half-dragging him up the stairs of the rooming house, waiting as he puked his insides into the toilet, and finally throwing him into his bed, Roméo was ready to head out. It was almost two o'clock in the morning. Ti-Coune lay curled up in the single bed, his hands tucked under his head. For one brief moment, Roméo could see the little boy that Ti-Coune was so many years and lives ago.

As he got into his car, he couldn't stop thinking about what Ti-Coune had said. Were two people now dead, killed by asphyxiation that was *not* accidental? The Montreal police had not mentioned the second recent homicide. By traumatic asphyxiation. What was going on here? What was Hélène Cousineau's connection to Rosie Nukilik? Was Hélène even alive? Was she in danger? Roméo's head was spinning with fatigue and too many possibilities. Too many tabs open in his brain. He glanced at the time. Marie was a very light sleeper, and he would certainly disturb her coming in at this hour. Sophie could sleep through a war. Roméo decided to go home to his daughter. But as he drove through the deserted, snowy streets of Montreal, he couldn't help but think: did they have a serial killer on their hands?

# Thirty-Three

DANIELLE CHAMPAGNE HESITATED just a moment, and then she pushed the heavy door open. Everyone—including her Chief of Curation for E-Content, her Beauty Director, and Strategies for Lifestyle Director—was on their feet, smiling and applauding her enthusiastically and without a trace of irony, as far as she could tell. The deal she just negotiated to expand into the northeast US market was huge. There was also talk of opening two actual retail stores of curated exclusive products for women and men in two cities. Toronto was a done deal. New York was more elusive, but Danielle felt certain that would eventually happen. She was in no big hurry just now. *La Vie Champagne* was rocketing into the stratosphere of success and Danielle was trying to enjoy the view. One of the issues on the table that morning was to finalize the name for the Toronto store. Danielle didn't want her name on the store at all, but her associates felt differently. She didn't want to become like Oprah—her face on the cover of every issue of her own monthly magazine. Would she call it "D"? Or

"Danielle"? That was a kind of narcissism that made her a bit uncomfortable. As the two young interns popped open several bottles of champagne and poured them into the waiting flute glasses, Chloé cleared her throat and stood at the head of the enormous table. Once everyone had their glass in hand, she raised hers to Danielle.

"To good sex, good sleep, good coffee, and great BIG GONADS!"

All the women in the room laughed. Her television interview had gone viral. There were memes of Danielle repeating those words over and over again. There were photo-shopped images of her and a horrified Donald Trump comparing her hands to his. Hers were much bigger, of course. There was her and Vladimir Putin or Kim Jong-un or Mohammed bin Salman looking down between their legs and Danielle celebrating her clear victory with triumphant upraised arms. The women all bowed their heads to Danielle, lifted their glasses and then sipped at the champagne. The interns glanced around nervously to see if anyone's needed refilling. Not at ten o'clock in the morning.

Danielle wet her lips but not much more—she needed to be clear-headed for the day—and gestured for everyone to take their seats. Chloé began to hand out the material for the meeting, giving each woman a glossy champagne-colored folder. Laptops opened. Phones were placed within reach of nervous fingertips. Danielle went to the side table to fetch herself a croissant to go with the champagne. An intern hastened over to her with a cloth napkin. Danielle thanked her, asked her to please make her a double espresso, and took her seat at the head of the table.

Her CFO was walking them through a very thorough report on quarterly projections, but Danielle's thoughts had minds of their own. Her eyes felt as though someone had held a hot blow dryer to them, as she'd slept very little the night before. Again. When she had finally fallen into a fitful sleep, she'd had another disturbing nightmare. She was with her ex-husband in his red Peugeot sports car, and he was driving much too fast. Danielle begged him to slow down, but he refused. Instead he lurched off the highway and headed directly towards a lake. When they approached the huge pier that seemed to run halfway across it, he drove the car onto it even faster. Danielle wanted to jump out, but they were going too fast and she was too terrified. Her ex anticipated her plan to escape and hit the door lock. The next thing she knew, they were flying off the end of the dock and hitting the surface of the water hard. Then they were underwater, and she was desperately trying to open her door, but the pressure made it impossible. He had managed to escape, though, and she was alone in the car as it slowly sank to the bottom of the lake.

She woke up to the sound of her own moaning, her face soaked with tears.

Danielle opened her eyes to the droning of her CFO's voice and realized she must have nodded off for a minute, as Lise was already concluding her report. As she stifled another yawn and willed herself to keep her eyes open, the door to the boardroom began to open silently. Thank God, here was the coffee at last. The young woman bumped the huge door open wider with her hip and Danielle expected to see a tray of coffee appear as she turned around. But there was no tray. No coffee. And she wasn't the intern. It was another woman. She had dead-straight, long, black hair and was wearing a white parka zipped up to her throat. She stood motionless, staring directly at Danielle, her eyes a luminous black-brown. She didn't move, but a suggestion of a smile began to form on her gaunt face. It was her. It was Rosie Nukilik.

Danielle gasped out loud and covered her face with her hands. No one really seemed to notice except Chloé, who hastened to Danielle, and leaned over her.

"Are you all right?"

Danielle slowly lowered her hands. Too frightened to open her eyes, she hesitated a few seconds.

"Danielle? Can I get you something?"

By now, everyone had turned away from the PowerPoint on the screen and towards Danielle. She slowly opened her eyes and forced herself to look towards the door. Rosie Nukilik was gone. The intern appeared with her coffee, and Danielle lifted the cup to her lips with trembling hands. She had to get clear, had to get some sleep or she would completely fall apart. Danielle hated sleeping pills, but she resolved that night to take them and fix this once and for all.

Penelope, her marketing director, started her presentation on the extraordinary claims of a new weight-loss product based on maple tree water that *La Vie Champagne* was looking at, but then Danielle noticed her mouth kept moving and no sound was coming out. She suddenly felt like the air had been extracted from the room, and there was a high-pitched ringing like someone striking a tuning fork. Was she going to faint? She dropped her head into her hands and tried to breathe through whatever this was. Her eyes felt stuck shut. She *knew* Rosie was back in the room. She could feel her. When she finally opened her eyes, Rosie was sitting at the other end of the table in Penelope's chair. Rosie was still wearing her parka, and continued her examination of Danielle with that same half-smile on her face. Danielle forced herself to stand up and half-staggered to the door, giving Rosie a wide berth. She managed to get to the washroom down the long, carpeted hall without passing out.

The water felt amazingly restorative. She splashed and splashed it onto her face and ran it over her wrists. She clutched at the edge of the cold sink. If she could just stay still for a few minutes, the ringing would go away and she could get clear. Danielle had tried to watch the news—had tried to read what little coverage there was in the paper about Rosie—the same photo of her was used again and again, in her beautiful white parka with the embroidery, a broad, toothy smile on her face, looking directly at the camera. But that's as far as Danielle could go. She just could not know any more about this woman or she would go completely off the deep end. Danielle heard the swish of the bathroom door open. She knew it was her. No, it wasn't. This was absurd. There are no fucking ghosts. She was just exhausted. *Epuisée.* Nothing left. Still, she could not bring herself to open her eyes. She heard an intake of breath.

"Danielle? What's going on? Are you sick? Can I call you a car to take you home?"

Relieved, she opened her eyes to a sincerely stricken-looking Chloé, who watched Danielle's reflection in the mirror. She didn't move, just held onto the sink and kept her eyes steady on her assistant's face. Chloé took a step toward her with an outstretched hand, but Danielle waved her away.

"I don't know what to do."

Chloé didn't know what to do, either, so she continued to stand there. Her boss leaned heavily against the wall, then slowly sank to the bathroom floor and hugged her knees tightly to her chest. Chloé joined her on the floor, tucking her tight skirt under her bum. Danielle stared ahead of her, unable to make further eye contact. The words fell from her in such a catharsis of relief and shame.

"I've done something terrible. And I don't know what to do."

Chloé reached out for her boss's hand and gently held it. She would have to get back to the meeting soon, though. She discreetly checked the time on her phone. She decided to wait three minutes before she returned to the room and declared the meeting adjourned.

# Thirty-Four

"*LIKE LOVERS, Tahiti and her islands in French Polynesia are meant to be embraced...*"

Sitting before her iPad, Gennifer Moran scrolled through the article from a high-end travel magazine. It was full of island paradise clichés, but when a place really was an island paradise cliché what else was there to say? She had considered going to Panama, or Vietnam, or Australia, or Hawaii, but Tahiti sounded like the place for her. Jean Luc had promised her anywhere in the world, and she was going to take him up on the offer before things got too busy again and she couldn't get away. It looked like the island of Tahiti itself was a place to avoid, but Bora Bora and Moorea seemed gorgeous. She thought of those exquisite paintings Paul Gaugin painted of Tahitian women. How shocked the art world in Paris was of his *embracing* of this culture and especially its beautiful young women. She looked out the window at a very different scene from a South Pacific Eden. It was a bitter, nasty day, and people were rushing by just trying to get to their destination, leaning into the wind, their coats clutched at their necks. The door to the café blew open a with a blast of cold air, and a young woman stood there tentatively for a few moments before she began to unravel the over-long scarf around her neck and remove her mittens. That must be her, Gennifer thought. She let the young woman scan the room for at least a minute before she raised her hand to call her over. The girl lifted her head in recognition and headed to the small, round table for two.

After a bizarrely polite exchange about the bad weather and how cool this café was, Gennifer decided to get down to business. She made sure to discreetly push the record button on her iPad.

"So. What is it you want?"

Brittany returned the stare with the same dispassionate gaze. She had eyelash extensions that were so long she looked like a cartoon cat. Her nose was too big for her small face, and her parents should've seen to those teeth.

"I want justice for my friend."

Gennifer stirred the foamy milk in her second cappuccino, and let it drop slowly from her spoon. "Justice! Justice for *what*, exactly?"

Brittany glanced around the café for a moment, and leaned closer. "For the sexual assault on my friend."

"Your friend is mistaken. Nothing happened to her."

Brittany pushed her coffee aside. "I want you to draw up a contract for her. The one you promised her? Remember? On *Nasty Women*. Now I see who it's named after."

Gennifer smiled. "Ooh, ouch. *That* hurt. And what's in this for you?"

Brittany closed those long, silly eyelashes and opened them again. "I would like fifteen thousand dollars."

Gennifer tried very hard not to laugh out loud. Was this

a *shakedown*? This idiot had watched one too many lousy movies. She put her hand on Brittany's for a moment, then withdrew it. "Do you know how many little slut girls we see like you in just one *week*?"

"We'll go to the police."

"We understand that…you all want to make it. It's not easy here in Montreal—especially in the English market. You are all fighting for little crumbs from a little pie that *we* get to share as *we* see fit. I understand your…frustration. I understand the *attraction* of going after a man like Jean Luc. He has an extraordinary charm, and power can be intoxicating—"

"He's a disgusting, pathetic old man who likes to rape girls. I know my friend wasn't his first. Maybe she'll be his last, though."

Gennifer started looking through her bag for her wallet.

"Listen. I was in the room with the two of them the entire time. We interviewed her for a few minutes and realized that she just was not the right person for the role. She stormed out of the room, and that is the last we saw of her. That's it, that's all."

"That is NOT what happened!"

Gennifer summoned the waiter. "Why isn't your friend here now with you?"

"Are you kidding? She doesn't want to see *you*. She'll wait to see you in court if she has to. She asked me to come and… represent her."

Gennifer leaned her elbows on the little table and laced her fingers together like she was about to pray. She smiled at Brittany. "She doesn't even know you're here, does she?"

Brittany puffed herself up as large as she could. She straightened her back and looked evenly at Gennifer, but before she could respond Gennifer stood up from the table, closed her iPad, tucked it in her bag, and shrugged her coat onto her shoulders. "It's girls like you—who make false accusations—who give *all of us* a bad name. Do you understand? Contact me again, and we will have your ass in court so fast your friend will *really* feel like she's been assaulted."

Gennifer tossed a twenty-dollar bill on the table and walked out. She waited until she had turned onto Ste. Catherine street and stepped into the entrance to Forever 21 before she made the call. "Hi. Yes. I just had the meeting. There should be no more trouble." She waited for him to respond. "Yup. We're all good...." She hesitated. "Wait—Jean Luc? I wanted to tell you—"

But the voice at the other end had already left the conversation.

# Thirty-Five

ROMÉO AND STEVE POULIOT made their way through the endless stream of students flowing by, in all shapes, colors, sizes, and languages. They passed mothers dragging tired children by the hand, passed idling window shoppers, elderly walker-pushers, bustling businesspeople who always looked like they were talking to themselves, but in fact were talking into their ear buds. Roméo was always impressed by the eclectic parade of human experience in such a concentrated space—the metro level of Alexis Nihon mall. What did Marie call it? *Anthrodiversity.* He could see why Marie loved her job so much—there was an endless supply of people to watch, and Marie was a people-watcher and a self-described professional eavesdropper. He often joked that she would've made a good detective, if only she wasn't squeamish about blood and didn't find guns abhorrent. Roméo had noted the beggars just outside the metro turnstile, but none had asked for money. All but one was passed out on pieces of cardboard, their faces turned away from the uninquisitive crowds. Only one was awake and held out a filthy hand, but she seemed half-hearted in her appeal for change. She looked to be about sixty years old, but Roméo knew she might be half that age. Living on the street took a merciless toll, sometimes aging people shockingly beyond their years. He wondered if Steve Pouliot was thinking the same thing: could one of these poor souls be the next to die?

As they entered the Canadian Tire, Roméo was struck by the sheer immensity of it. He hadn't been to one of these stores in quite some time, and the onslaught of choice made him a bit queasy. Before they'd been in the place a minute, a cheerful young man had tried to sell him a credit card, then backed off when Steve Pouliot asked him where they could find the floor manager. Another clerk was summoned, and she disappeared to the back of the store. Roméo wondered if she'd ever return again. Steve Pouliot was picking up and putting back several items in the discount bin. Something called Sham-Wow, three-for-a dollar gloves, and oddly, a flashing red heart attached to a windshield scraper. Roméo suddenly remembered Valentine's Day was looming. He noticed that the store was already moving the winter stuff out and preparing for spring. That seemed terribly hopeful, given that it was early February and twenty-two degrees below zero outside. He idly picked up a scraper and wondered if Marie would find it funny. When he looked up again, a very tall and burly middle-aged man was standing before them with a gold nametag that read *ISAAC* pinned to his left breast. He had a full head of unruly, graying hair and a face with regular, even features except for a rather prominent cleft chin. As the two policemen introduced themselves, he looked from one man to the other impassively, but what Roméo saw was clear distrust, perhaps even fear.

They sat on white plastic chairs at a white plastic table in one of the cheaper coffee-pastry eateries in the open mall. Although Steve Pouliot fit neatly and comfortably into his seat, Roméo and the tall man sitting across from them spilled out of theirs and had to tuck their legs in sideways so as not to trip every customer passing by. The two policemen drank their coffee black, but Isaac Blum shook three sugar packets into his and stirred nervously. He glanced at his watch twice, but said nothing. Steve Pouliot opened a black file on the table. Isaac Blum pointedly did not try to see what was in it.

"Monsieur Blum, we understand that you deliver tea and sandwiches to indigent people every Monday and Thursday morning. Is that correct?"

Isaac nodded and said "Yes, that is correct."

"We know that your area of…interest is in and around Cabot Square, Shaughnessy Village, and sometimes Little Burgundy."

Isaac confirmed that as well. Steve Pouliot pulled a photograph from the file and turned it to face the man.

"Do you know this woman? Her name is Rosie Nukilik."

Isaac picked up the photo and examined it for a respectable amount of time. There was a slight hesitation and a quick dry swallow before he replied, "No. I don't know her."

Roméo knew right away that Blum was not telling the truth.

"Are you certain you have never seen this woman?"

Isaac repeated his denial of ever having known or seen Rosie Nukilik.

Isaac Blum sipped at his sweet coffee and glanced at his

watch again. Roméo noted that he was someone who was acutely aware of the time. Steve Pouliot closed the first file and reached for another. He perused it for a minute before returning his attention to Blum. He slowly pulled out a second photograph.

"Do you know this man?" Isaac glanced at the photo and averted his eyes immediately. "We apologize for the...graphic nature of the picture. It's the only one we have."

Blum cleared his throat twice and said, "I do know this man. Well, I don't *know* him, but I have met him."

"Where did you *meet* him?"

Blum dry swallowed again. "From...around. I knew him and his girlfriend. We never talked much. Those two kept to themselves, mostly."

Steve Pouliot nodded and replied casually, "He was murdered last Thursday night."

Isaac Blum dropped his head into his hands. "Oh my god."

Steve Pouliot waited for him to say something else, but nothing else was offered. He continued, "The man's name is Christian Bourque, and his girlfriend identified you as the man who led her to the body of Mr. Bourque."

"I didn't know there was a...a body there!" It was the first time he had raised his voice. "I just told her that this guy—I don't know his name—I saw him and...Christian...heading off in the direction of this church—I heard that church was a good place to bed down. A safe place."

"What did *this guy* look like? Did you know him? Did you ever see him before?"

Isaac shook his head. "He was white, very tall, clean-shaven—or, no beard. And wearing a blue parka."

"You may as well be describing yourself. What else can you remember about him?"

"Nothing. It was nighttime. In winter. He...looked like everyone else. Except he was taller than average. He and... Christian just walked out of the square heading west. The dog was with them, of course—"

"Did the man seem afraid of the dog? Or the dog afraid of the man?" Roméo asked abruptly.

"I don't know. No, it didn't seem that way. Why do you ask that?"

Pouliot shifted in his little chair and redirected the questioning. "You said you knew Christian Bourque and his girlfriend, Nia Fellows. You spent time with them, and...followed Christian that night, right?"

"No! I just happened to be there—"

"But that wasn't your usual schedule. Why were you in Cabot Square that night?"

Isaac checked his watch again. "You said fifteen minutes of my time. I have to get back to work—"

"Why were you in Cabot Square that night?"

"I worked a late shift and decided to wander over and see that everyone was okay. It was very cold. I was worried about...some of the people I...know there. That's all."

Roméo was starting to feel quite annoyed by this man.

"Tell us again about your relationship with Christian and Nia. Why would a man of some...fifty-odd years hang around with—"

"I don't hang around with them!"

"Why were you so *interested* in them?"

"They're just *kids*. Just good kids who got unlucky with

who their parents are. And the…dead boy suffers from mental illness. Many homeless people do, you know."

Steve Pouliot took over from Roméo and looked at Blum directly and evenly. "According to your record, it seems that you really *like* kids."

Isaac Blum's entire body changed its language. It had been talking cautious cooperation, but now it was speaking fearful defiance.

"What are you talking about?"

"You were charged with sexually interfering with a nine-year-old child in your school when you were a teacher—in… two thousand and seven."

Isaac Blum inhaled deeply, trying to control his anger.

"Those charges were later proven to be false. The child was very angry because I had separated her from her best friend in the class, so she…made up a story that could hurt me. I was completely exonerated."

Steve Pouliot only pretended to read the notes in front of him, because he already had them all memorized.

"You were not in fact exonerated. The charges were dropped because they ended up taking your word over the little girl's. In those days, that happened much more often than it does now."

Isaac Blum suddenly seemed completely deflated. "They dropped the charges in the end, but it didn't matter. I was ruined."

"And *that's* why you don't work for any of the official organizations that help the homeless. You can't. You have a record."

There was a long, silent pause. Roméo leaned in, and asked gently, "Why are you so…driven to help others?

Especially people who can be very, very difficult. People who often don't have the…wherewithal to show any gratitude. Or often, the…ability to turn their lives around." Roméo took the last sip of his tepid coffee.

"I lost everything. I lost my wife. My kids. My house. My life. I was drawn to people who'd lost everything, too."

Roméo cracked a small, sympathetic smile. "It must be exhausting, discouraging work. Trying not to burn out must be a constant challenge."

"I witness such need every day…I can't *not* do anything." He looked at both policemen squarely. "Just because you can't save them all doesn't mean you shouldn't try."

Steve Pouliot then pulled a third folder and opened it on the table. He showed Isaac a new photograph. It was of Shannon Amittuk, the Inuit woman who the police claimed had hanged herself, but whom Steve and Roméo suspected had been murdered. "Do you know this woman?"

Roméo watched as Isaac Blum's eyes softened for an instant. He knew her.

"No, I don't think so."

Roméo watched him carefully. "Look again."

Isaac closed his eyes for the briefest of moments, as though recalling or perhaps erasing her memory. He reopened them and looked at the picture.

"I first met her just outside Cabot Square after a shift one day. She tried to bum a cigarette off me, but I don't smoke. She told me she'd come down from Nunavik to visit her sick mother." He sighed deeply. "She was…she was an outgoing, friendly girl, who was living with a friend in Lachine. She was, a very *naïve* person, though, you know?" The policemen nodded. This was a very different man sitting before them.

"Then a few weeks later, or maybe a month or two, I see her with this guy. He's been hanging around Cabot Square for years, and he preys on young, vulnerable Inuit and First Nations women, getting them hooked on crack and then into the sex trade. I see it all the time—he's a predator." He pointed a finger at Steve Pouliot.

"You all know about him and have for years. Why don't you guys do something about *him*? Why aren't you interviewing *him*?"

"What's his name?"

Isaac Blum dismissed the question with a contemptuous snort. "Jim. Bob. Pierre. Bozo the Clown. It doesn't matter. There's more where he came from."

Roméo looked carefully at Isaac Blum.

"So what happened with Shannon?"

"A few weeks after…that…she approached me again. She was much thinner, so…diminished…like there was no light in her eyes left. Like there was no one home. But she still smiled at me and…she offered to give me a blow job for ten bucks."

"Did you take her up on the offer?" Steve asked with no trace of sarcasm.

Isaac looked at his watch. "I have to get back to work. We're short two people on the floor and a shift change is coming up."

Roméo nodded and Isaac Blum bent himself out of his chair and stood up. He was at least as tall as Roméo.

"Mr. Blum, if you have not told the truth here today, we will find out. Expect to be questioned again soon."

Isaac smiled grimly. "I have told the truth. Every word of it."

Roméo and Steve Pouliot watched him walk off and then get swallowed by the throngs of shoppers hustling to stores before heading home for supper. They returned to their notes and began to compare their impressions of the Good Samaritan. Isaac Blum hastened back to Canadian Tire and made a beeline for the cavernous stockroom in back where his closet-sized office was. He closed the door and locked it. Then he took out his phone and methodically deleted every single photo he'd taken.

# Thirty-Six

"PEPPA PIG! PEPPA PIG! PEPPA PIG!" Nicole LaFramboise actually covered her ears as her two-year-old son, Léo, marched around her and demanded she let him watch yet another episode of his favorite cartoon. She loved her son. He was the beating heart of her life, and for the last two years and nine months, her *raison d'être*. But sometimes she really wished she could send him to his daycare when he was running a low-grade fever. Like today. But almost as soon as she wished it, she felt guilty. What kind of a mother wanted her kid away from her when he was too sick for *garderie*? Sometimes, she also wished the daycare was open on the weekends. What kind of mother wanted her child gone on the only two days they had all to themselves? A bad mother, that's who. A mother who didn't really want to be a mother. A mother who didn't deserve to have such a beautiful, healthy baby. But maybe a mother who'd had no days off. None. For the last three weeks. She had also been fighting a flu bug all week, and today she actually felt okay—but she was behind on her work, both at her job and her house chores. It always seemed to Nicole that single motherhood was one long race.

Just as she was about to drag her exhausted but triumphant body across the finish line, someone moved it a bit further.

That morning she had woken up with Léo at 5:30, made him warm milk, tried and failed to get him to sit to read him a book, let him bat his Nerf ball at her head for about an hour, fed him breakfast and a dose of Tylenol, and did two loads of laundry with him hanging off her hip. She washed a week of dishes, took three more Tylenol for herself, and then played another hour of Ride Mommy. This was also after she had patiently answered his hundredth "*Pourquoi, maman?*" about everything she did.

"We have to do the laundry now."

"Why?"

"Because our clothes are dirty, and we like to be clean."

"Why?"

"Because we feel better when we're clean."

"Why?"

"So people won't say peeyoo, you stink! to us."

"Why?"

And on and on and on. She had finally resorted to letting him watch *Peppa Pig* on her iPad, which Léo knew how to use better than she did. Nicole felt guilty again for doing so, but she was dangling at the end of her rope and just had to finish reviewing all the documents. She had them all neatly and carefully laid out on the coffee table in her living room, while Léo sat next to her on the sofa, sedated by the virtual world he was watching.

She was focusing on the cold case homicide Roméo had assigned to her specifically—Chantal Lalonde-Fukushima. Nicole's team had already re-interviewed everyone who would still talk to them. She'd sent them to talk again to friends, teachers, and family. Everyone's story was consistent. Chantal was a type-A high-achiever who spent most of her time studying. She didn't do drugs. She didn't have a boyfriend. She did have aspirations to be a model—but only to make money to put herself through school. Her parents lived comfortably but modestly, and paying tuition at a fancy school was out of the question. She liked dogs and had pestered her parents about getting one. Her mother had kept almost all of her things: her little music box by her bed. Her well-loved stuffies. Her Judy Blume books and even her textbooks from grade eleven. She would have graduated from high school that spring.

But how Chantal ended up raped and dumped in the St. Lawrence river that Friday night remained a complete mystery. Despite re-interviewing her friends, no one really knew her whereabouts that night. Her mother said she was going to study at a girlfriend's—which seemed odd for a Friday night—but not for Chantal. The girlfriend testified that they had not made plans at all for that night—so no one noticed she was missing for almost twenty-four hours. Her body wasn't found for several days.

"*Maman?*"

"*Oui, mon amour?*" Nicole answered without taking her eyes off her work.

"*Maman? On peut aller dehors?* Can we go outside?"

Nicole didn't answer. She was minutes away from skimming the last of the files.

"*Maman!*" Léo whined, pulling on her arm.

"*Deux minutes, mon amour.*"

Suddenly, Léo leapt from the sofa and onto the coffee table, kicking all the documents and papers across the living room floor. "I want to go outside!"

He jumped down from the coffee table and ran through the papers, like they were a leaf pile he was kicking through.

"LÉO!!!! *TABERNAC*! WHAT DID YOU DO?" Nicole grabbed her son who was still stomping on and scattering the years of collected work. She sat him down hard—too hard—on the sofa and ordered him to stay put. He began to cry. So did Nicole. She held him to her, rocking him in her arms so tightly he began to squirm away. As he watched his mother wipe her tears away, her son got quiet. Léo sat on the sofa, sucking his thumb, while Nicole got on her hands and knees and started to clean up the mess he'd made—dumping the papers, reports, and handwritten notes randomly into the box. She'd have to sort through the whole thing later that night when Léo went to bed. But as she picked up one photograph dated the year Chantal died, she noticed it was taken at some kind of party, and in the photo was a face she recognized. He was much younger, of course, but he had his arms around two young women and all three were smiling and laughing. It was the very well-known producer, Jean Luc David. Standing behind them, but not posing for the photo, was Chantal.

What was she doing there? Had anyone noted this before? Nicole leaned back against the sofa and forced herself to remember a conversation she'd had. It was a vague memory of someone—maybe a girlfriend from college—telling her about Jean Luc David's legendary parties, and how the cops covered up for him for years of debauchery and legally dubious activities. Chantal seemed like the last person on earth to end up at one of those, but maybe her modeling ambitions led her there? Nicole peered at the photograph again, then placed it carefully aside. This was worth looking into further. She looked at the files scattered all over her living room floor, and then suddenly kneeled over to her son and hugged him to her.

"If it wasn't for you, I wouldn't even have seen this, *mon Léo. Merci.*"

Then Nicole got to her feet, held out her hands and said, "Let's go play outside."

# Thirty-Seven

"YOU DID *WHAT?*" Michaela's voice was an amplified shriek as it echoed in the empty stairwell where she was leaning against the corner wall, talking on her phone. Brittany described again her encounter with Jean Luc David's assistant. She hadn't meant to tell Michaela, but her conscience finally got the better of her and she confessed what she'd done.

"How the fuck could you do that, Brittany?"

She had embroidered the story though in the retelling; she recast herself as the selfless crusader—much tougher, much more defiant, and only looking out for her friend. She mentioned the contract she tried to get for her. She did not mention the 15,000 dollars she asked for herself.

"I was doing it for you, Mika—"

Michaela interrupted her. "But you didn't *tell* me. And now they're going to think it was all a lie because you asked for a *contract.*"

Brittany's voice hardened. "I wanted something good to come out of it. Make that fucker *pay.*"

Michaela tried to control the sob that threatened to choke the words from her.

"But the only one who will pay is *me!*" The last word was like the wail of a forlorn child.

"Mika, I'm really sorry. I had no idea you'd be this mad." Brittany's voice broke and then she began to cry.

"Don't you start crying. Don't you *dare* start crying, Brittany!" But her friend couldn't get any words out. Michaela hung up. She just stood in the stairwell, staring blankly at the wall. Then she sank to the floor and started to sob.

As Marie headed along the seventh-floor corridor, her head was full of her class that had just finished. Four students had done their oral presentations that morning, and Marie had been pleasantly surprised. One girl with more piercings than Saint Sebastian had discussed whale evolution, explaining how whales went from small hooved mammals who could swim and walk on land to the titanic blue whales we have today. Another one who claimed to be a militant omnivore discussed conflicting attitudes about the whale hunt. Were whales just another resource to be harvested? That's how the Japanese saw them—no different from the cows or pigs the people in the West eat voraciously, and who are subjected to horrific lives before they are slaughtered. At least, he argued, whales lived a free life on the open sea until a whaling harpoon ended it.

Marie remembered being in Tokyo many years earlier and being repulsed by people chowing down on whale tongue, whale heart, and whale sushi. Her friend had urged her to try it, but she just could not. He pointed out that food preferences and prejudices are almost entirely cultural constructs and reminded her that she loved bacon and pigs were highly intelligent animals—at least as smart as whales. That relationship didn't last very long.

Another student explored why whales didn't get cancer. They should, as cancer starts in a cell that is abnormal, so it would follow that the bigger the mammal, the more cells there are, the more the risk of developing cancer. But it seems that the bigger the body, the less likely it is to develop tumors. She explained this was something called Peto's Paradox. Whales have tumor-suppressing genes, so comparative oncology is studying them to determine how these genes work and if they can be applied to humans.

Marie's last presenter, a very sweet but very shy student whose cheeks turned bright pink when Marie called on him, did the old standby—whale echolocation—the ability to observe an environment using sound. He explained that toothed whales send clicks and whistles out to bounce off nearby objects and return information about them by measuring the amount of time it takes for the sound waves to return. This information allows these animals to find food, navigate their surroundings, and become aware of danger. He added at the end that blind humans have been known to use echolocation to see their environment, and even sighted people can learn the skill. Marie was thrilled to see her class sincerely impressed by this whale trick. She reminded them that other animals echolocate too and asked them to think of the bats who catch thousands of mosquitoes on a hot summer night using this ability. Most of her students had never even seen a bat.

The seventh-floor hall was always very quiet, as it was lined with many of the science labs. Occasionally a few students in white lab coats would emerge from one, talking excitedly about something on their way to the elevators. Marie decided to take the stairs down to the library when she heard the sounds of someone crying. Sobbing, really. She stopped to locate the sound and realized it was coming from the stairwell she was headed for. It wouldn't be the first time Marie had heard a distraught student on those stairs. It seemed to be a popular place to fall apart. Marie hesitated. She didn't want to intrude, and even more, she didn't want to have to deal with whatever had happened to this student. Probably a breakup tale of woe. Valentine's Day was next week, and it was often the time that boys (for the most part) chose to break up with their girlfriends so they didn't have to get a Valentine's gift before dumping them. Marie had observed this mating phenomenon for years. But the crying was so completely gutting that Marie followed it into the stairwell.

Very gently, she asked, "Hi. Can I do anything for you?"

The young woman looked up, and then quickly averted her face. To Marie's shock, it was Michaela, her student who'd gone AWOL.

"I'm…I'm okay." She tried to wipe the tears from her face with her hands, but she was sodden. Marie pulled a mostly clean tissue from the bottom of her bag and handed it to her.

"Do you want me to leave you alone?"

Michaela nodded slowly. "Yes, please."

Marie went to the door and hesitated. "Michaela? You are not alone. Whatever it is, whatever is happening to you,

I'm here to listen. And help in any way I can, okay?"

"Professor Russell—wait!"

Marie let the door close and turned around. "Do you want to tell me what's going on?"

After some hesitation and resistance, and in a voice so mortified it was almost a whisper, Michaela told Marie what happened to her. She did not say who her rapist was. She did not share all the details—those were too horrifying and shameful to tell anyone. Ever. Marie felt her shame—it was palpable.

"It was my fault. I was so *stupid* for going there."

"No one goes to a party and *expects* to be raped. You are not stupid. You were *not* asking for it." But Marie knew intimately that no matter how many times a rape victim was told that, it took a long time to believe it. Michaela was no exception.

"I should have known there was something wrong with the whole thing. Why would a guy like that—" Michaela cut herself off.

"A guy like what?" Marie asked gently.

Michaela shook her head. "I don't want to say who he is."

"Okay."

Marie shifted her hips slightly to ease what was becoming pain from the hard floor.

"It's okay, Professor Russell. I'm all right. I'm sure you have to get to a class—"

"Please call me Marie. And I don't have to be anywhere but here right now."

They sat in silence for several minutes. Michaela sighed deeply once.

"Did you go to the police?"

Michaela hesitated. "No."

"Did you keep any…um…evidence?"

Michaela looked at Marie, tears filling her eyes again and nodded. She didn't say what she'd kept.

"That's good. That's very good, Michaela."

"But it doesn't matter. I'm not going to say anything. I can't. I'd have to tell my parents, and I can't. I can't tell my father. He would die."

Marie was always moved by how girls wanted to protect their fathers from such a thing—it was such an ancient, biblical impulse. Shield the father from the shame, or the idea of their daughter being defiled in such a way. Those patriarchal roots ran so very deep.

"You don't have to tell anyone until you want to, Michaela. I think you're very brave for telling me."

Marie started to sweep a loose strand of damp hair from Michaela's face, but withdrew her hand. "Would you like to go and see the counsellor downstairs?"

"No! I don't want to see a counsellor. I can't do that right now. Do you understand?"

"Yes, I do."

"It would make it…real."

Michaela bowed her head as though she was about to pray. Then she took another deep breath. "He's a very famous TV producer. And writer. And director too, I think."

Marie said nothing.

"I wanted to meet him because he…because I'm a writer and I act, too. I wanted to meet him to try and give him a script—like have the chance to actually put it in his hands. I'm such a fucking *idiot*."

Marie started to refute that again, but Michaela cut her off.

"And my so-called friend just informed me she tried to cut a *deal* with him—I say nothing and he gives me a *contract*." The last word came out in a garbled sob.

"I'm sorry—*what* did she do?"

Michaela explained as best she could that Brittany had basically tried to blackmail him.

"Who is this man, Michaela?"

She took another cathartic, deep breath. "Do you watch Netflix?"

"Sometimes. Yes."

"Have you ever watched *Nasty Women*?"

"Oh, god. Yes—I love—" Marie stopped herself in time.

"It was him. Jean Luc David."

Marie's jaw fell open in shock. "It doesn't matter who he is, Michaela, you have to go to the police."

"No! I can't do that. And you cannot tell anyone, Professor Russell. Please. Not *anyone*. Promise me you won't tell anyone!"

Marie very reluctantly said, "I promise."

Michaela started to cry again. This time, her whole body heaved in uncontrollable sobs. Marie and her teaching colleagues were never supposed to touch their students. In fact, they were never supposed to be alone in their office with a student unless the door was open. But that morning, Marie took the tiny, weeping Michaela in her arms and held her like a child.

# Thirty-Eight

THE DAY WAS VERY WINDY but sunny and mild for February, so he pulled the heavy hood from his head, as he was out of her line of vision now. He loved watching people who had no idea they were being observed. He noted their physical flaws, the idiosyncrasy of their gait. Were they slouched, hunched, erect? Did they walk pigeon-toed or splayed like a ballerina? What was their comportment? Fast or slow? Athletic or awkward? He liked to catch them picking their noses, or adjusting their underwear, or in winter, slipping and falling on the ice and then pretending like nothing happened. Sometimes if he observed someone for a while, he made up backstories for them—imagined what their house looked like, what they ate in front of the TV, what they had looked like in grade one, what they looked like having sex, what they looked like when they were sleeping. Watching complete strangers was one thing, but he particularly enjoyed watching people he knew. There was an intimacy and vulnerability between the observer and observed that he savored.

He especially enjoyed watching her. There she was, her mitts tucked under her armpit, awkwardly trying to put up posters on a lamppost. *Lost Dog! Chien Perdu!* He figured someone at the shelter was nice enough to print them for her and give her some duct tape. She was struggling to press the poster against the surface, then rip the tape, then make it stick. Of course, they weren't sticking because it was too cold, and he sympathized as she tried to add more tape so they would. Should he go and help her? The wind was snapping at the paper now too, and several posters that slipped from her hands went fluttering down the street. She watched them blow away, realized there was no point in chasing them, and tucked the remaining ones back into her plastic bag. She pulled a half-smoked cigarette from her pocket and struggled to light it in the wind. He remembered that feeling of the first inhalation. That delicious first hit of nicotine that slowed the world down. Forced you to take a step back. Reset. Of course, he didn't smoke anymore. That was a defilement of the body he had abandoned many years ago. It was a shame she was poisoning herself, as she was still very pretty even though these days she looked rough. Of course, the girl looked so much like *her*. There were thirty or so years between them, but it was remarkable. He watched as she exhaled the smoke from her cigarette through her nostrils. Did she not sense she was being watched? Had she recognized him that night? It had taken almost all his willpower not to tell her everything. He wanted to tell her that they would *all* be better off, now.

He knew that many people had told Nia to give up the search for the dog—just for the time being—for her mental health. But he knew she never would. And if she was focused on finding just the dog—that was good. Nia dropped the butt on the sidewalk and crushed it out with her heel. Then she looked up and gazed directly at him. He flipped his hood back up. But there was no recognition, no awareness in her eyes. Then she just turned and headed up the street. He crossed over to her side of the street and checked his watch. 10:59. She would probably be heading to the metro to get a little money. He followed her down the block, but she suddenly turned into the gate to the college. This was unusual. Was she going to put up posters there? In all these years since he had graduated, he'd never once gone inside, and he wasn't going to start now. He decided to let her go. The wind on the corner of Atwater and de Maisonneuve was often ferocious on a normal day, but now it was actually howling viciously through the wind tunnel the buildings created. He continued south and headed towards the market. He had other fish to fry.

# Thirty-Nine

ROMÉO DROVE ALONG the southwestern slope of Mount Royal, through the neighborhood of upper Westmount, for decades described as the richest in Canada. In spite of himself, Roméo still marveled at the homes he passed—palatial stone mansions with grand staircases separating them from the street, all certain of their own importance. Marie always said they looked like mausoleums, but some were more fancifully Victorian, featuring wraparound balconies and bell towers. One he passed had an enormous greenhouse attached to it, as well as tennis courts and a fully loaded hockey rink. Another had twin stone lions—almost the size of the ones in Trafalgar Square—on either side of its imposing front doors. Once the home of only the wealthiest Anglo Montrealers, upper Westmount now belonged to a more mixed *arriviste* crowd. But the legacy of white, Anglo privilege was there in every cornice, cupola, turret, and brilliantly chandeliered drawing room, still enough to get the blood boiling of every die-hard separatist in the province.

Roméo descended Belvedere Road, turned down Mount Pleasant, and hit the brakes hard, as a middle-aged, probably

Filipina, woman crossed the street with a dog twice her size who pulled her along in bursts of frustrated, boundless energy. She held onto the leash with both hands, and still couldn't completely restrain him. It was dog-walking hour, and almost on cue Filipina nannies emerged from these homes to walk the family dog. It was the time of day called *entre chien et loup*—when the light is so dim you can't distinguish a dog from a wolf, or the safely familiar from the unknown and dangerous. In February in Montreal, that was about five p.m.—just before their employers expected supper to be ready and waiting for them, the kids' homework done, and the house spotless as well. Roméo made sure the woman got to the other side of the street safely and watched her wait patiently as the dog stopped to squat and deposited a huge poop on the sidewalk. He pulled away before he had to witness her picking it up in a little plastic baggie.

As Roméo continued cautiously down the steep hill towards his destination, the contrast between these two possible worlds never failed to shock him. If you walked a straight line from this part of upper Westmount due south towards the St. Lawrence river, you would hit Cabot Square, less than two kilometers away. Roméo imagined how the people who lived in these castles would fare if they suddenly found themselves living like the homeless there. They wouldn't survive the day, he thought. Not even one day.

Roméo circled the narrow, congested streets near Ti-Coune's rooming house looking for a place to park. Cars were plowed into snowbanks every which way, and every empty space he spotted either had a fire hydrant or plastic orange cones warning any hopeful driver away. He flicked off the radio in frustration. Once again it featured the crowing orange rooster from south of the border, and the indignant hens who had to react to every new outrage. Roméo couldn't listen to another minute of him. Instead, he pulled away from the anarchy of Montreal streets in winter and into an empty construction lot beside another new condo project going up where the old Children's Hospital used to be. He quickly checked the messages on his phone—one from Marie, one from Sophie, one from Nicole, and one from Ti-Coune, suggesting they meet at the Cock and Bull instead of his little room, which he claimed was too depressing.

Roméo thought this was a terrible idea given how dramatically Ti-Coune fell off the wagon there last time. He shook his head in disapproval, but messaged Ti-Coune that he would meet him there, as they had agreed to compare any more information on the search for Hélène, and whatever light that search might shed on the Rosie Nukilik case. Roméo pulled out of the lot and headed towards the bar, reviewing the details of the various cases again. Rosie Nukilik knew Hélène Cousineau somehow—at least enough that she had her photo in her pocket and Roméo's cell number on the back of it. Who else but Hélène would have written that? Maybe any number of people—maybe the photo of Hélène standing at Beaver Lake was no more than a piece of scrap paper to hastily scribble a number on. But Roméo didn't think so. He felt certain there was a connection, however tenuous, between the two women. That older bartender with the orange hair also knew Hélène and thought she might be a bartender herself. Since then the trail had gone ice cold. Had Hélène left Montreal? Was she in some kind of danger related to the murder of Rosie? Or did that have absolutely nothing to do with her? Rosie also knew Isaac Blum. Or Isaac knew

Rosie in some way, Roméo was sure of it. What was she to him? Someone to save? Someone to use? Someone to squeeze the life out of? Was he carrying the kind of rage *that* required? He could be. He said he had lost everything, and those who have nothing to lose can be dangerous—like one of those murderers Roméo had played in a production of *Macbeth* in grade ten at Outremont High. He never forgot one of the lines they say just before they go off and kill Macbeth's best friend, Banquo. *I am one, my liege, whom the vile blows and buffets of the world hath so incensed that I am reckless what I do to spite the world.* Roméo smiled as he remembered who played the other murderer—none other than Ti-Coune Cousineau. Roméo remembered that Ti-Coune was so nervous the night of the show that Roméo had to say all his lines. Ti-Coune just stood there and tried to look menacing.

As Roméo turned onto Ste. Catherine street and gunned his car towards a parking spot opening up, he thought of the other homicide victim. Christian Bourque was not part of the Cabot Square crowd—he and his girlfriend, Nia, hung out closer to the new shelter on Park Avenue. But both Rosie and Christian were asphyxiated. Christian had a dog that had gone missing. It had probably run for its life but was now most likely dead. And what about the guy who Isaac Blum described walking off with Christian, most likely to his death? Blum was the only one to have seen him. Did he even exist at all? The forensic evidence was scarce. They'd found a few fibers from a generic jacket that could have been purchased in any one of fifty stores. There were so many boot prints near Rosie's body once the ambulance guys had left that the evidence was contaminated and useless. Anything near Christian's body had been obliterated by snowfall. The only traces of DNA they'd found were from Nia holding him in her arms and from the dog.

But they did know a few things: the killer was strong. Sizable. Almost certainly male. The murders were not random in the sense that homeless people were his targets, and the *modus operandi* was the same. He wondered again if there was a serial killer on the loose, and what his motives were. Was he on some kind of perverse personal mission? To do what? "Clean up" the streets?

Roméo thought about the so-called "Starlight Tours," where the police take Indigenous people they pick up off the streets for a "drive" in sub-zero temperatures and dump them on the outskirts of the city. Where they would freeze to death. To the twisted thinking of those police officers, that was social cleansing. Was it possible that this killer was a cop? One of his own? Roméo knew that in Montreal, racial profiling was notoriously common—people of color—especially Black and Arab—were arrested four times more frequently than people who were not. But Roméo also knew that Montrealers called the police to intervene on racialized people more than others. Was it only police racism or a xenophobic impulse so engrained in people that they saw a threat when none was there?

The Cock and Bull pub was almost empty, except for a couple of hardcore VLTers staring slack-jawed at the fruit spinning into view on their screens and a greasy, gray-haired geezer playing pool by himself. Behind the bar was the bartender he remembered from his last visit, although her hair was now evenly dyed bright blond, and her eye makeup was a little less Cleopatra and more Marilyn Monroe—if she'd lived long enough to be a *grandmaman*. The snake tattoo that coiled down her forearm was hidden by a skin-tight, sparkly black sweater. She spotted Roméo immediately and smiled warmly. Then she disappeared into the back room. Ti-Coune was bent over a drink, staring hard at nothing. Roméo put a hand on his shoulder in greeting and pulled him out of his thoughts.

"*Salut, mon grand.*" Roméo pointed at Ti-Coune's sweaty drink. "*C'est du Coca Cola, j'espere? T'as vraiment caller l'original l'autre soir.*"

Ti-Coune smiled ruefully. "*Ouah. Je veux pas avoir mal au cheveux.* I'm not drinking tonight." But he sure didn't seem happy about it. Roméo reached into a bowl of peanuts and dropped a few into his mouth. As he chewed he reminded Ti-Coune about the play they were in way back when. Ti-Coune couldn't remember any of it.

"*Anh? M'en souviens plus. T'es tu certain?* Are you sure?"

Roméo nodded. "*Ah oui, mon ami. Monsieur Shakespeare. Meme en l'anglais de la Reine Elizabeth!*"

Ti-Coune smiled grudgingly again. "Me, I prefer to forget about those days. They weren't so great."

Roméo and Ti-Coune weren't exactly friends in high school. Roméo was a star hockey player and dutiful student. Ti-Coune was an undiagnosed dyslexic and already a delinquent. But they both got beaten up regularly by the adult men in their lives—Roméo by his father, Ti-Coune by his mother's various boyfriends. There was solidarity in their shared shame and anger. Roméo sometimes wondered if Ti-Coune had PTSD from his childhood—he'd heard a psychologist recently on Radio Canada suggest that many children did and were never properly treated for it.

"I'm sorry, Jean-Michel. But so far, I've found nothing about Hélène. Except this connection to the dead woman. A possible connection."

Ti-Coune stared down disconsolately into his glass.

"And me, I found nothing neither. Maybe I'll head back up to Val David. *Ma chienne me manque.* I miss my dog."

Roméo tried to catch his eye, but he wouldn't return the glance.

"*Pis? Ta blonde?*" Roméo asked if he missed his girlfriend.

Ti-Coune finally looked at Roméo. "Hélène is gone. I don't know where, but I know she's not in this fucking city anymore."

Suddenly the bartender appeared before them, and Roméo ordered a club soda. In solidarity. As she handed it to him, she leaned a very impressive pair of breasts onto the bar in front of Roméo. Ti-Coune gave a low whistle.

"You're still in town, Detective Inspector."

Roméo nodded and sipped at his drink. "There's nothing quite like Montreal in February."

She reached into her décolletage with two red-nailed fingers and withdrew a folded piece of paper. "I have a message for you."

Roméo was trying very hard not to stare where he shouldn't. It was a challenge.

"This girl came in here a few nights ago. I saw that she was…a Native person, and so I thought, why not ask her if she knew this this Rosie Niku…Niku…The woman who was killed. I told her you'd been here looking for some information. She told me…that she was Rosie's *best friend.* But no cop has even come to ask her about Rosie."

She rested her hand on Roméo's and slid the paper

between his long fingers. "She didn't want to talk to the police at all, but I told her you were different. This is her number. She is expecting your call, and she will only talk to you."

Roméo looked up into the eyes of the bartender. They were a deep brown, outlined with jet black eyeliner and watching Roméo with amusement under those same painted on brows. She smelled of jasmine and flat beer.

"My number's there, too. Just in case you need my help."

Roméo reached into his wallet and left two twenties on the bar. "*Merci, Madame.*"

Ti-Coune was staring at the wall of liquor in front of him like he could empty every bottle right then and there. He looked like Captain Haddock from the Tintin books when he desperately needed a drink—choking and sweating with the thirst for it. Roméo grabbed his arm and pulled him off the stool. "Come on, *mon chum. Allons-y.*"

But Ti-Coune shrugged him off and slid back onto his seat. "I'm staying here."

Roméo took his arm again, but Ti-Coune shoved him away. Roméo knew better than to force him. When it came to man versus booze, booze usually bats last.

# Forty

THE VIEW OF LAC ST. LOUIS from the living room window that ran the length of the entire enormous room was quite spectacular, as a full moon illuminated its frozen surface so brightly it looked like it was almost daytime. A fire crackled convincingly in the fireplace, which had been painstakingly built by a family of stonemasons she had tracked down living in the little village of Ste. Lucie in the Laurentians. The grand room was made more intimate by the overstuffed armchairs in rich fabric the color of pomegranates, the intricately carved coffee table that had once been the door to a derelict temple in Thailand, and the several cashmere carpets she'd bought on a trip to Turkey when she'd made her first million dollars. The gorgeous bouquet of fresh gardenias she had received that morning from Sidney filled the entire room with their cloying fragrance. But Danielle didn't even see or appreciate any of it. Instead, she was drinking her fourth Negroni and staring at a gigantic television screen while she obsessively changed channels. Despite poring over every newspaper and online source she could find, there was still little information about the girl, and even less on the investigation into her death. Did she have parents who were grieving for her? A husband? Did she have a *child*? *Children*? What little the news covered didn't include anything personal, anyone speaking out for her. She turned up the volume on *Say Yes to the Dress*, and watched the store manager trying to fit a very small wedding dress on a very large woman. She changed the channel. A woman was sitting in her living room, piled high with garbage and papers and about twenty cats milling around. She changed the channel again to a young couple wandering around a gorgeous house in the tropics somewhere. Home porn. She could settle on that for a few minutes. Danielle needed sound. She needed voices who didn't know her, stories so removed from her experience that she could pretend a little longer that that terrible night had never happened. She needed to be anesthetized by the irrelevance of television, because if she wasn't, she kept hearing and feeling the horrible thump of her car as she hit that girl. She swallowed the last of the Negroni, opened her laptop and erased her search history again, terrified they could somehow find all this on her computer and arrest her based on that alone.

She looked at her phone again. She could ask to speak to the officer in charge and just tell him what happened. Just like that. She should never have left the scene of course, but she was convinced she'd hit a dog and the storm was too violent, too extreme to stop. He would understand. She would have to turn herself in. Go to court. Pay a fine. Maybe go before a judge and receive a sentence of a few years, which they would—what was the word? Postpone? Commute? Because of who she was in her community. Commune. Community. Were those words related? Of course she should have called her lawyer. Why didn't she call her fucking lawyer right away? Because her lawyer was her new boyfriend, that's why. Who Danielle was pretty sure wouldn't be too impressed with her. Who she was supposed to be out with tonight. When she called him to cancel he sounded more irritated than hurt. He'd made a reservation at L'Epicurien three months ago, and tonight was finally the Big Night.

So maybe that would come to an end, too. She had said she was sick to her stomach, and that at least, was true. She mixed herself another Negroni and began to pace up and down the huge room, oblivious to the lunar spectacle outside. She closed her eyes and thought at least she hadn't told Chloé, although she'd come close. So close. But when she looked up into Chloé's eyes, which were empty of anything but admiration and affection for her, she just couldn't.

If she actually told someone, then she'd have to accept that it might really have happened. But her need to confess was unbearable. She could talk to a priest—maybe the one who ran her little parish in La Pocatière, who had given her first communion and taken her first confession. But he had been arrested a few years ago for assaulting several boys at the boarding school he worked at. She could tell a friend, or one of her sisters, but just the idea of them first *judging* her and then maybe feeling pleased that something terribly unlucky had happened to her and not them was even more unacceptable.

Danielle lay down flat on her back on the plush cashmere rug and tried to breathe. Her head was spinning from the last drink. Maybe she could call anonymously. She could call from a phone booth—were there even any pay phones anymore? And say…what? Disguise her voice and say she did it? The couple on TV were sitting in two beach chairs leaning in for a kiss as the sun was setting over the ocean. Guess they bought the house. Just do it. Like the Nike ads. Get it over with.

Danielle suddenly got to her feet and grabbed her phone. She knew the Station 12 phone number off by heart. But the phone buzzed in her hand, startling her. Julie. Julie was calling. Danielle hesitated and then pressed *accept*.

"*Maman?*"

"What's wrong? Are you all right?"

Julie was at her best friend's house for an overnight movie party, and would never normally call her. She could hear shrieking in the background, and Julie's voice was shaky.

"*Maman?* I…I just got a call." More screams and now laughter in the background. Danielle felt an ocean of relief.

"I got a phone call from a funny man with an accent—he sounded like the mawwage man in *The Princess Bride*—remember him? He called from Oxford university—I am accepted to Oxford—in modern languages and linguistics! *Maman?* Did you hear me? I got into Oxford! *Maman?*"

"Oh, Julie. *Je suis tellement fière de toi.* I am so proud of you."

The rest came out in a torrent of words. She was accepted to Pembroke College. She could now apply for scholarships, but of course they would not cover even half the costs.

"*Maman*, he asked me to confirm my acceptance soon. I want to say yes now! Can I say yes now?"

Danielle nodded her head, but the words hadn't come out yet.

"*Maman? Allo?* Are you there?"

Danielle said yes, she could tell them yes. She couldn't hear the rest of the conversation, because Julie and her friends who she had just shared Danielle's answer with, were all screaming and laughing.

"*Merci, Maman! Merci, merci MERCI!!!! Je t'aime!*" she paused to catch her breath. "I'll tell you all the details tomorrow. Oh, I don't think I'll be sleeping tonight!"

The call ended with a loud, smacking air kiss from Julie. Danielle put the phone down and fell back onto the sofa. Her daughter was on her way into a big life. And Danielle was not going to let anything stop her.

# Forty-One

THE SNOW DANCED AND SWIRLED around them depending on the whims of the wind, which seemed to be undecided about which direction it was coming from. Roméo and Marie strolled through *Notre Dame de Grace* park, enjoying the soft drifts of powder under their boots, the snow falling like diamonds in the light of the streetlamps. They held hands, or at least mittens, and leaned against each other playfully as they meandered towards Marie's house. They were both pretty tipsy—Marie from the bottle of wine she had mostly drunk by herself, Roméo from the two beers and two scotches he'd accompanied their supper with. Apparently, they had both needed to drink.

Roméo had gone over the Rosie Nukilik case in detail with Marie—thinking out loud for the most part. Marie wanted to know everything, and he filled her in on the details Annie Qinnuayuak had provided. He asked her again what she could remember about Rosie.

"I mostly remember her wandering around the mall, you know, looking in shop windows. Once or twice I noticed her in the lineup at the Tim Hortons, because her parka was so exceptional and beautiful, especially compared to most of the students, who all feel they have to wear those identical Canada Goose jackets."

Roméo smiled at the memory of seeing so many of them in "uniform" at the mall.

"Was she with other people? Is there anyone you remember her hanging around with? Getting into an altercation with? An argument?"

"No. Not at all. I'm sorry. Once, or maybe twice, I noticed she was with another young woman—Inuit, as well. They seemed to laugh with each other a lot. Just like two normal women enjoying being young and…just being with a good friend."

Marie closed her eyes and shook her head. "Every time I think of her just…left there like that, I feel sick to my stomach." They both sat in silence for a few moments.

"And what about this boy found near Dawson? What is going on?"

"It would seem he was the victim of the same person, with the same MO. But there seem to be no other connections between them—other than they both spent time around Cabot Square and the mall. Bourque has been living on the streets for years, but to our knowledge, Rosie Nukilik had not."

"It's so terribly sad about that boy, too."

Roméo drained the last of his scotch and gestured for the check.

"He had a dog who apparently never left his side—it's gone missing. The girlfriend is desperate to find it."

"Oh my God, I hope she does."

As they waited to pay Roméo got her up-to-date on the Hélène Cousineau situation—which was to say up to nowhere. They slipped into their coats and said good night to their waiter. Besides The Decision, each of them had something more they needed to talk about—but the walk home to Marie's gave them a few more minutes of undiluted pleasure. Marie stopped to show Roméo a perfect snowflake that had landed on her black mitten. Every Canadian has done this a hundred times, but there was always a feeling of awe in the moment.

"At the center of almost every snow crystal is a tiny mote of dust. Did you know that?"

Roméo shook his head. "I did not."

"It can be a speck of volcanic ash, or even a particle from outer space. *Imaginez vous.*"

Roméo took her hand back and continued their walk.

"I know that every snowflake is unique—no two snowflakes are alike."

Marie smiled. "On a molecular level, yes they are. Each ice crystal has a unique path to the ground. Each floats through different clouds of different temperatures and varying levels of moisture, which means it will grow in a unique way. But it's hard to believe that in the trillions of snowflakes that form, no two form in exactly the same way."

"Thank you, Professor Russell."

Marie gave Roméo a little push. "Well, you made an assertion that is not factual, Detective Inspector Leduc."

He gently shouldered her back, then caught Marie in his arms. Roméo leaned down to kiss her, but both of them had so much winter snot dripping from their noses that they each turned away at the critical moment. They both wiped it away with the palms of their mittens and laughed. Marie pulled Roméo down the park's snowy walkway. "Let's go home."

They didn't even make it to the bedroom. As soon as they got in Marie's front door they'd kicked off their snow boots, peeled away the layers of winter clothes, and fell into each other on Marie's living room sofa. It was short, a bit feral and yet sweet. Now Marie lounged under a poofy duvet, regarding the trail of discarded clothes from the front door. That kind of urgency didn't happen much anymore, but it certainly was delicious when it did. Roméo returned from the kitchen with two glasses of single malt whiskey. He had tied Marie's scarf around his waist. Marie threw the duvet over her head in mock shame.

"Oh my God. I didn't even close the living room curtains."

Roméo went to the window and quickly drew them. "That must've given the neighbors a thrill."

Marie accepted the glass of scotch. "Two old farts doing it? I'm not sure *thrill* is the right word."

Roméo lowered his very long body back onto the sofa and took Marie in his arms under the duvet. They both sipped at their whiskey and stared at the perfectly symmetrical flame of Marie's gas fireplace. The gravel-voiced Leonard Cohen sang through their speakers about dancing to the end of love. They were suddenly quiet, each separated by their respective preoccupations. In all the evidence Roméo had pored over he knew he'd missed some clue to the identity of the killer. He had messaged Steve Pouliot about interviewing Rosie Nukilik's friend, Charlotte, and was waiting for an answer. But answering texts on Saturday date nights was forbidden. When Roméo was working a case, he hated getting distracted by anything. Or anyone. This laser-focus of his had destroyed his marriage. His wife's sleeping with her high-school sweetheart hadn't helped much either, but Roméo knew that his neglect and focus on his job to the exclusion of all else had propelled Elyse right into Guy's arms. He would not let that happen again.

"Roméo?"

"Mmmnnn?"

"Are you awake?"

"Of course I am. I just closed my eyes for a minute—I'm a bit sleepy from the scotch. And. Well. Seeing as I'm an old fart now, according to my girlfriend. That's what happens to us old farts after sex."

Marie pulled her arms out from under the duvet, sat up and rubbed her face. Then she took a breath and turned to face Roméo. "I have to tell you something."

"Okay."

"It involves breaking someone's confidence—"

"Then you shouldn't say anything."

"I promised to say nothing." Marie chewed on her thumb cuticle. "But I think it's too important a...situation to respect that. I think public safety trumps it."

Roméo was sitting up now and looking intently at Marie. "Tell me."

Marie told Roméo everything she knew about Michaela and her assault. Roméo was silent for several moments. Although he had arrested the serial rapist and murderer William Fyfe years earlier, the horrors of his crimes were still fresh for Roméo. He took Marie's hands. They were cold.

"I am so sorry that happened to your student. It was brave of her to tell you. Am I to assume if she swore you to secrecy that she did not report the assault to the police?"

"Yes."

"Did she get treatment? Report it to a doctor? To a sexual assault prevention center? To anyone?"

"No." Marie hesitated. "Only me—that I know of."

Roméo exhaled and ran his hand through his unruly hair. "Do you know if she kept any of the…evidence?"

Marie sighed. "She said she took pictures of her injuries. But she took a shower and I think tried to scrub all traces of him from her—including using mouthwash and brushing her teeth."

Roméo muttered something to himself.

"What did you say?"

"There might still be something to test. If she kept her underwear, for example. His DNA might be on it. But that doesn't prove rape. It only proves that he touched her and then her underwear."

"There was blood. She is…was…a virgin."

"Jesus." Roméo slowly rubbed his eyes for several seconds. "How many days ago did this happen?"

"Last Friday night—so eight days ago."

Roméo shook his head. "That's not so good."

"Can you do something? If we can persuade her to press charges? I think she will—she's just too traumatized right now. And she hasn't even told her parents."

"She has to come to us. But it won't be a slam-dunk because she has little physical evidence, and she waited too long to come forward. It may be a case of he said–she said. I just don't understand. She's a smart woman, isn't she? Why didn't she go to the police? Why didn't she report this?"

Marie sat up and moved away from Roméo. "*Smart*? What's smart got to do with it? Men rape smart women. Men rape stupid women. Old women, young women, ugly women, pretty women. You know that more than *anyone!*"

"Maybe I didn't express myself precisely." Roméo switched to French. "I thought that girls—women—these days knew, or at least were told to *never* get rid of evidence. To always get a medical examination. So there's a record. Somewhere."

"Believe me, you don't always think so clearly and—and *logically* when someone has just forced his dick into your mouth. Or your vagina. Or your anus. Or all three. You just want to make it all go away."

Roméo tried to take Marie's hand again, but she pulled it away.

"I know, Marie. I know."

"No. You don't. Michaela was angry at herself for getting raped. At *herself*—for putting herself in that situation—"

"I understand that. She goes off alone with a powerful man. In retrospect, she must feel very naïve and stupid—"

"WHAT?" Marie slipped off the sofa and stood up with the duvet gathered around her. She punched off the music. Roméo was left sitting there with just her scarf on.

"So she was asking for it?"

"I said," Roméo grabbed a cushion and clutched it to his stomach. "That I can see *why* she feels that way—NOT that she *should* feel that way. At all."

"Well, thank you for that, Camille Paglia."

"Who?"

"A so-called feminist who said that a girl who lets herself get dead drunk at a fraternity party is an idiot—she said feminists call this blaming the victim, but she called it plain common sense—putting all the responsibility on the woman not to provoke or arouse a man in any way, or to always be on high alert. I mean. No wonder with attitudes like that, more women don't come forward—"

Roméo answered very gently. "Marie. I am not the enemy."

"Sometimes it feels like all men are. Men like Jean Luc David are protected by the system, by their power—so they can assault women with impunity—"

"Not impunity. They can be punished—but women must speak up. And we have to make it *safer* and easier so they can come forward with no shame and no fear, of course—"

"Yeah, well it's hard in this rape culture—the whole system creates and supports these guys."

"Not all men are rapists, Marie. And this idea is so… alienating to normal men. Men who aren't rapists. Men who are trying to understand—"

"I'm not talking about all men. I'm talking about a culture that normalizes and trivializes sexual violence. It's all rigged in favor of the rapists—"

"Marie, there has to be high evidentiary standard in rape cases, because we still believe people are innocent until proven guilty. In rape cases, beyond a reasonable doubt is sometimes hard to prove—so often a prosecutor will not bring the case to trial—hence the need to preserve the evidence—"

"Why don't we believe women when they say they were raped? If you had spoken to Michaela, you'd know every word of it was true."

"Not all women *always* tell the truth. There has to be a trial. It is fundamental to our system—"

"I know. I heard you the first time."

Roméo's phone suddenly buzzed and vibrated, almost moving itself across the coffee table. He glanced at it, but of course didn't answer. Marie snatched the phone and looked at the caller ID.

"It's Nicole. Your ex."

"She's not my ex."

"You slept with her—had sex with her. There was a clear abuse of power there."

"We had consensual sex. Once."

"But you were—are—her boss. Maybe she felt she had to have sex with you—to stay in your good graces—and make detective sergeant."

"Fuck off, Marie."

Roméo never swore. At least never at her. Marie was shocked. And a bit ashamed that she had provoked him to it. Roméo did not like to gossip and never kissed and told. But he felt a powerful urge to now.

"Let's just say that she was a very willing participant. If anyone was coerced. Or pressured? It was me. Not her."

Roméo's phone beeped that a message had been left. It was Nicole LaFramboise. Her ears must have been burning red hot. He wondered what would trigger a call from Nicole at ten o'clock on a Saturday night. But he sure as hell wasn't going to answer it. Marie sat down next to Roméo and took one of his hands in hers. She rubbed his long fingers, the carefully trimmed nails, the bump where he'd broken two knuckles that had never properly healed.

"We've been putting up with this shit for way too long. My generation just shut up and took it, you know. But this generation? I want it to be way better for them. I never want to hear a woman like Michaela ever again say *she* was stupid for *letting* it happen. I never want to hear ever again that she's ashamed to tell her father. Do you understand?"

Roméo shook his head. "I can't change the world. I can't fix the system overnight. It's imperfect, I know. But I don't agree that this situation is impossible, or that the system is so misogynistic that it doesn't want men like this to be punished. If you can manage to get Michaela to go to the police, then I will do everything in my power to get her case into the hands of the best team I know. That's what I can do."

Marie kissed the top of Roméo's broken hand. "Then for now, that will have to be enough."

But as Marie leaned back into Roméo's arms, she was not at all certain she could persuade Michaela to break her silence. She had also not told Roméo what Michaela's girlfriend had done to extort some money from that man. What effect would that have on the case if it ever even went forward? Marie needed to think. Alone.

"I'm going to take a bath. Will you be coming up soon?"

Roméo eased Marie out of his embrace. "I'm going to just sit by the fire here for a few minutes."

She kissed his forehead and with the duvet pulled around her shoulders, headed a bit woozily upstairs. The two dogs stirred from their sleep and got unsteadily to their feet. Barney opted to stay with Roméo, but Dog yawned, stretched and padded after Marie. Roméo drained the dregs of his scotch and picked up his phone to check the message from Nicole LaFramboise. She had just asked him to call her back. Marie stopped, her hand on the banister of the staircase, and turned back to Roméo.

"Why would the killer go after someone who has a big dog? I mean…wouldn't the dog be protective? Why would he take such a risk? What if he's after the dogs?"

# Forty-Two

The uneven snowbanks along the side of the condo construction site looked like someone had spilled buckets of blood on them. But it was just the squalid reflection of the red police car lights staining the blanket of whiteness. A feeble February morning sun was just coming up, casting a surreal yellow shadow over the entire chaotic scene. Detective Steve Pouliot hastened to keep up with Detective Cauchon, who was crossing the street to the crime scene at a surprisingly fast pace. He had finally decided to get fully involved in these so-called *Homeless Murders/Assassins Sans Abri!* as *Le Journal de Montréal* was ghoulishly calling them. There was much more attention being given them by the press and media now, so Cauchon was suddenly all over it. The story of Christian Bourque's missing dog, and the loving girlfriend who was determined to find it had been picked up by one of the city reporters, and now they were all in a feeding frenzy on that meal. A missing dog was so much more appealing than a couple of dead homeless people. Steve Pouliot noted that the scene had been securely cordoned off and was being overseen by at least a dozen uniformed officers. He headed towards the ambulance on Cauchon's heels.

A pair of paramedics were leaning over a stretcher, one adjusting an oxygen mask, the other pulling a reflective emergency blanket over the man and belting him onto the gurney. Cauchon didn't even need to show his badge, but Pouliot did. The big man leaned against the ambulance bumper and got the lowdown on what had happened. Steve Pouliot discreetly bent over the man. The victim looked to be about sixty years old, but it was hard to tell. They had found no ID on him. His face was quite deeply browned and lined by the winter sun and exposure. There was embedded dirt in the crow's feet at his eyes, and in the scruffy gray beard that grew in patches on his jaw and cheeks. It looked like some frostbite had gotten the tip of his nose and ear lobes. The paramedic explained that although he was slightly hypothermic and in shock, his vital signs were good. His eyes were closed, but he was conscious. Steve Pouliot felt his heart beat a little faster. They finally had someone who could perhaps identify his assailant. He couldn't wait to let Roméo Leduc know. He pulled out his phone to send a text, and suddenly his wrist was wrenched away. The man had grabbed him. He looked up at Steve, his eyes wide open and terrified. With his other trembling hand, which was attached to an IV bag, he pulled away the oxygen mask. Steve Pouliot leaned in closer so he could hear.

"*Mon chien*? Whersh mmme dog?"

"Pardon? What did you say?" The man had just a few teeth left in his mouth and was very hard to understand.

"*Mon...mon...CHIEN!*"

The paramedics hastened to the man, and started to ask Steve Pouliot to step aside, but the man grabbed him even harder.

"He said…he said to me. He said, 'I will help you. Don't be scared. Help is coming—'"

The man had a thick accent that Steve couldn't quite place. He had to listen very carefully to make out what he was saying.

"Then he…SAT…on me and…and…choked me. But I, I am a fucking veteran of…of…Vietnam, okay? I know how to, how to move some FUCKER off me!"

He tried to sit up, but the paramedics eased him back onto the stretcher.

"Where's my dog? Where is she?"

He began to whimper. "I think he took her. I think he took MY DOG!!!"

Steve asked a cop on duty if a dog had been found. He shook his head.

He returned to the man, whose eyes were closed again. A few tears had escaped them and were trickling down his cheeks.

"*Monsieur?* Did you know the man who attacked you? Did you recognize him at all? His face? His voice?"

The man answered very slowly, as though every word was now an effort.

"I didn't see. His face. But. I knew his voice. Know his voice." The man made a painfully shallow inhalation, and the paramedics stepped in. The oxygen mask was back on, and they moved to close the ambulance doors.

"Where are you taking him?"

"The General. It's closest."

Steve Pouliot jumped down from the back of the ambulance before the doors were slammed shut. They had a victim who might be able to identify the attacker. They had a face. Someone with a memory. A survivor. Steve Pouliot pulled his jacket tighter around his neck, and his hat over his ears. There was a nasty dampness in the air. Snow would be coming soon. He headed towards where he'd left Detective Cauchon but stopped abruptly in his tracks. Detective Cauchon was holding forth to a scrum of reporters and TV cameras. He didn't even glance Steve's way. Not once. Steve Pouliot made his way out of the three-ring circus and immediately texted Detective Inspector Roméo Leduc.

# Forty-Three

"BONJOUR, BOSS! *Comment ça va ce matin?* Did you get my message last—"

"Yes. I got it."

There was a brief hesitation. "Oh. Okay....Did someone get up on the wrong side of the bed this morning?"

"*Non, pas du tout.* What do you have for me?"

"It's just that you sound a bit...weird. Is everything all right?"

"Everything is fine, Detective Sergeant LaFramboise. What do you have?"

Roméo glanced over at Marie, who was busy in the kitchen frying up some eggs and bacon. Noah was running around being chased by his aunt Ruby, who was now popping out from behind the sofa and startling him into fits of shrieking and giggles. Ben and Maya were drinking coffee like their lives depended on it. Young parenthood. One of the greatest tests of character Roméo had experienced.

He stepped out for quiet into the living room. Nicole's tone chilled to officially professional.

"Well, Detective Inspector Leduc. I went through all

the Chantal Lalonde-Fukushima case files. I rechecked all the interviews and had the team re-question the family and a few friends, as per your suggestion. Then, quite by chance, I discovered a photograph of Chantal with this guy. Jean Luc David." Nicole knew that Roméo wasn't much into popular culture, and certainly not a binge-watcher of television series. He still had a VCR, for God's sake.

"Do you know who he is?"

"Yes. Of course I do."

Nicole realized that even Roméo couldn't avoid the thousands of words written about this guy, and his picture in every Quebec tabloid newspaper, along with significant worldwide exposure.

"I'm wondering if there's a possible link between Jean Luc David and the girl who was murdered." She explained that Chantal had aspirations to be a model, and Nicole had a hunch that maybe she'd gone to one—or possibly more—of his parties and just hadn't told anyone. She also told Roméo what her college girlfriend had said about him, and the rumors of his infamous debauchery that were circulating in those days.

"I think he's cleaned up his act significantly. He has a couple of grown kids, a brand new wife, and settled into domestic bliss. At least for show. But…."

Roméo's heart began to pound. "But?"

"Well, I did a little digging, and it turns out that David pled guilty to one count of sexual assault in nineteen ninety-seven, and was sentenced to one year of probation. He appealed, and his sentence was reduced to an *unconditional discharge*—which left him with no criminal record. Get this—the authorities felt he was too important in Quebec to be compromised in any way—too big to fail, you know?"

Roméo nodded his head, but made no audible reply. Nicole pushed on.

"That way, he was still allowed to travel all over the world. Basically, the powers that be did not want to clip his wings in any way. He was just too important to the Quebec *brand*." Nicole made an exhalation of disgust. "Unbelievable. *Deguelasse*."

"There's no real evidence at all connecting him to Chantal, is there?"

Nicole's voice sank. "No, boss. None."

"Who did he assault in 'ninety-seven?"

"An eighteen-year-old woman. Girl. From St. Lambert. On the South Shore of the city. That's all I know."

"I want you to pull all but one guy off the other cold case team for now and get everyone on this. Get Robert to go over every possible link to the girl and David that you can. Every old photo, every newspaper article. Re-interview whatever high-school friends you can find. Someone must know something."

"Okay. Got it."

"I want this pursued vigorously, Nicole. Okay? Everyone piles on, understood?"

Nicole watched as Léo dumped the entire box of mega blocks she had just tidied back onto the living room floor.

"Yes, boss."

"I want the DNA testing from the Fukushima case pulled and check to see if David has DNA on file. Got it?"

"Yes, boss. Thy will be done."

There was an awkward pause.

"Is there anything else?"

Roméo thought of the conversation with Marie the night before.

"No. Nothing for now."

Roméo ended the call and stepped back into the kitchen. Marie was trying to coax Noah into eating a piece of orange. Noah was in his highchair, entertaining everyone by dropping bits of his breakfast on Dog's enormous head, while Barney, Marie's much smaller pug, kept hurling himself at Dog's head to lick it off. Ruby, Ben, and Maya were all watching him and laughing themselves silly, which only encouraged him to do it more. Roméo tousled the mop of silky black curls on Noah's head. Marie took the spoon from him and explained gently that the food was for his mouth, not Dog's head. Roméo felt a sudden pang of guilt that Sophie was not a part of this. Marie always invited her for these Sunday brunches and special family events, but she usually sent her excuses at the last minute. Roméo knew she often felt alienated at these gatherings of Marie's family, even after two years. He didn't know why. Roméo resolved that next time, he would just go and get her, and insist that Sophie join them. Marie was still wiping her grandson down and briefly looked up into Roméo's eyes. She could see that he wanted a word with her, so she handed the soggy mess of food and paper towel to Ben and wiped her hands on her pajamas.

"What is it?"

"Do you think you could speak with Michaela Cruz again?"

"I hope to. Why? What's happened?"

Just as he was about to answer, Roméo's phone beeped in his pocket. He fished it out and checked the screen. *Another attack. Looks like our guy. Victim survived. Has a dog. Gone to Montreal General hospital.*

"I have to go."

"What? You haven't even eaten breakfast—I made you a special vegan plate of woodchips!" Marie protested.

Roméo kissed Marie's lips very lightly. "I have to go."

"You will call me later and we will continue this conversation, right?"

Roméo nodded and threw his coat and hat on. He patted his pockets and checked that his gloves and keys were there. By the time he looked up and went to wave goodbye, Marie had already returned to the kitchen. Roméo watched as they all chatted and laughed with each other. The family circle had just closed up tight again.

# Forty-Four

*Monday afternoon*
*February 11, 2019*

ROMÉO SQUINTED THROUGH the windshield of his car trying to make out the road through the relentlessly falling snow. Another blizzard was pummeling Montreal, the third in as many weeks, but Roméo felt a strange relief. After several winters of freakishly warm weather and green Christmases, maybe all this snow meant climate change wasn't as dire as all the scientists were predicting, and he could deny its inevitability a little bit longer. He glanced over at Steve Pouliot who'd been quiet since Roméo had picked him up outside the station. He was working at getting his right thumbnail chewed down to the quick. Being lowest on the food chain at Station 12 probably left him on edge much of the time. Plus, everyone probably knew Pouliot was cooperating with Roméo despite the Sûreté du Québec being the enemy.

The victim had finally been identified as Travis Hall, sixty-seven years old. He had suffered two broken ribs, and a fractured hyoid bone in his throat. He was very, very lucky to be alive. Pouliot had taken a statement from him for what it was worth. The attack had left him so traumatized he'd had a psychotic episode and was largely incoherent. The nurse had explained that he was quite heavily medicated for pain and anxiety, and that Pouliot would have to wait twenty-four hours at least. Roméo peered through the windshield.

"Did you know that the Inuit have something like fifty different words for snow?"

Steve Pouliot stopped chewing long enough to say "No."

"The word for recently fallen snow is *qanittaq*—not sure of my pronunciation there."

Pouliot nodded but his index finger was now being worked on.

"And *qanniapaluk* means a very light falling snow, but in still air. Quite poetic, isn't it?" Roméo leaned in closer to the steering wheel. "Language adapts to people's need to express what is most important to them. I guess I should have looked up the word for snow coming down at you like an avenging angel of hell."

Pouliot stopped gnawing on his hand and looked at Roméo. "You like to read, don't you?"

Roméo smiled. "Yes, I do. Always have. Why? Do you?"

Steve Pouliot shook his head. "I like to *do* things more."

"Such as?"

"I'd like to catch this fucker."

Roméo thought of a local newscast he'd watched that morning. They'd interviewed several homeless people from around Cabot Square. They were really scared now. The threat of violence—being beaten, robbed, or assaulted was always a reality of life on the street. But now, the thought that there was someone actually targeting and killing homeless people was terrifying. Veteran street people who'd never go to a shelter were doing so for the first time. Night patrols had doubled their numbers. The SPVM, in response to media pressure, were organizing a special squad of police officers to put on the case. But Roméo knew that the killer could strike again at any time, and most certainly would.

Charlotte Paloosie sat on one of the white plastic chairs at a white plastic table inside the enormous room at the Le Foyer shelter. Next to her was Annie Qinnuayuak, the shelter worker Roméo and Steve had interviewed there a week earlier. Roméo had arranged for Annie to join them, as he felt that was a safer and more appropriate way to approach Rosie's friend. He had also asked Charlotte's permission before he brought Steve Pouliot inside. She was nervous around the police, and Roméo noticed she never looked at Steve once. For some reason, she made direct and open eye contact with Roméo. He felt perhaps he had Annie to thank for that.

"Charlotte, thank you very much for coming to talk to us today. Especially in this snowstorm."

"That's okay. I'm pretty used to them."

A guarded smile formed on Annie's face, but she said nothing.

"So, we'd like to just go right to asking you a few questions. Is that okay with you?"

Charlotte nodded. Her dark brown eyes bore into Roméo. Straight to his heart.

"Can you tell us how you met Rosie?"

"I was at Roasters—you know, that restaurant in the

mall? At Alexis Nihon? I used to go there a lot, because one of the waitresses there was real nice, and she always asked us questions about home, and how we were doing here in the South, in the city. And like, she always managed to get us a bowl of soup, or a dessert for no charge."

Roméo smiled and held up a finger to pause her for a moment.

"Sorry—may I ask what brought you here to Montreal?"

"So I could go to school here. At Dawson College. They got a special program for First Nations and Inuit people…to transition to college. It's really great. The teachers are so nice. There's not much opportunity for…higher education back home. There's one school with grades one to twelve, but hardly anybody goes after grade nine." Charlotte looked down at her hands. "And we had a lot of…suicides…so, I really needed to get out."

Roméo had been horrified to learn that the suicide rate in Inuit communities was ten to twenty times the national average. The loss of their land and traditional life, the devastation to their communities had made suicide epidemic. *Especially amongst schoolchildren.*

"I was billeted with these real nice people. But, anyway, I didn't finish my first semester."

"Can you tell us why?"

Charlotte hesitated, then continued. "They really tried to make it work for me. The people were really nice. But I didn't know anyone, and I was too homesick. I missed my brothers and sisters. I missed the quiet up there, you know? And everyone here was, like, so different in their thinking. We got in a discussion in class about the seal hunt—I took this class—Humanities, I think it was—and we read this guy's book who said eating animals was immoral. For my people, the hunt is…it's what keeps us alive, even if we can get food from the South. It's our blood. It's who we are."

Roméo remembered the commercial seal hunt was effectively and finally ended by a huge protest movement led by Greenpeace and French actress Brigitte Bardot and continued by Beatle Paul McCartney. He remembered photos of them on the ice floes, cuddling baby harp seals and excoriating people who hunted them. The Inuit have been hunting seals for many generations, but they never hunted the baby white-coated seal pups targeted by the anti-sealing campaigns. Still, the ban had a devastating effect on their local economy. Roméo knew he had never realized how crucial seals are to the Inuit way of life.

"That must have been real tough for you."

Charlotte glanced over for just a moment at Annie.

"Yeah, well. Like I said. I didn't make it through the term."

Annie Qinnuayuak briefly touched the top of Charlotte's hand.

"But Charlotte has decided not to give up. She's going to go back in the fall semester."

Roméo nodded. "I'm so glad to hear it. So you met Rosie Nukilik at…Roasters?"

"Yes. She was just sitting by herself, and we started talking. She was pretty reserved, but really like, serious and funny at the same time, you know? Anyway, she told me she was from Salluit, which is like a really small community north of where I'm from."

Roméo remembered from his quick Wikipedia search that Salluit means "The Thin Ones" in Inuktitut, the language of the Nunavik Inuit. The name came from a time, long ago, when some Inuit were told the region was rich in wildlife. Yet when they arrived, they found almost nothing to eat and, as a result, suffered near starvation.

"I'm from Kujuuag—it's only like eleven thousand people, but it's a big city compared to Salluit. So, we started telling stories about coming south to a real city, and how we didn't know how to do nothing here. Like, there's no traffic lights in Nunavik, so when Rosie first came here, she didn't know how to cross the street. She said somebody had to show her how! Rosie told me all the stuff she did since she came down here with her sister that she was embarrassed of." Charlotte started to giggle, and then just as quickly, stopped herself.

"I told her about how I just walked into this girl's room at the place I was staying, and the girl freaked out on me. Like, freaked out. Up north, that's what we do—no one ever knocks or nothing. You just go right on in to someone's place. It was a small thing, but I felt really stupid about it."

Charlotte looked down at her sweater and picked a stray piece of fluff from it. She had very small, capable hands that looked like they'd seen some hard work.

"We used to make each other feel less homesick, you know, by telling stories." She hesitated. "Like, in Nunavik, most everyone loves to golf—well, the men do—but they also stick their hunting rifles along in their golf bags in case a caribou or a bear or a seal came along. We laughed about that." Charlotte looked at the two policemen and felt the need to explain.

"Because now, some of the animals are a lot harder to find. My grandfather said it's changed so much."

Roméo had read everything he could on Nunavik. And the Arctic North. Besides the social problems, climate change was accelerating at a pace scientists had not even predicted.

The Arctic was warming four times faster than the rest of the planet, and Nunavik was experiencing the effects earlier than anywhere. Caribou herds were dying off. Winter fishing was harder, too, since the water didn't reliably freeze over the way it used to just a generation ago. Maybe the most terrifying was that the permafrost was melting for the first time in thousands of years, which then released more methane, a greenhouse gas, than they could even measure. It's like the Inuit were the most extreme victims of colonization. Again. Roméo suddenly felt dizzy with the immensity of it all.

Annie Qinnuayuak decided to interject. "Charlotte, can you tell us a bit more about what Rosie was like?"

"She really loved her sister, Maggie. They were real close. Maggie was her big sister, and looked out for Rosie. She told me that once that her uncle tried to…mess with her, and Maggie came home and just about killed him. So when Maggie got sick, Rosie came down here to be with her—for her treatment."

Roméo continued. "And she was staying at this Aboriginal Women's Residence?"

"Yes. She liked it there okay."

"Did Rosie have other friends that you knew?"

"Not so many, I don't think. I warned her about hanging out in the square, because that's where a lot of Inuit go anyway. But there's guys there—who…target girls like us. They're like, waiting for us. So, she stayed away. But then, her sister died. And for Rosie, it was like her world ended. I told her to get back up to Salluit, you know? I told her to get out of the city because it wasn't good for her. For us. I was staying because I wanted to try another program at the college, but for Rosie? I saw her a few weeks after her sister passed. She didn't look good. She lost a lot of weight, and her eyes weren't clear. She was still pretty drunk from the night before."

Charlotte got quiet for a few moments. Annie Qinnuayuak took her hand this time and asked, "Would you like to take a little break?"

Charlotte shook her head and looked directly at Roméo, and finally at Steve Pouliot, too. "I wanted to tell you before that she was a real good piano player."

Annie nodded in agreement.

"Like, sort of amazing. We went over to the waitress's apartment one night, and Rosie sees that she has this old piano—I mean it was pretty crappy—it had broken keys and everything, but Rosie just went and sat down at it and just knew how to play. You know when someone suddenly does something unusual, or has this like…talent you're not expecting? She just played these really great songs. Like, straight out of her head."

Roméo smiled at Charlotte. "She sounds like a really wonderful person, Charlotte."

"She is. She was."

Roméo looked briefly through his notes. "What was the waitress's name?"

"Helen. Or…*Hélène*? Like the French way to say it. You don't pronounce the 'H.'"

"*What?*" Roméo realized he'd almost shouted. "Do you know her last name?"

"Um. No. I just knew her as *Hélène*."

"Do you know where we can find her to talk to her?"

"No. I haven't seen her in a while—maybe five or six months?"

To Annie Qinnuayuak's and Steve Pouliot's surprise,

Roméo reached into his pocket and pulled out his cell phone. He scrolled through it, then held it up to Charlotte.

"Is this the waitress Hélène?"

The girl took the phone from Roméo's hand and peered at the photo. "Yeah. That's her. Maybe when she was a bit younger?"

"Sorry—where was her apartment?"

"Someplace on Lambert-Closse—I can find the address, I think. It was just a little place, pretty basic but okay, you know. Clean. We went over maybe a couple of times to watch Netflix, or just hang out—"

Roméo would go to Roasters and check employee records. He would find Hélène.

"Did you meet other people there?"

"No. It was just us." Charlotte thought for a moment. "Wait, there was this guy once."

Roméo felt a *frisson* of anticipation. "Who was this guy?"

"He dropped by one night to visit Hélène. We weren't sure if he was her boyfriend or something. Like, I think he sure wanted to be. He was pretty nice—like, pretty friendly and curious about me and Rosie. Maybe more to impress Hélène? He was really complimentary about Rosie's piano playing. He said she was *gifted*. Anyway, they seemed to hit it off."

"What did he look like?"

"Um. He was very tall. Like, huge. And white, an Anglo-Canadian type of guy. He seemed like a military guy. He had very good—what's the word? *Posture*. Like he had a stick up his ass." She giggled again. "Sorry."

Roméo's *frisson* had become a chill. "What was his name?"

Charlotte frowned. A few moments later she said, "I can't remember. I'm sorry. I only met him the one time—"

"How old was he?"

"I'm not so great with figuring out people's age. Maybe forty? Or maybe fifty? Sixty?"

Roméo took a silent deep breath. "Please try to think of his name."

"I can't remember. I'm sorry!" Charlotte tugged nervously on strands of her thick, black hair.

Roméo turned off his recorder and reached across the table to shake Charlotte's hand. He thanked her for being so brave in coming forward and told her how helpful she had been. He also reminded her that she might be asked to look at a few photos. He was hoping this mystery man might somehow be tracked down. Roméo and Steve Pouliot stood up and started to gather the many layers of clothes to prepare for the storm outside. Annie and Charlotte were talking with each other quietly—Annie probably just checking in on her, Roméo suspected. He touched Charlotte very gently on the shoulder and said, "I'm very, very sorry for what happened to your friend." Then he beckoned to Steve Pouliot and they headed towards the door.

"Do you know what happened to Rosie's dog?"

Roméo stopped in his tracks. "Rosie had a dog?"

"Yes. After Maggie died, like I said, Rosie really fell apart for a while. I don't really know half of what she got up to." She took a breath. "But then, a while later, she found this little lost dog—this ugly little thing. It looked like a little white weasel—or rat—I mean, we'd talked about the dogs up in our communities—how sometimes we were really scared of them, but Rosie, she just fell in love with it. I guess she kind of gave it the love she missed for her sister. She had to hide it because she wasn't allowed a dog at the place she was staying. I don't know what happened with that. The next I heard was—" Charlotte's voice faltered. "That she'd been hit by a car. And died."

Roméo recalled what Ti-Coune said about Nia Fellows and her boyfriend—something about a dog missing. And Steve Pouliot had told him that in the most recent attack the survivor was desperate to find his dog. What was going on here? Was Marie right? Was the killer after the dogs? Stealing dogs? For what possible reason? For medical experiments? For fighting? For some other awful way to use them? It was certainly not unheard of. But why would he have to kill their owners first?

# Forty-Five

DESPITE BEING ADVISED TO GIVE UP the search for Hamlet, Nia had spent the entire afternoon at The Bunker scrolling through rescue shelter websites. Everyone kept saying he should have been spotted by now, but Nia knew they really meant that Hamlet was probably dead. What if someone had found him after he'd been wandering for a few days and then brought him to a shelter? What if someone had kept him for a few days, and then decided he was too much trouble and dumped him? She checked the SPCA website daily and had again called every single shelter within a radius of 100 miles. Nothing. Because some of the local media had publicized Nia's situation, The Bunker was fielding dozens of calls a day from concerned dog lovers and the workers were now starting to get quite annoyed by the whole thing. There were actual human beings at this shelter who were struggling through every day, but a missing dog got the passionate attention of the city. Many of The Bunker's intake workers knew that for the most part, these concerned citizens meant well, but they also felt that their priorities were pretty screwed up. Therese, one of the older counsellors, was keeping a close eye on Nia. She had brought up her case with the rest of the team, and they all agreed that now that she was not tied to Christian anymore, she might start to turn her life around. Therese had checked Nia's school records in the Eastern Townships; her IQ test score was exceptionally high. She had been a gifted student as a child and then went off the rails in high school, after her parents were arrested. Diagnosed with OD—oppositional disorder—and possible borderline personality, Nia had resisted all forms of authority. Whenever The Bunker counsellors gently raised the possibility of going back to school, Nia just laughed and responded with some variation of, "Most of the really smart people I know—I mean the *really* smart ones? Don't do so well in that so-called 'real' world. As in school. Christian was brilliant. Off the charts. It didn't do him much good, did it?"

No, Nia had to focus all her energy on finding Hamlet. Because if she didn't, she would have to think of other things, like Christian's parents, who had come to get their son's body and return him to South Porcupine. A meeting had been arranged with them, which Nia had agreed to in spite of her gut screaming at her not to. The mother was alarmingly normal. She looked like any middle-aged lady in any little town anywhere—including Rockville where Nia had grown up. She looked nothing like the monster Christian had described. The three of them sat uncomfortably on the edge of the plastic chairs in the Private Room and spoke very little. The mother didn't hug Nia or try to comfort her in any way. The father actually shook Nia's hand, like they had just agreed to some kind of deal. Nia examined their faces to see how terribly they were grieving. Maybe Christian's death was a relief to them. She wanted to be kind. She wanted to forgive them for their sins against him, but she couldn't. She knew too much. She told them that Christian was a lovely, generous, and thoughtful man who had been trying very hard to navigate his life. She told them she loved him very much. What else could she say, really? Certainly not the truth about how he felt about his entire life with them. The mother had opened a little plastic baggie of Christian's—what was the word?—*effects*. Nia asked if she could keep Christian's ring—it was a silver signet ring he would twist on his beautiful ring finger when he got agitated. His mother smiled very briefly at Nia, and said no. That ring had been his grandfather's and it would go back to the *family*. Nia wanted nothing else.

She thought about her own family. Her mother had somehow tracked her down, called for her at The Bunker and left a message. *I am so sorry for what happened to your friend. Please call me.*

One day she had felt so low and so entirely alone that she almost did call her mother. Then, for some reason, she remembered one summer night when she was about eight years old, when she was supposed to be asleep. She heard cars slowly approaching along their long gravel driveway, and when the passengers in the back seats got out, Nia could see they had blindfolds on. She thought it was some kind of game her parents were playing with their friends. Blind Man's Bluff? A surprise birthday party? She only learned years later that that's how their customers arrived at her house—they were never allowed to see where their suppliers lived or how they got there. When they tried to convince Nia that they just had drugs for their own infrequent use—they were not *dealers*—Nia knew the truth. And so did everyone else. She lost everything. Her parents. Her home. Her dog, Heathcliff, and her two cats, Franny and Zooey. She had lost her school and pretty much all her friends. And what did she get instead? A foster home where the woman's fat husband pinned her against the washer in the laundry room and shoved his hands up her skirt while his wife was making supper ten feet away. And that was just the introduction to foster care. So, no. Nia would not be calling her mother.

Nia went to warm up a cup of tepid tea in the microwave. Her eyes were going all squiggy from staring at the screen too long and too intensely. Just as she was returning to the computer, a hand restrained her.

"I think I found your dog."

It was Claude. He actually lived in a little town called St. Calixte, northeast of Montreal. He stayed at The Bunker when he came into the city to beg, often bringing his two dogs with him. The guy was down on his luck—his truck was seized for unpaid parking tickets, and without it, he lost his moving business. But he had a *home.* And he'd had a *truck.* Nia didn't like him much and so mostly avoided him, as she suspected the dogs were just props for his begging business. He knew it, and consequently was always trying to ingratiate himself with her.

"What do you mean?"

He pulled her over to another screen and scrolled down to a wall of dog photos. It was a no-kill rescue shelter Nia had not seen before. In some place called l'Épiphanie.

"Look. Isn't that Hamlet?"

On the screen appeared a photo of a dog, looking quite disconsolately and timidly up at the camera. His name was "Buddy," and the site claimed he was a rescue from a Korean dog farm. Nia peered at the screen. Enlarged it. Looked at all the angles. Her heart started to pound. It *really* looked like Hamlet. His collar was different, and he seemed thinner. But this dog had the same bizarre big torso and stubby legs as Hamlet. What were the odds that he had such a doppelganger?

"Where is l'Épiphanie? Do you know where that is?"

Claude nodded. "It's about forty-five minutes northeast of here. Maybe an hour." He moved a little closer to Nia. "Shit. If I had my truck back, I'd take you there."

Nia quickly jotted down all the information and printed out the picture of Hamlet. She had to get there as soon as possible, but she knew the bus service in those little towns was sketchy, and according to the Google map, it looked like this place was outside of town in the middle of exactly nowhere.

"Can I use your phone?"

"I don't have a phone. Can't afford it."

Nia smirked at him and gestured for him to hand it over. Claude reluctantly pulled it from under his shirt where he'd hidden it inside his belt. "Don't tell anyone. They'll all want to be using it."

Nia found the crumpled piece of paper that she'd stashed away in her backpack and tapped in the number.

"Hi. It's me. Nia. I think I've found my dog. Can you take me to him?"

# Forty-Six

"IF YOU CHANGE YOUR MIND about pressing charges, it's not too late. Please call me." Michaela lay on her side in the same fetal position she'd been in for several hours, replaying Marie Russell's messages over and over. She had left several since yesterday, imploring Michaela to call her back, but they now seemed to have stopped. She rolled onto her back and looked around her little room, washed golden yellow with the setting winter sun. Nothing in it felt like her. Nothing in it mattered. Her stupid photos of her friends from elementary school tucked into her vanity mirror, mementoes from her high school—her dried wrist corsage from prom and the numerous awards and trophies she'd won for academic excellence. The stuffed animals she just couldn't part with lined up in her window. She felt like burning all of it. She replayed the assault over and over in her head, wondering what she could have said or done to stop him, and why she was the one he raped. Was it so obvious to him that she was a perfect target?

What did that say about her—feminist that she was. Stupid enough to go to a man's fucking office alone.

Michaela had tried to get back to her normal routine. She got up and showered every morning. She dressed herself, and got some food down her throat, but she tasted nothing. She felt nothing. She went back to her classes at school— because if she blew this semester then *he would win* totally and completely. And Mika could not let that happen. Would not let that happen. She would not be a *victim*. Except nothing made sense. Why was she going to school when a rapist was free to live his life? Why was she talking to these people in class who knew nothing about what had happened to her? Why was she even studying or writing endless idiotic essays? What was the point? She tried to stay calm and in control, but whenever she saw Brittany she felt like throwing up. Nothing made any sense at all. There was no point to doing *anything*. Despite Marie Russell assuring her that she would be there for her, and that her partner was a policeman who very much wanted her to come forward and break her silence, Michaela was far from convinced. Still, Michaela gathered every ounce of the little energy she had, slowly roused herself to a sitting position, and pulled her laptop closer. She decided to do something—something very Michaela. More research.

*One woman in three has been the victim of at least one sexual assault from the age of sixteen. Slightly more than eight in ten victims know their assailant—close to seven in ten victims were sexually assaulted in a private residence. And only one out of twenty sexual assaults is ever reported to the police, who often dismiss and minimize the case or dissuade the victim from pressing charges. If their case does makes it to court, they often endure a brutal cross-examination that often re-victimizes them.*

No wonder that most victims never even bothered reporting the crime. Michaela read on. *Forty percent of women with a physical or mental disability will be sexually assaulted at least once before they turn eighteen. Over seventy-five percent of Indigenous girls under eighteen have been sexually assaulted.*

The statistics were shocking. And until just nine days earlier, they were only that—numbers. But Michaela also thought about the systemic misogyny of the justice system, where sexual violence is the only crime where the idea of consent is examined to prove that a crime has been committed. If someone is physically attacked and injured they don't begin the court case by asking the victim if they *wanted* to be attacked. In rape cases, the prosecution has to demonstrate beyond a reasonable doubt that there was no consent, and as a result, the victim is positioned as a potential liar from the beginning of the legal process.

Through her closed door, Michaela could hear the sounds of life from downstairs. Her mother expertly chopping something. Her father's low drone, punctuated by short bursts of her mother's laughter. He probably had a beer in his hand and was going over his day for her. If she…if she told them—that would mean it really had happened. There would be no going back. Would they ever look at her the same way again?

She slowly got up from her bed, tucked her unbrushed mess of hair behind her ears, put on a cleaner top, and opened her bedroom door. Now she could hear her parents doing what they did every weeknight at six o'clock. They were playing *Jeopardy*—loudly declaring their mostly wrong answers at the TV. Michaela put her foot on the first step, hesitated, and then began heading down the stairs to her innocent parents.

# Forty-Seven

*Wednesday*
*February 13, 2019*

"*TABERNOOSH, IL FAIT FRETTE!* It's too fucking cold!" It was twenty-four below zero outside, and Ti-Coune Cousineau was scraping away the frost on the inside of the windshield with one hand and steering the car with the other. He had borrowed this crappy old Honda Civic from his old "friend" from the Cock and Bull pub after Nia had called him and asked for his help. The heater and defroster didn't really work, and Ti-Coune could barely feel his feet anymore. It also stank of beer, weed, and some other disgusting thing he preferred not to identify. He was feeling grumpy and fervently wishing he himself could have a beer right about now. "I told you we should've gone another day."

"I couldn't wait another day," Nia snapped. She glanced at this strange old man from the bar who was putting himself out for her and softened. "I really, really appreciate your doing this for me. Give me the scraper. I can do that while you're driving."

They hadn't talked much once they'd found themselves in the car and realized the journey was going to be epic given the car's many challenges. Despite a provincial law that said all vehicles had to have snow tires on by December 15, the car's tires were almost bald all-seasons, and Ti-Coune felt like they could go skidding into a ditch at any moment. It wasn't a good feeling. What did feel good, though, was getting farther and farther from Montreal and further into the Laurentian boreal forest. They had passed the little town of l'Assomption, named for the assumption of the Virgin Mary directly into heaven Ti-Coune remembered from his grade one catechism class. Now they were driving past the sign for the golf course in l'Épiphanie.

"Do you know what *l'épiphanie* is?" Ti-Coune asked as he peered through the hole in the windshield frost that Nia had temporarily cleared.

"That's when the wise men came to visit Jesus, isn't it? On the twelfth day after Christmas?"

Ti-Coune glanced at Nia and smiled. "Not bad. I thought your generation had no religion at all."

"I didn't. I mean, I was raised to be very anti- *any* religion. But I read a lot. I read the entire Old and New Testaments when I dropped out of high school. For some crazy reason, I thought there might be some answers there. Boy, was I wrong."

"When I was a kid, and they said the three wise men brought gold, frankincense, and myrrh, I always called it Frankenstein. Used to make my teacher laugh."

"An epiphany means something else too, you know."

"Oh yeah? What does it mean?"

"It's like the moment when a person is suddenly struck

with a life-changing realization, which changes the rest of the story. It often starts with a small, everyday experience that shows something much bigger."

"I never heard of that."

Nia grabbed the scraper again and went at the windshield on her side of the car.

"You ever had one?"

Ti-Coune nodded. "*Oui, ma belle*. I had a few. One big one, two years ago. But I'm not sure the rest of my story is changed yet."

He suddenly made a sharp right turn. "That's the road to St. Esprit—according to Google, it's down this way."

The car fishtailed a bit on the icy dusting of snow caused by the frigid temperature. Ti-Coune slowed down and pointed to a road sign indicating the next town.

"The Saint Esprit." He said with English pronunciation.

"Who got the Virgin Mary pregnant through her ear."

Ti-Coune started to laugh. "*Anh*? What did you say?"

"The Holy Spirit got Mary pregnant through her ear so her…um…sexual organs could remain intact. So she could still be a virgin. That's very important to Catholics, by the way."

"*Mets-en.*"

"What does that mean?"

"*Mets-en*? It means…oh…it means in English—*put more. Say it more.*"

"Maybe it means…you can say that again!"

Nia and Ti-Coune both chuckled at yet another unique Quebecois expression. Then they both got quiet and watched the road ahead, unfolding before them in a straight line of blue-whiteness punctuated with the odd forlorn farmhouse.

"I hope they have your dog."

"Thanks." Nia added nothing further. She didn't want to even entertain the possibility that they might not.

"I hope you find your sister. Hélène? What is she like?"

Ti-Coune was so slow to respond that Nia thought he might not. Then, he took a deep breath and said, "She's the toughest person I've ever known—she is like those toy clowns, you know the kind they buy for kids to punch? But no matter how hard you punch it, it always comes back up to face you again? That's Hélène." He tried not to look at Nia, as he felt he might cry. "And she saved my life. Many times."

He composed himself and glanced at Nia briefly, but then returned his eyes to the road ahead. "She is also very beautiful. She looks a bit like you—or you look like her."

Ti-Coune instantly felt her entire body tighten. He shouldn't have said that. Did she think that was a come-on? "I'm not into young girls, okay? I like you. I like dogs. That's it, that's all. Okay?"

"Okay."

They drove in silence for several more minutes along the St. Esprit road. Suddenly Ti-Coune braked the car to a stop, threw it into reverse, and backed about 500 feet up the road, the car whining all the way.

"I saw a sign. I think we passed it."

Nia glanced back over her shoulder until Ti-Coune stopped and put the car into drive. Nailed on a tree, half-hidden by branches and handwritten in uneven letters in what looked like black marker was a sign that read La Crèche>>.

"That's IT!" Nia whipped around excitedly in her seat. "Turn here."

"*Crissti*. They really don't want you to find it, *anh*?"

Ti-Coune turned the car down the road that cut a thin line through a dense swath of balsam trees and continued along for another ten minutes or so. There was absolutely nothing around them. There were no other cars, no houses, no gas stations, no *dépanneurs*. Only the trees and the snowy road. Ti-Coune drove carefully along it, looking for signs of human life. Suddenly the road just ended. They peered through what was now the already diminishing light of early afternoon, trying to make its way through the dense foliage. Then Nia saw it.

"Look! There's a house! Right through there, see? Wait, there are two houses!"

Ti-Coune turned the car into the trees and along a very narrow, snow-packed driveway. He aimed his tires into the two deep ruts that led them towards their destination.

Before them was a basic prefab bungalow, and behind it they could just make out a few outbuildings. As they got out of the car, Nia reminded Ti-Coune of what they'd agreed to say, just in case "Buddy" had been stolen.

"Remember, we're here to adopt a dog. We saw the one named Buddy on the website and thought he could use a home."

Ti-Coune quickly took out his phone and thumbed a quick text. There wasn't much power left on his phone. "Okay. You do the talking."

As they approached the modest house, the front door opened, and framed inside it was an extraordinarily tall person. Nia gave a little wave and announced why they were there. As they got closer, they realized the person was in fact, female, although it wasn't easy to tell. She had on what they used to call a red lumberjack jacket that was faded with age and gray with wear. She had on a pair of baggy overalls tucked into decrepit winter boots with the tongues hanging out over the laces. Her long, gray hair was matted and looked like a toddler had glued it in patches to her head. She stared at them balefully. "You need an appointment to visit the dogs. You didn't make an appointment." And with that, she slammed the door. Nia marched right up to it and knocked hard until the door reopened. In her heavily accented but serviceable French she said, "We don't have an appointment, but we drove all the way from Montreal to find a dog. To choose a dog."

The woman looked Nia up and down with disdain. "You don't just choose a dog. A dog chooses you." But she nodded at them to come in the house and directed them toward her kitchen table. A little dog who looked like a scruffy white rat scrabbled after her as she disappeared into an adjoining room where a TV was on very loud. She returned moments later with a few crumpled papers. "Fill these out. Name, address, phone, and why you want a dog." Then she disappeared into a different room through a curtained doorway, with the little white dog on her heels.

Nia and Ti-Coune looked at each other, eyebrows raised, and shrugged.

"Is that a man or a woman?" Ti-Coune whispered.

"I'm not sure—but a woman, I think. The voice."

"*Elle lui manque des bardeaux.*"

Nia looked at him quizzically. "Ehm. She's missing a few.... I don't know the word in English."

Nia smiled and started to fill out the forms in earnest, while Ti-Coune took in his surroundings. The kitchen was small and despite the appearance of the woman of the house, remarkably tidy and clean. Immaculate, even. The little table they were seated at had a worn but spotless floral tablecloth, and on it were a white Scotty dog saltshaker and a black Scotty dog for the pepper. There was almost nothing on the walls at all. Not a photograph, not a cheesy still life painting, not a little sign with a stupid saying like "It's beer o'clock somewhere." The only thing hanging on the wall was a calendar. It advertised an auto parts store, and had a sexy woman bent over a car wearing very short shorts and a bikini top, winking at the viewer. Except someone had drawn a thick dog collar on her in pen, and two X's over her eyes. It was very disconcerting. Nia finished filling out the form and watched Ti-Coune checking out the kitchen. He very much wanted to see what was in the fridge but restrained himself. The giant woman had not returned.

"*Allo? Madame? Allo? Madame, vous êtes là?*" Nia called out to the back room, but there was no response. Only the loud ticking of a wall clock beside the fridge. "*Allo?*" Nia wandered through the rest of the house. "I've finished filling the paper out. Can we go see the dogs?"

There was no answer. Ti-Coune put his coat on and gestured to Nia to do the same.

"I don't have a good feeling here. I think we should go."

Nia and Ti-Coune went back out the front door towards their car, but Nia broke away to circle around the house to see what was in the backyard. There was still no sign of the woman who had greeted them. Suddenly, there was an explosion of barking, whining, and yapping dogs. Nia started to run towards the sound, while Ti-Coune trudged along the path through the snow behind her, on alert for any sign of human life. Ahead of them was a small building hidden in a copse of trees, and there Nia saw the first dogs—maybe a dozen of them in a huge enclosure, with individual dog houses lined up like on a suburban street, and a few tree stumps and old tractor tires embedded in the snow for them to play on. Several started to bark at her and Ti-Coune, but their tails were wagging and their ears perked forward. One ran up and down from corner to corner trying to get their attention, while another stood on his hind legs against the fence and whined at them. They all seemed happy and in good health. But Nia did not see Hamlet. Ti-Coune let a one-eyed pitbull lick his fingers through the fence, then heard Nia call to him.

"Jean-Michel! I think there's another kennel here. I can hear more dogs!" Ti-Coune jogged toward Nia's voice. When he'd caught up with her they walked together through a large shed towards the sound of more barking.

"Oh my God, that sounds like Hamlet!" Nia started to run, and before she knew it, she was in a similar dog run to the last one, but this one had a tin roof and was completely enclosed. But there were no dogs to be found there at all. Ti-Coune followed her inside. "Nia? Please stay with me here. Nia!"

"I can hear him. I'm sure that's his bark." And then, there he was. Hamlet. He hurled himself at the fence separating them, jumping up and down, crazy with joy at the sight of Nia. She fell to her knees and tried to touch him through the fence. They were both crying. Ti-Coune left them there and went back to the metal gate they had come through. It had somehow locked behind them. He suddenly felt sick to his stomach. Had someone locked them in? This outdoor cage with no heat, no shelter? He called several times for the woman, but his voice just echoed in the windless, frigid air. Nia got to her feet. "What is it?"

"It's locked. The gate is locked."

"What? That's not likely. Let me try."

Nia pried at it, rattled it, and finally bashed at the lock. It was impossible to open. Ti-Coune began shouting for help to the woman again, and Nia added her cries to his. No one came. Hamlet paced frantically back and forth along the fence that separated him from Nia, never taking his eyes off her. Ti-Coune did the only thing possible. He pulled out his phone to text Roméo. But his phone was dead. The cold had just killed the battery.

# Forty-Eight

SHE WONDERED WHAT HAD HAPPENED to him. For close to seven years now, *Le Bon Samaritain* had come every Monday and Thursday to pick up day-old bread and charcuterie that was otherwise destined for the garbage bin and taken it to distribute to the homeless. In all those years, she could count on one hand how many times he had not shown up. It was now Thursday afternoon, and Madame Yvonne was just tidying up after the feeding frenzy of the lunchtime rush. She was trying to restore some order to what was left of the neat rows of bread she had so lovingly and carefully stacked at six o'clock that morning. Thursdays were usually very busy, and she always looked forward to Monsieur Blum and his gentle, polite small talk before the madness of her day began. She read somewhere that it was these small human interactions, courteous, polite exchanges of no great importance, that made a society healthier and saner. Isaac Blum was one of the people who made it better. Madame Yvonne had customers who'd jostle and elbow each other out of line for the last *pain rustique* or one of Chez Babette's famous *croissants aux amandes*. Isaac was always a gentleman, and he tipped very well. She had prepared a bag of day-old bread and pastries for him anyway and hoped that he hadn't caught the second round of flu that was laying waste to every employee at the bakery and half the city. Madame Yvonne sat heavily in the chair where she always took her break, and slipped her shoes off her aching, swollen feet. She was getting too old for this.

Isaac Blum sat in his ancient armchair watching the thick paper curl into the blue flames of the fire. He had removed every photograph from his wall, and every bit of information he had collected over the years would soon be now gone, consumed in minutes. He had seen so many come, some go back, and so many die or disappear. He watched the photos he'd taken of Shannon disappear. And then her friend, Vickee. There would be no evidence of any of these girls. Not the kind he collected. He had spent so many years trying to make a connection with them, especially after his own children were taken from him.

The day after Isaac was falsely charged with sexual interference, his ex-wife took their young son and daughter and flew home to Brazil. She informed Isaac she was never coming back to Canada, and he'd never see his kids again. He had followed them down to Sao Paolo, but his wife came from a powerful and connected military family, and they closed ranks. Isaac was forced to leave without his children and without even seeing them or saying goodbye. They were grown up now, maybe even with families of their own. Were they Brazilian now? Or back in Canada? Did they ever, ever think of him?

He tossed the photo of Nia he'd taken months ago into the flames. She never let him in. Maybe because she had always had that boy with her—they were hermetically sealed in their affection and loyalty to each other. Isaac thought of Shannon again, and the crack burns he'd seen on her arms that day, the brand her pimp had given her. He had spent so many years listening to their stories, their heartbreak, their memories of better times. Some of them. Some didn't have any memories of better times. They devoted themselves to obliterating all memories—to living in the ever present. Listening to them made him feel part of something bigger, and he desperately needed to feel bigger than himself. He had only wanted some record that they had existed—and mostly for the girls he felt were in real danger. Didn't everyone have the right to exist? To be treated equally? He knew that society's answer to that was, in fact, a resounding no.

He peeled away the last photograph on his wall. Of Rosie Nukilik, lying on her back, her head resting on her arm like she was just having a rest, frozen solid. He dropped her into the fire as well. He felt terribly, terribly deflated and sad. But he had no choice. His…behavior could be misconstrued. Once you make a mistake, you pay forever. Or they make you pay forever. This is what Isaac had learned. He had already been punished once for something he hadn't done. He was not going to let that happen again.

# Forty-Nine

ROMÉO WAS SUPPOSED TO ACCOMPANY Steve Pouliot to interview Travis Hall, the survivor of the most recent attack by the "homeless killer." But as Roméo was on his way to the Montreal General hospital, he got a call from Marie. Joel and Shelly her "next door" neighbors (who lived a good fifteen-minute walk from her house in Ste. Lucie) had called to tell Marie that her little house in the woods had been broken into. Again. They had been snowshoeing the trail behind her place when they heard the alarm. When they arrived, they saw that her front door was smashed in and a snowdrift had gathered inside the foyer. They assured her that they'd shoveled out the snow, nailed a piece of plywood to the doorframe, and called the local police. But Marie needed to get up there as soon as possible, and Roméo had offered to drive her because Ruby had borrowed Marie's car to go to a study break retreat in the mountains near the Vermont border.

Now Marie and Roméo were on their way "up north" on highway 15, with about forty-five minutes to go, just passing the gargantuan shopping mall in Blainville (or "Blandville" as Ruby called it), that ran alongside the highway, identical to every other shopping mall the world over. Marie gazed out at the sky, which had been a luminous blue all day, but was now already deepening into a deep cobalt as the afternoon wore on and the sun began its slow descent on the horizon. They passed a billboard with a giant close-up of Danielle Champagne's handsome face and her upraised index finger demanding an end to conjugal violence with a ÇA SUFFIT! Marie thought it was a brilliant campaign. She knew that despite her great success, Danielle Champagne herself had been a victim of domestic violence, documented in horrifying detail in the wildly popular autobiography she'd published a few years earlier. Good on her for using her influence and success to try to do something about it, Marie thought. They were just coming up to St. Jerome where Roméo had his precinct office when Marie took his hand and pressed it gently.

"Thanks for this."

Roméo nodded and squeezed Marie's hand in response. "*Il n'y a pas de quoi.*"

Marie watched the box stores of St. Jerome clustered along the highway fall behind them. "Who do you think it was? It can't be the Thibodeau twins again. They're still in jail, aren't they?"

The Thibodeau twins were part of a local and legendary family of criminals who earned a living breaking into the houses of rich weekenders in the upper Laurentians. They famously had escaped the law for many years, until two years earlier when they finally got caught red-handed. Marie's house had been a target in that criminal shopping spree as well.

"They're still in jail, but I heard their younger cousins from Rawdon are in the business now. They seem to have passed their family values on to the next generation. It's quite heartwarming, isn't it?"

"Those fuckers. It's not like I have anything left to steal." The twins got Marie's TV, a few bottles of scotch, and an old laptop the last time they'd robbed her.

"Who knows? Maybe this will lead to something really positive."

Marie looked at Roméo balefully. "Oh yeah? Like what?"

He glanced at her for a second and then returned his eyes to the road ahead. "Like…meeting the love of your life."

Marie and Roméo met for the first time when her house was broken into, and Roméo came to investigate. It was certainly unusual that a Detective Chief Inspector with the Sûreté du Québec would investigate a local B-and-E, but there had been a murder in the area, and Roméo thought they might be related. As it turned out, they weren't. Marie's involvement in that case involved a connection to the victim that dated back to her childhood growing up on the West Island of Montreal.

Roméo could still palpably remember the feeling the first time he saw Marie. She was crawling out from under her bed where she had hidden some precious jewelry that, as it turned out, the thieves did not find. When she looked up at Roméo with those brown eyes that just penetrated right through him, he had what could only be described as a *coup de foudre*—love at first sight. Marie also later admitted that when he took her hand to say goodbye that day, she hadn't felt anything that electric and erotic since high school.

Marie took his hand again. "I guess I should thank the Thibodeau twins for bringing us together, right?"

"You can always do it in person—I think you can find them in the Bordeaux prison. You could be one of those women who writes to inmates and ends up falling in love with one."

They continued along in silence for a few more minutes, each lost in the delicious memory of that first encounter. A distance sign for Ste. Agathe loomed on their right and disappeared.

Marie released a deep sigh. "I really miss Louis, you know?" Louis Lachance, the local *homme à tout faire* who charged next to nothing, did solid work, and was totally reliable had once come to fix her burst pipes on Christmas day.

"I felt like I always had someone looking out for the house. And for me, too of course—when I'm alone up there. At least if he was in the home in Ste. Lucie he could hang out with my mom." Marie's mother, Claire, had been moved to a residence in Ste. Lucie so Marie could visit her more easily. She was now in the middle stages of Alzheimer's disease.

Roméo raised an eyebrow. "Your *maman* and Louis?"

"Why not? Old people fall in love."

Roméo decided not to remind Marie that her mother couldn't even recognize her much of the time, let alone Louis Lachance.

"Of course. Look at us."

Marie punched him gently on the arm. "I mean *very* old people. Elderly. I love the idea of them sitting on the porch, holding hands, drinking tea, chatting about this and that."

Marie was sometimes acutely aware that she was ten years older than Roméo, who looked ten years younger than he was. It sometimes made her feel very insecure, like the entire glorious ride they were on could be cut short at any time. Roméo glanced at her for a moment and then asked, "Have you heard from your student?"

"No. Nothing. And I've left several messages."

"I wanted to tell you that Nic—Detective LaFramboise—may have…found something on him—"

"WHAT? What do you mean?"

"Nothing is at all confirmed yet, and it's very speculative, so don't get too excited about—"

"That fucker. Michaela has to come forward—for her own healing—and we have to nail him—"

"Marie. Listen. Michaela has to go through a very difficult process here—she may not be ready—"

Roméo was interrupted by a ping on his phone. A text message. From Ti-Coune Cousineau. *I'm with that girl Nia—with the dead boyfriend. She lost her dog. We think we found it at this shelter—in l'Épiphanie. We're here. My phone's about to die.*

Ti-Coune had attached the Google map coordinates to the text.

"What is it? Anything important?"

Roméo showed her the message on his phone. "I wonder how this happened."

"He sent the directions to this place."

"Yes."

"Let's go, then."

"What? No, I'll drop you at your place, and I'll maybe go check it out on my way back to the office."

"Roméo. What if it *is* the missing dog? What if there's some connection to the killer here? We should go now and check it out."

Roméo laughed. "We? There's no *we* here. I'll drop you off at your house, and then I'll meet you up there later." He hesitated. "I will go, if I decide there's merit, okay?"

Marie narrowed her eyes at Roméo. "No. Not okay. You're going, and I'm coming with you."

Roméo raised his hand in protest and shook his head.

"Marie, I am not allowed to bring you with me. It's protocol. *Pas de question.* I'll drop you off at the precinct in St. Jerome, then. We're five minutes away. I can get one of the officers to drive you to your place."

Marie turned and glared at Roméo. "Rosie had a dog. Christian had a dog. This last victim had a dog. You know there's something going on here. What if this is connected to Rosie's murder? I'm coming. I'm part of this too, you know. Let's go."

Roméo muttered something softly and abruptly steered his car into the U-turn lane reserved for police in the middle of the divided highway. He stopped to attach the cherry light to the top of his car and then pulled into the southbound lane right back in the direction they'd just come from.

It took them some time to find the place. Like Ti-Coune, Roméo drove right past the obscure La Crèche sign to the shelter and had to backtrack to find the right road. Roméo finally directed his car down the long and narrow snowy lane. He hadn't said a single word to Marie since they'd turned around near Sainte Therese, still furious with her for insisting on coming along. They both saw the house up ahead at the same time and pointed it out to each other simultaneously. Roméo pulled his car as close to the building as he could without risking getting stuck in the deep snow. He turned off the engine, took the keys, and turned to Marie.

"This is police business that you have no part of. You will sit in this car until I come back for you. *Under no circumstances* are you to leave this car. Do you understand?"

"Yes."

"Promise me you will stay here until I return."

"I promise."

He looked directly into her eyes for one long moment, and then pulled open his door. Roméo breathed in the frigid air, infused with the smell of woodstove smoke. He realized how much colder it had gotten—the tiny hairs stuck to the inside of his nose as he inhaled, a telltale sign of well below zero temperatures. He pulled his hat lower over his ears and as Marie watched his progress through the windshield of the car, Roméo trudged through the snow towards the front door of the house.

# Fifty

STEVE POULIOT WAS USED to the other cops asking him to retrieve something they had deliberately placed out of his reach, so he'd have to use a chair or ladder to get it. Then they made sure the ladder disappeared, so he'd have to ask a taller cop for help, while his Neanderthal colleagues chuckled in chorus. Some of the older ones made fun of his neatly trimmed beard and mid-fade crew cut—the requisite rookie look. One of Cauchon's buddies just referred to him as *la tapette* or pansy, an old Quebecois slur. Pouliot was reminded again and again that homophobia was alive and well in the SPVM despite all the sensitivity training they'd all been forced to take.

Several just referred to him as *le nain*—the dwarf. They also enjoyed dreaming up other ways to torment him—including old chestnuts like ordering a dozen extra-large pizzas for the precinct on his credit card that they'd snuck out of his wallet, or each taking turns urinating in his locker. Pouliot was used to bullies—his diminutive size and implacable nature had made him the object of much cruelty over the years. That was why he had trained since he was eleven years old in the various martial arts, earning a black belt in both Karate and Krav-Maga—the martial art that has no concern for an opponent's well-being, favored by the Israeli Defense Forces. When a colleague imaginatively called him a gay dwarf in the parking lot of the precinct, Steve forced him into a snowbank by twisting his arm within a millimeter of breaking and made him swallow a great big mouthful of yellow snow—another favorite "prank" of bullies past. That had kept everyone at the station quiet for some time.

So he was a bit surprised to open a gift box on the seat of his cruiser that morning to discover a reeking pile of what was clearly human shit with a little note attached: *Un petit cadeau pour tes amies Esquimaux! A little gift for your Eskimo friends.* Steve took a photo on his phone of the attached note and the contents of the box, and then deposited it in a trash can. Then he entered the precinct office to the obvious stares and snickers of his colleagues as he headed towards his desk, saying absolutely nothing and betraying no emotion whatsoever on his face.

Roméo Leduc had texted him earlier to say that something urgent had come up and he would have to delay the interview with Travis Hall until later that afternoon. Steve decided to wait for Roméo. Meanwhile, he had a couple of hours to kill and brooded over how best to use them. Should he try to figure out which of his colleagues had put that gift in his car? He would probably learn their identities soon— idiots had a way of betraying themselves and each other. It was just a matter of time. Instead, Pouliot decided he would do everything in his power to catch the fucker who'd run over that poor girl in the tunnel and left her for dead. No one else here gave a flying fuck about the fate of Rosie Nukilik. No one had had even bothered to double check the work done on the hit-and-run, so Steve decided he would reexamine the CCTV footage of the tunnel. Even though Cauchon himself had said it was hopeless, Steve Pouliot wasn't so sure.

Less than three hours later, he had a hit from the CCTV data he'd sent off to a friend in Toronto. According to the coroner's report, he figured the estimated time of death was at the most two hours after the collision, so he narrowed down the traffic to about two dozen cars. Then he whittled away at that list down to the cars whose plates could be read more clearly by the LPR technology his friend had run the data through. That left five. A Dodge Ram pickup, a Subaru Forrester, a Toyota Rav 4, a Hyundai Elantra, and a Lexus Infiniti. He decided to check the Infiniti first for no other reason than it was by far the most expensive of the vehicles. It was registered in the name of Danielle Champagne, which seemed very familiar to him. When he looked her up online, he was reminded that she was some kind of feminist fashion maven and author. The chances were very remote that she was his "man," but as Steve Pouliot wrote her information down, he decided he would pay Madame Danielle Champagne a visit first thing in the morning.

# Fifty-One

THEY HAD NOTHING LEFT. No voice. No strength. No warmth. Nia and Ti-Coune had shouted, screamed, demanded, pleaded, and finally kicked the fence repeatedly for over three hours, to no avail. Nia was convinced someone would hear them sooner or later, but Ti-Coune knew how very remote this place was. Very deliberately so, he guessed. Now they were both squatting on their haunches in the snow, back-to-back, keeping an eye out and trying to stay warm. Nia could no longer really feel her feet, and Ti-Coune's fingertips were frozen. He hadn't even worn gloves.

"Jean-Michel? We'll freeze to death if we don't keep moving. Let's keep walking."

He nodded and struggled to his feet. Then he pulled Nia up, and started pacing the length of the fence, swinging his arms back and forth to force some circulation to his fingers. He watched Nia's shallow breaths dissipate in the frigid air. The sun was almost down, and the temperature would soon plummet. They were in a dangerous situation now, and Ti-Coune felt like an idiot. Why the hell did he allow himself to get talked into this? Did he think he was playing the fucking hero for this girl he hardly knew? What kind of a loser *does* something like this?

He looked over to the next enclosure where they'd first spotted Hamlet. Even Hamlet had given up pacing the fence with Nia and had retreated to the warmth of his doghouse. Ti-Coune could just make out his face, resting on his paws, his eyebrows twitching as he followed Nia's every move.

"They can't just leave us here. Like this. I mean, someone is gonna come. Right?"

Ti-Coune smiled wanly. "Sure. I think so. Maybe Roméo will get my text."

Nia searched his eyes for any reassurance and found none. She knew they were in trouble, too.

"Maybe that…person at the house will come back here. She didn't seem like, like a killer. Like she wanted to kill us. Right?"

When Ti-Coune didn't respond, Nia started jogging around the perimeter of the enclosure, pausing to stamp her feet every few seconds. She was trying very, very hard not to cry. So was Ti-Coune. Suddenly, she stopped and turned to him excitedly.

"Maybe we should dig a snow cave. Don't those insulate you? Protect you?"

Ti-Coune lifted his frozen hands to her. "What should I dig with? My elbows?"

Nia jogged over to him and looked into his face. His eyebrows, lashes, and scraggly beard were coated with frost. The snot on his thin moustache had frozen into small white icicles.

"I'll dig. And then we can get inside it and use our body warmth to keep our core temperature up. I saw it on *Naked and Afraid*."

Ti-Coune looked at her, confused. "You saw it on *what*?"

But Nia had already moved to a corner of the enclosure and started frantically digging at the snow like a dog digging for a bone. Hamlet continued to watch her.

"Now you know what it feels like." The disembodied voice came out of the whisper of wind, somewhere near the locked gate. Ti-Coune turned to the sound of the voice. It was close. But he couldn't see anyone. Nia stopped digging, panting from the exertion, and got shakily to her feet. She peered into the direction of the voice but could see nothing.

"I *am* sorry. You shouldn't have been able to find us. But, you *were* very persistent."

"What WHAT feels like?" Nia shouted.

They heard the snow crunching under the person's feet as he took a few steps closer. "Freezing to death, of course."

Nia ran closer to Ti-Coune, and grabbed one of his frozen hands. Hamlet was out of his house and running back and forth against the fence, whining. Suddenly the other dogs started their chorus of barks, whines, and yowls.

The man must have done something, like blown a dog whistle—because just as suddenly the dogs went silent. Even Hamlet stopped and sat, his tail wrapped around his huge body and truncated front legs.

"This is all a misunderstanding. These dogs back here? They are never, *never* to be put up on the website. These are the special dogs that I rescued myself, personally. She *knew* they weren't supposed to go on the website. She knew. You should never have come here. But now, here we are. What am I going to do with you?"

Ti-Coune stepped closer to where he heard the voice. "You're going to unlock that gate and let us go back to our car and get the fuck out of here. And we will tell no one about the whole thing. That's it, that's all."

Suddenly, they could make out the silhouette of the man as he stepped into the beam of light cast by the spotlight on the kennel. "*You're up shit creek without a paddle, my boy.*" The voice chuckled. "That's what the Man used to say to me when he sent me to the cage."

"What cage?" Nia asked. "What are you talking about?"

Ti-Coune ran closer to the voice. "*S'il te plait, tabernac. Je gèle.* We just want the dog back."

"Oh, I'm not giving you the dog back. He's staying here, where he's safe and cared for. I am never giving any of them *back*." He paused for a moment, and they could hear his breath catch with emotion. "Do you remember that beautiful boy who froze to death a few months ago? Froze to death outside the metro, because his stupid *owner* didn't care enough to give him up and find him a proper home? No. He kept him out on the streets, and that beautiful boy? He died."

The man stepped closer. Nia could still not make out his features, but she could see something vertical in his hand. Was it a stick? Was it a gun? A rifle?

"When I saw that story on the television, I knew that it was finally time to do something. Really do something, after all these years. I wanted all those poor animals to know—help was on the way."

His voice was just on the edge of being familiar to Nia. What was it? Soft-spoken. Higher register. Almost feminine. She forced herself to think, but just couldn't place him. Yet.

"She was the one who first made me think about saving

the dogs. She cried over it. Said something should be done. That it wasn't right. I thought. I will fix this. I will help."

"What the fuck are you talking about, man?" Ti-Coune asked, his voice weaker now.

"Why are people so cruel to animals? All they want is to love you. Unconditionally. They don't make *choices*. They have no control over their lives. I know what it's like to have no control, believe you me! But, you people do. You choose to keep those dogs on the street—living like, like garbage. Have you seen one with its paws frozen off? Its pads frozen to the sidewalk? What that looks like?"

Nia drew closer to the fence and the voice. She was so close to knowing who he was. She was sure of it.

"Sir? I am sorry you feel our dog was…abused. But we *loved* him. And we took good care of him. He had a good life with me and…me and Christian."

The face turned and he took another step closer. "You look so much like her. That's how I first noticed you. Do you remember?"

"Like who?" Nia asked gently.

"I told her about the Man. She was the only one who really understood, because she came from hell as well."

Ti-Coune shouted into the near darkness. "*Christi*! I'm frozen! Let us out of here and we'll talk—"

"When they asked me, years later, why didn't you *tell* anyone? Why didn't you escape? I thought every kid went home to a cage. I thought every kid wore a collar and was tied to a tree. That's why I never told. Because I thought it was normal."

"Sir? My friend here—is very, very cold. Could we—"

But he kept talking. "When they…arrested the Man and my mother, they were only sentenced to two years. Two. Years. After nine years of my life. My only companions for nine years were the other dogs. That's why when that dog died, I had to help. They saved me."

Nia went up to the fence and stared directly into the face she still couldn't quite see. "Dogs are so important to homeless people, too. They're often the only thing keeping us alive—the only animal we can trust. Like you with your dogs. We don't want to ever hurt them. They save us, too—and maybe we save them?"

Ti-Coune was now slumped in a corner of the dog run, hugging his knees to his chest. He wasn't talking anymore.

"Please. You can keep Hamlet. You can keep them all. Take good care of them all. It's important what you're doing. It really is. Just *please* let us go inside."

There was no response at first. And then suddenly, the man flicked on a floodlight and stepped fully into its the beam. Then he shone his flashlight on Hamlet.

"Well, hello there, gorgeous."

Nia gasped, and then in the most even voice she could muster, she said, "It's you."

Roméo Leduc trudged along the narrow snow path towards the faint light in the distance, careful to make as little sound as possible. Something felt very awry here. He slipped his gun from his shoulder holster and, just to be cautious, pulled back the safety. As he approached a series of outbuildings, he could hear voices going in and out of earshot depending on the direction of the wind,which had picked up. He turned in the direction of the speakers. One woman and one man. He inched closer. There was a very big man in the shadows, clearly growing more agitated, speaking to the girl, Nia. Another figure lay hunched against the fence, not moving. She was begging him to let them go. Roméo held his gun directly in front of him and stepped forward. Just at that moment, the wind direction must have changed, and suddenly the dogs picked up his scent. There was an explosion of barking, yapping, and howling dogs. The man stepped back into the shadows and disappeared. Roméo ran to the fence and turned on his flashlight. The entire dog run was illuminated, but the man was gone.

"Nia! Get Ti-Coune on his feet now! Make him walk. Now. DO IT!"

Nia ran to Ti-Coune and started punching and pushing him, but he refused to stand up. Roméo held the flashlight high above his head, and with his gun cocked and the dogs still barking hysterically, he ran towards the kennel.

This was ridiculous. She'd been sitting in the car for a good ten minutes, trying not to look at her phone. To distract herself, she was trying to appreciate the neon streaks of fuchsia the setting sun was painting across the sky. But the more she thought about it, the sillier it was—they were at a dog shelter, for God's sake, not the hideout of the Hells Angels. What would it hurt if she were to just step out of the car and take a little look around? She opened the car door and immediately heard the dogs. At the same moment, Marie was quite certain she saw a curtain in the window of the house flutter. So someone was watching her.

Roméo stepped cautiously into the damp and close, doggy warmth of the kennel, and inched carefully past the dogs who watched him, oddly silenced by his presence. He looked around for a light switch but couldn't find it. The beam of his flashlight illuminated a swath of the kennel quite effectively, but the corners were in darkness and he was on hyper alert for any sound that would betray where the man was. Roméo knew he was at a dangerous disadvantage—he was on the killer's territory, which he knew intimately, it was almost completely dark, and he was armed as far as Roméo could tell with a 22-caliber hunting rifle. The man had seemed familiar to him—something in his voice—and then Roméo remembered where they'd met. He followed along the wall, his empty hand feeling along it for the light switch still, trying to control his breathing and pounding heart.

"Why did you have to come here?"

Roméo heard the click of a rifle's safety being released.

"Drop your gun, please. And flashlight. Now."

For one nanosecond Roméo thought he'd take a shot. But there was purpose in what the man said. Lethal purpose. He dropped his gun into the sawdust on the floor. It landed with a small thud. He thought of hurling the flashlight at the man's head, but instead dropped it as well.

"Now please put your hands on your head and walk straight out that door."

Roméo did as he was told, his mind racing with possible counterattack. Nothing seemed plausible at that moment.

"Could you please let the girl and her friend inside the kennel? I think they're both severely hypothermic. Do you want their deaths on your conscience?"

"They should've minded their own business. Same as you. Then, we'd be good. All of us."

"You killed her boyfriend. You stole her dog."

"Stop right here."

"And why Rosie Nukilik? What did she ever do to you?"

The man hesitated. "She couldn't take care of the dog. It would've been dead in weeks. It was just a matter of time."

Roméo turned around to face the man. "You can't bear to see dogs suffer? Is the suffering of dogs, not humans, intolerable to you?" Roméo watched the rifle carefully. The man handled it easily. He had clearly hunted before.

"Humans have control over their lives. They make choices. They are the only species that enjoys the suffering of other sentient beings. I could not watch another human enslave a dog to his life. We'd all be better off if we as a species were entirely eradicated."

Roméo shook his head. "I have to admit a big part of me agrees with you there."

"Could you get down on your knees, please?"

Roméo did not like where this was going. His heart was pounding hard enough to make his breath catch. He struggled to get down on his knees with his hands on his head.

"Did you meet Rosie at your friend's place? What happened to your friend, Hélène Cousineau?"

"You shut your mouth—"

"Did you…do something to her? Did she deserve to be punished too?"

"I said, shut your goddamn mouth."

"Did you know that is her brother over there freezing to death?"

The man paused for just a moment, then quietly commented. "Good riddance, from what I heard."

"What did you do to Hélène? Did you kill her, too?"

Almost before the last word escaped Roméo's lips, he felt the force of an animal hit him. He fell back off his knees, and into the deeper snow. The man was straddling his chest, squeezing the air out of him. Roméo flailed away, but he knew he was in deep trouble. The man's strength was feral. Roméo knew he only had a few seconds. The man leaned over him and whispered into his ear, "I'm so sorry."

Just as Roméo was letting it all go, all of it, and accepting the calm and peace that came with that release, he felt a thump and then another, and the terrible pressure ceased. As he struggled to get air back into his lungs and up to his brain, he opened his eyes for a second, and there was Marie standing over him, a bloodied log in her hand, staring at him wild-eyed and screaming for him to wake up.

Roméo watched the entire *denouement* unfold like it was a police action movie with the sound on mute. There was Ti-Coune being loaded into an ambulance, looking small under the emergency blanket, his hands folded across it and wrapped in enormous white bandages. Roméo was relieved to see he was conscious. There was a very large person, a woman, he thought, sobbing and cradling the big man's bloodied and bandaged head in her lap, begging the SQ officers to let her into the ambulance with her brother. There was Nia Fellows, also under a metallic emergency blanket, but clearly in better shape than Ti-Coune. A very large and strange-looking dog was in her arms, looking up at Nia in worship, and licking her entire face every few seconds. Suddenly, the paramedic ripped the blood pressure strap from Roméo's arm and gave him a terse thumbs up. Still, Roméo knew several ribs were broken, and for some reason he was still having trouble hearing anything clearly. Roméo turned to see Nicole LaFramboise appear beside him, a phone to her ear and directing the first ambulance off to the hospital. He could see that the CSI vehicle was just arriving and would soon secure the entire area for evidence. Roméo was very grateful for the call he made to Nicole in St. Jerome before he headed out to the wilds of l'Épiphanie.

And then, there was Marie. He could see that Nicole was now sitting next to her in the back of a third ambulance, looking right into her eyes and nodding at something Marie said. She took Marie's hand and gave it a squeeze. Then she stood up and headed over to welcome the CSI team. Roméo tried to smile as Marie approached him. She looked about as shocked as someone would who'd just beaten a man with a log. Roméo thought he had never seen anyone more beautiful in his entire life, real or fantastic. Marie sat next to Roméo, gently touched her head to Roméo's chest, careful to avoid any pressure where she knew he was hurt, and sobbed.

# Fifty-Two

*Five days later*
*February 18, 2019*

WHEN A NUNAVIK RESIDENT DIES in a Montreal hospital, the government pays to transport the deceased person home. The same is often the case if someone dies in prison. But if the deceased had been living on the streets, it becomes the family's responsibility to pay to transport that person's body back north. Rosie Nukilik's mother had died six years earlier, and her father, who was grieving terribly, could not begin to afford to fly his daughter home—the price of a ticket to Nunavik was astronomically out of reach. Annie Qinnuayuak persuaded the Native Women's Network to pay for Rosie Nukilik's body to be flown back to Salluit to her loved ones, accompanied by her friend, Charlotte. The flight was the very next morning, so a small, symbolic funeral ceremony was being held for her in Cabot Square. It was a gloriously mild February morning, and the mourners had slowly peeled back the layers of protection each had worn and allowed themselves to be warmed by the sun. Rosie's friend, Charlotte, was delivering a tearful eulogy.

"I think a few of you here know that Rosie loved so many songs, and I wanted to sing one of her favorites, but I can't sing. Like, at all. So, I wanted to finish today with a poem she really liked and that reminds me so much of who she was. It doesn't rhyme or anything, but this really makes me think of Rosie and the kind of friend she was. Oh, I changed it just a little bit. I hope that's okay." Charlotte opened a piece of paper and began to read.

"I said: What about my eyes?
She said: Keep them on the road.
I said: What about my passion?
She said: Keep it burning.
I said: What about my heart?
She said: Tell me what you hold inside it.
I said: Pain and sorrow.
She said: Stay with it. The wound is the place the light enters you."

Charlotte slowly folded her piece of paper and returned in tears to the hugs of a group of girlfriends. Then an elderly priest solemnly took Charlotte's place and asked the mourners to join him in a prayer. Annie closed her eyes and tried to focus, but all she could think about was him—Peter LaFlèche. He had come to her two years earlier and offered to volunteer a few hours a week doing basic IT for Le Foyer.

He quickly and unobtrusively made himself indispensable. Within six months, they were able to offer him a tiny salary to work for them three days a week. He graciously accepted. Peter was kind, competent, and a generous team player. But to say he was guarded with his emotions would certainly be an understatement. The man revealed nothing about his personal or emotional life, and Annie had not inquired about that side of Peter because he was so necessary to her work, and he so clearly did not want to share himself. When Annie thought of what he'd done to Rosie and Christian Bourque—and now the police were saying perhaps others, too—she felt the bile rise to her throat and thought she might vomit. How had she worked with this man for two years and not seen the signs of a sick soul? How had she not known? Had she been south in the city too long? How long before her soul, too, became completely eroded, flayed to the bone? How many more bodies would she be sending home?

Annie had to put out so many metaphorical fires every day that she had little time to think too much—because if she did, she'd never get up in the morning. She tried to remind herself of all the good that they'd done, the success stories of people who'd gotten off the streets, found their way back home—alive, and if not exactly well, then *better*. She refused to see her people as perpetual victims, but as survivors. But still. She had allowed that—what was he? A monster? He wasn't born that way. Monsters are created. Annie had learned that Peter LaFlèche had managed to completely transform himself depending on the different roles he was playing.

At the Salvation Army shelter, where she found out he volunteered one or two days a week, he wore a full uniform. When he wanted to prey on and blend in with the people he served, he seamlessly became a street person. Annie thought of the stories her grandmother had told her, about the *Ijiraat*—shape shifters who could transform themselves into any arctic animal—bear, caribou, wolf, or raven—and who often led wanderers to their deaths. Many believed they were not inherently evil but misunderstood—and were the embodiment of the souls that had not found peace after dying. Although they could transform themselves to deceive their victims, they could not disguise their eyes, which were always red—whether they were in their animal shape or human. How had she not seen the truth in his eyes?

The brief service was just coming to a close, and the three dozen or so people were starting to shift and re-gather. Several Inuit community leaders were chatting quietly, and Annie noticed a few police officers had come out to pay their respects. Roméo shook Annie's hand and walked slowly and carefully back to Marie and Ruby who had both wanted to honor Rosie's life and memory. A few people continued to file past a little table covered in a piece of sealskin that held her framed photograph—a smiling Rosie Nukilik standing by the bay in Salluit, staring directly and joyfully at the camera. Next to her photo was placed a long and delicate flight feather of a snow goose. Also on the makeshift altar was a snow globe that Rosie loved, picturing downtown Montreal. There was also a dog-eared book of *100 Most Popular Songs for the Piano*, and a crinkled snapshot of Rosie together with her sister, Maggie.

Roméo watched as Isaac Blum left the service alone, without speaking to anyone, and headed towards Alexis Nihon mall. The word on the street was the Good Samaritan was no longer doing his rounds. He still wondered why Isaac

Blum had lied about knowing Rosie. Was there more going on with the young women he ministered to than they knew? Roméo followed Isaac's trajectory as he trudged back towards Alexis Nihon mall. Would that be it, then? Back to work at Canadian Tire, and all the possible healing he might have continued to do was over? Roméo scanned the dispersing mourners one more time, just to be sure. He kept hoping that Hélène Cousineau would show up.

"How are your ribs?"

Roméo smiled and gently touched his rib cage with both hands. "Better than they were."

Steve Pouliot nodded and held out his hand to Roméo. "I wanted to say thank you. For taking an interest. Maybe one day we'll be working together again."

Roméo raised one eyebrow. "You'd have to change teams. But you'd be welcome anytime with me at the Sûreté. Just let me know."

Steve Pouliot turned to leave and stopped. "Oh, I thought you'd like to know, as it hasn't officially been announced yet. They're forming a special investigative unit to look into the deaths of the two Indigenous women—Shannon Amittuk and Vickee Quissak. We'll be reopening those inquiries and several other cases that were never properly investigated."

"We?"

Steve Pouliot chewed thoughtfully at his thumbnail. "Yes. They've asked me to head up the unit."

"*Felicitations, mon ami.* That is very good news."

"Oh. I thought you'd like to know this, too. Your friend and mine, Detective Cauchon? He's been suspended with pay. Pending further investigation of his, um…attitudes and activities. The dinosaurs are dying off, Detective Inspector Leduc."

Roméo watched as Officer Pouliot turned on his heel and walked away. If the political timing is right, he thought, Detective Cauchon will be gone. And hopefully not to Tahiti, but maybe to Thetford Mines.

# Fifty-Three

THE FORMER ROYAL VICTORIA HOSPITAL sits nestled on the southeastern flank of Mount Royal, sandwiched between McGill University's science buildings and its football stadium. It is a Victorian relic, full of towers, turrets, and labyrinthine passageways. It is also now closed. When the government discovered that it would cost a fortune to renovate and update the 125-year-old building, they pulled up stakes and decided to amalgamate several hospitals into one super-hospital in NDG. The Royal Vic, as Montrealers commonly called it, fell into disrepair. There was the inevitable talk of converting it into condos, or a new student residence for McGill. But the new mayor had decided on another possibility.

Nia Fellows walked down the hallway that still looked very much like a hospital, painted toothpaste-green and eerily quiet. Hamlet's nails clicked on the floor as he followed closely on a leash beside her. A few volunteers were setting up a coffee station, and several others were unloading a vanload of clean donated blankets and sleeping bags. One or two nodded and smiled at Nia as she passed. She was focused on the figure standing at the very end of the corridor. He turned around when she called his name.

"Jean-Michel! How are you?" She kissed him gently on both cheeks, the standard greeting in Quebec.

He had clearly washed his long hair and combed it over into a ponytail to cover the widening bald spot. He looked tired. Before he could answer, she asked, "How is your hand?"

Ti-Coune raised his bandaged right hand and dropped it again. "*Ça faisait mal en ostie.* It hurt like hell, but now it's better."

"Jean-Michel. I am *so* sorry. I was really hoping that they'd got there in time—"

"*Inquiète-toi pas, madmoiselle.* Don't worry so much. I didn't really need those two fingertips anyway."

They both broke eye contact and waited awkwardly for the other to say something. Ti-Coune reached down with his good left hand and scratched Hamlet's head.

"*Salut*, Hamlet! *Ça vas mieux, mon pitou?*"

Nia and Ti-Coune moved to a more private part of the corridor, where Nia pulled up a couple of chairs. Hamlet sighed heavily at Ti-Coune's feet, put his big head on his paws and promptly fell asleep.

"I bet you didn't know that I was born here."

Ti-Coune raised an eyebrow and whistled. "*Pour le vrai?*"

"So, I guess I've come full circle. Me and Hamlet can stay here until we find permanent housing—"

"You can stay here with Hamlet? You're allowed?"

Nia smiled the widest smile he'd seen on her face yet. "Yup! This shelter is especially for homeless people with dogs."

Ti-Coune touched her shoulder softly. "*Chuis content pour toi.* That's good news." He was still struck by her uncanny resemblance to his sister, Hélène. Although he had not found his sister, he felt certain that she was alive and surviving some-where. He had put out the call to the universe, and maybe it would answer. For now, he'd have to be patient.

"Nia. I wanted to tell you. That, eh…I never had no kids, me. And, eh…I got this little house in Val David—that's one hour from here in the car." He cleared his throat once, and then again before he continued, his voice breaking ever so slightly. "So, if you are ever stuck, ever again, with no place to stay. You let me know. You got a place with me."

Nia reached down and scratched a groggy Hamlet to distract herself from the embarrassment of Ti-Coune's kind offer. She couldn't look at him right at the moment, because she didn't want to cry. She nodded, and very quietly said, "Okay."

"Hey, Nia, remember that little white dog? The one that looked like a rat? That was in the house at the shelter?"

"Yeah, I do—"

"You know, that was the dog of Rosie Niku…ilik? So anyway, I called Manon—*ma blonde*—my girlfriend, and she came to Montreal, and…she took the dog back to Val David to live with her."

"Jean-Michel, that is the *best* news."

"I would have like to take the dog with me, but my dog, Pitoune? There's no way. She's too jealous."

Ti-Coune then got to his feet, leaned down to pat her shoulder, and made his way down the hall towards the bright red *Sortie* sign. Nia was about to call out "*À la prochaine!*" to him, but the truth was she would probably never see Jean-Michel Cousineau ever again.

# Fifty-Four

*One week later*

SHE LOOKED UP FROM THE NEWSPAPER and gazed out
the window. Not that she could see very much, as it was opaque
with frost arabesques. The space heater she'd bought to bol-
ster her apartment's ancient heating system was on its highest
setting, but it couldn't keep up with minus thirty-five outside.
And shitty insulation. They'd told her Winnipeg was cold in
winter—but they were guilty of extreme understatement. It
made Montreal winters seem balmy. She watched a sleepy
winter fly rubbing its legs over the leftover eggs on her plate,
and then flicked it away. The newspaper was still open to the
double-page article she had read for the tenth time and would
pore over again. *ALLEGED SERIAL KILLER ARRESTED—
TARGETED HOMELESS—TO "SAVE" DOGS FROM LIFE
ON THE STREET.* It went on to describe how he targeted the
very people he was meant to help and castigated all the people
who didn't notice they had a serial killer in their midst.

Of course, there was the requisite deep dive into his
background, and all the horror of his childhood trauma was

described in lurid detail. Readers were going to eat it all up like the dogs he saved inhaled their food. She kept reading the words, but they just weren't registering in her brain. Peter LaFlèche. *Peter.* She'd known there was something very strange about him, but of course she did not anticipate *any-thing* like this. She remembered the night he first came into Roasters. A hockey game was on the TV and he sat alone at her bar and half-watched it while half-watching her. But not in a creepy way. They struck up what she would describe as a highly entertaining conversation about the people in the restaurant. He had made her laugh at the detailed backstories he imagined and narrated for each of her customers. They were incisive and funny but not mean. She appreciated that— it was too easy to be gratuitously nasty. He was smart, but he knew when to shut up, too. At the end of her shift he left her a very good tip, and most importantly, did not hit on her.

She didn't see him again for another week, when he returned to watch another game, and they fell into easy, but compelling conversation. She was flattered that he clearly found her attractive at her age and after the life she'd had.

Hélène looked at the grainy photograph of Peter the newspaper had dug up. He was handsome in a vapid, chiseled way. Like his face was waiting to be written on, when in fact, she learned later that he had already lived in hell. When had he first come over to her place? Maybe in April or May? She had waited weeks before she invited him, and even then she was wary. But he chatted easily with her while she prepared a simple meal, and he just *fixed* things. The first time it was a leaky faucet. The next, a torn screen on her window. Then her cheap vacuum cleaner. These were all things she was capable of fixing herself, but somehow never got around to them.

Slowly and steadily, he started making her life a bit easier, insinuating himself into it, until she almost *needed* him. He would drive her to Costco for a giant order of food and supplies because she didn't have a car. He would propose corny outings, like a tourist would do—a visit to St. Joseph's Oratory to see the crutches of all the cripples whose pilgrimage had "cured" them, or a paddle on Beaver Lake in a fake canoe. But he never asked her to sleep with him. She figured he was a closeted gay guy, or maybe asexual, although she didn't really believe such a person existed.

One evening, after he'd washed up the few supper dishes, and she was sitting on the sofa sewing up a tear in her uniform shirt for work, he sat next to her and took her hands in his. He was entirely transformed—suddenly he was like a child, stammering his words and avoiding eye contact. Like he was guilty of something. She felt so bad for him she kissed him. Of course, it didn't end there. They had sex that night—it couldn't really be called making love, as it lasted about three minutes and she hadn't gotten anywhere close before he came. Afterwards, he was in the shower for what seemed like an hour. When he finally came out, he *thanked* her. And left her apartment without saying another word.

Hélène leaned over the newspaper, ran her hands through her coarse, thinning hair, and could not avoid remembering how things had unfolded from there. The day after the sex, he showed up after her shift at work, and insisted on seeing her home. When they arrived there, she was able to convince him that she was exhausted and needed to go straight to bed. She asked him to give her some space and agreed to an evening out with him the following Saturday.

A pattern developed. Peter would pick her up a few days

a week after work, take her home, and then stay for supper and sex. It was always fast. She was never satisfied, and he never knew. Hour-long showers. But still the conversation was amusing, and he was unfailingly kind.

One evening, he hadn't shown up at her work, and she felt enormous relief—like she could breathe deeply for the first time in weeks. She headed home with a skip in her step and dreamed about the long bath she'd take and the *Nasty Women* bingeing she could do. But when she arrived at her little apartment—she noticed his boots first, on the little rubber mat outside her door. That was the first moment when she felt…was it fear? Resentment? Rage? It was then she knew for certain that she was in a situation.

When she thought about Rosie—even *thought* about Rosie—she felt like she might pass out. Hélène put her head in her hands and breathed. Sweet Rosie. So lonely for her family, mourning her sister who had died unexpectedly from some kind of hospital infection. Rosie would sit at the bar, and Hélène would listen to her stories of home—tried to imagine what twenty hours of daylight was like in the summer, and the twenty-hour darkness of those winters. Rosie told her about her grandmother who knew how to do *everything*—who could survive the end of the world if she had to—and how her mother had died of diabetic shock. Hélène had no family at all—except a brother she avoided because of the company he kept. She was well out of that scene, once and forever.

Hélène always gave Rosie a beef barley soup if they had it, and Rosie would talk about the country food that everyone in her village shared so no one would go hungry. Not like here in the city. Hélène often tried to persuade her to go home, but Rosie *wasn't ready yet*—a euphemism for Rosie had fallen into the life in Cabot Square. Hélène stood up and began to pace her tiny kitchenette. *Why* had she let him in that night? She had already told him it was over, whatever *it* was. Changed the lock on her door after he'd had the key made for himself. But he had been so polite, and seemed so himself, or at least his old self. She felt that perhaps with the two girls there it would at least be almost *normal. Had she used those girls for protection that night?*

She remembered how he had charmed Rosie and her friend. How he'd gone on and on about Rosie's playing that broken keyboard. How he said he could get one for her—he had a friend who had one to give away. She felt like ripping her hair out when she thought of him *luring* that girl with stupid promises. *Is that what had happened?* Hélène closed her eyes and tried to banish the idea, but she knew better. And the dog. Oh my God, the dogs. She had thought the little dog was a wonderful idea. Rosie was really turning things around for herself, and once Rosie got the dog Hélène thought having something to love and take care of would heal so many wounds. She encouraged her to get it, but told her if she saw any signs of suffering then she'd take it away. She had no idea that it would lead to Rosie's *murder.*

Hélène reread the horrible account of his treatment as a child. He had revealed some of this to her in sporadic mono-logues, but by that point, she was too afraid of him to have any empathy. She knew that he was following her, watching her, because he would turn up by coincidence in impossible places. One day, he showed up at Roasters during the happy hour rush, asked the manager very politely to turn down the music, and in front of all her customers got down on one knee and proposed to her. He had a ring and everything. A diamond. Hélène was appalled. She covered as best she could, mumbled a yes, and resolved at that very moment to get out of Montreal.

Should she have gone to the cops? And said what? That a creepy-but-damaged guy was obsessed with her? That he'd broken into her apartment? Hélène knew there was no point going to the cops, as they were useless. Besides, she had a record. The last time she'd had to get a restraining order it was against a cop she'd dated. Needless to say, his buddies hadn't enforced the order. The only way to get away from him had been to disappear. And she had. Why hadn't she called Roméo Leduc? Because he had no jurisdiction out west. Besides, she hadn't seen him in years. But she had given Rosie his number, written on the back of that photo Peter had taken and had printed out for her to put on her wall. Hélène told Rosie to call Roméo if there was trouble. *Or anything that worried her.* Or anything that she needed. Did she somehow *know* something was going to happen to Rosie?

Hélène carried her congealed eggs on the plate and dropped it into her tiny sink. She peered out the little kitchen window. Through the frost she could just make out her neighbor getting her two little kids to daycare. They were stuffed into snowsuits so thick they could barely move, so she grabbed one under each arm horizontally and carried them to the car.

Hélène had offered to help her out a few times, as she had no partner and often seemed overwhelmed. But her offers always drew a terse nod and a "thanks, anyway." Hélène glanced at the old-fashioned clock on the wall that had been left behind by the former tenant. She had fourteen minutes to get to work. She went to the bathroom and started to apply her mascara and eyeliner. She looked at herself in the mirror. Here she was. In Winnipeg. She'd left no forwarding address, no number, no clue at all as to where she was heading. Here, absolutely nobody knew her real name.

# Fifty-Five

THE TOASTS JUST KEPT COMING. *À la belle Margeaux! Plus belle que jamais!* Jean Luc David basked in the joy and satisfaction of his successful 40th birthday bash for Margeaux. He had managed to get almost all of her oldest and dearest friends to the party, each one astonishing her even more as they arrived one by one and embraced her. The room was full to bursting, and he particularly enjoyed watching all these people from such different parts of his life come together to celebrate his wife. There were a few local stars, and a few wannabees, but for the most part, the attendance was stellar—especially since the two leads in *Nasty Women* had surprised him with their presence. They were busy pretending they weren't as famous as they'd become through the series. Jean Luc glanced around the "head" table as it were. A few of his older friends joked about how Margeaux would have to be changing *his* diapers soon, and then punctuated their hilarious observation with drunken belly laughs.

Only his close friends would laugh at him like that—no one else would dare. He smiled pleasantly, nodded his head, and lifted his glass. *Laugh, you idiots. Look what I'm married to.* Margeaux smiled along with them, but she still wasn't pregnant, so any talk of diapers was painful to her. He could practically hear her biological clock ticking out loud. Sitting near his wife were two of his three children. He was thrilled they had attended, as neither really liked Margeaux, but both liked his money and his connections. Charles, his handsome and earnest firstborn, was an environmental activist who was hoping to run for municipal office in the next election. And next to him, giggling and leaning into her brother, holding her flute champagne glass aloft was his precious, his treasure, his middle child, the brilliant Ariane. She would be writing her bar exams soon. Jean Luc dreamed of working with her one day, side by side, and Ariane had not said no. His youngest, Paul, had not even responded to the invitation. He had taken his mother's side throughout the divorce and subsequent lawsuit and had not spoken to his father in almost six years. He ran a used record store in Verdun, and smoked so much weed he'd lost all ambition, all sense of urgency in his young life. Jean Luc felt sorry for him. Still, he was his son, and he was lost. The situation irked him.

He suddenly got to his feet, lifted his glass and tapped delicately on it with a spoon. The room slowly began to quiet down, as his guests peremptorily interrupted their conversations and turned to Jean Luc David to listen.

Just as he opened his mouth to toast his wife yet again, he noticed a disturbance at the other end of the room. As he looked to see what was going on, he noticed two uniformed police officers, standing alongside a woman. A cop. A Sûreté du Québec cop. What the *fuck* was going on?

"Jean Luc David? A complaint of sexual assault was filed

against you on February seventh of this year. Maître Remy Roussell of St. Jerome district has deemed the evidence sufficient. I am placing you under arrest." Jean Luc didn't really hear the rest. He stage-whispered to Pierre, his lawyer, to call his firm. He watched as the entire room, all 148 guests, went silent, except for a ripple of chatter asking what was happening, *qu'est-ce qui se passe?* Detective Sergeant Nicole LaFramboise took his two hands and crossed them in front of his crotch while she closed the handcuffs.

"You're starting all this shit up again? This is ridiculous. I am the victim here. I will sue the pants off the fucking SQ," he spat at Nicole.

She paused and smiled. "You do that. And when you're done, you can sue the SPVM as well. I believe there are a few other women who would like a date with you in court. Oh, do you remember Chantal Lalonde-Fukushima? No, you probably don't, I bet. She went missing after one of your legendary parties and turned up in the Saint Lawrence river. We have a few questions for you about her as well."

A uniformed policewoman read him his rights. He continued to threaten Nicole and the entire police force. Then he looked back at a stunned Margeaux and his son Charles. "Don't stop the party. This is a mistake. And someone will pay, let me tell you. I will be released in a few hours. *À tantôt, mon amour.*"

What Jean Luc David didn't know at that moment was that one other woman had come forward and accused him of sexual assault. A young woman from Montreal named Michaela Cruz. They led him away from the head table as his open-mouthed guests followed his progress, between the two cops, towards the exit to the restaurant. He caught the eye of his daughter, Ariane as she hastened over to him and asked what she could do.

"Call Gennifer. Gennifer Moran. Now."

Los Angeles to Tahiti. It took seventeen hours in all. Not bad. Especially since she'd booked first class for the flight from LA to Papeete and could spend that leg drinking champagne from real glass flutes and curling up in her sleep pod with four movies in the docket she hadn't had time to see. The first meal they'd served had been extraordinarily good, almost as good as the meal she'd missed at The Party. That was followed by a hot, soft face cloth, a little jar of quite expensive moisturizer, toothbrush, mouthwash, and a sleeping mask. All paid for so generously by her boss. Her former boss. She'd booked her flight back home to Montreal for mid-April, but Gennifer didn't know when she'd be coming home. Maybe never.

# Fifty-Six

HE HAD A CONCUSSION. From the blow to his head by the cop's girlfriend. He had been unconscious for thirty-seven minutes, they told him. She could've *killed* him, if the log she hit him with had been one inch closer to the left temple. He'd had a terrible headache and couldn't think of looking directly at any light. They had finally taken the restraints off him the day before, after he kept begging nonstop for hours for a proper shower. To be able to wash himself properly. He was filthy. Once they let him wash, he figured they thought he'd just vomit it all out, his traumatic past, what led him to do it, why he couldn't be fully responsible for his actions.

Despite the concussion, a veritable army of psychiatrists, psychotherapists, social workers, and neurologists from the Pinel Institute where he was being held—wasting all that precious public money on him—spent the last five—six?—days asking him question after question, to determine his fitness to appear in court and face the criminal charges laid against him. *Did he understand the nature of the charges laid? Could he clearly communicate to his lawyer? Is he aware what a trial is and that it might take place?*

He refused to speak at all. He thought perhaps his silence, along with the concussion, should keep them off his back for a while, until he figured out what to do. He could only hope and believe that they hadn't arrested his sister Janey, and that she was still able to care for the dogs at La Crèche. He had to believe that, because if he didn't, he would go out of his mind. The thought of all those beautiful trusting boys and girls wondering where he was, what had happened, when he was coming back, had nearly driven him truly crazy. But Janey was so fragile, and without him he feared she would simply revert to her old behavior—a lifeless abdication of all responsibility to anyone, including herself.

Then the social workers would swoop in again, the vultures, and she'd be off to the home again. He *had* to get out of this, but it was hard to focus. Whatever they were giving him were causing vivid, terrifying nightmares of the kind he hadn't endured in years. Palpable, visceral moments from his past kept coming back to him, sometimes during the day as well when he fell into a court-ordered drug-induced sleep. This was typical of these so-called healers who ethos was first do all the harm they'll let you get away with.

He looked up at the holes in the ceiling tiles. He looked out the tiny, filthy window and tried to see something. Anything. But it was all gray with winter smog and general negligence. Her windows were like that—if he hadn't cleaned every one of them that third time he visited. He couldn't imagine how she'd left them like that, but then he couldn't imagine her leaving him, either. Without a word. Like he was a fucking piece of gum under her shoe she had to scrape off and drop in a garbage can. When he got out—which he would—he would find Hélène and prove himself to her. Again.

He checked the time on his monitor. They would be back again in twelve minutes, for more stupid questions and his continued silence. In the meantime, he reached under his mattress with his liberated hand, and pulled out an envelope. In it were letters from several women—who were very *passionate* supporters. They had been smuggled in to him by a friendly member of the cleaning staff—a very pretty girl who couldn't have been more than twenty years old. She was a dog lover, too. He opened one of them and began to read the first few sentences one more time.

"*Dear Peter, I want to thank you, from the botom of my heart, for saving all those beutiful animals off the streets. They did nothing to deserve that life. There are no laws which protect them. You are the law. I think YOU are a grate hero—*" Suddenly his door opened and he could hear the chatting voices for a few seconds before they turned to him and their tone shifted completely. He had just enough time to refold the letter, hide it with the others, and rearrange his face to that of complete and utter indifference.

# Fifty-Seven

MARIE HAD GONE FOR A SKI that morning alone. Well, almost alone. Dog had followed her as he always did, doggedly and directly behind her, every now and then stepping on the backs of her skis, which often sent her stumbling forward over the tips. It was an annoying habit, but she appreciated his presence nonetheless. Although she'd skied solo for years now, and although he could be a hazard, she knew it was safer if Dog was with her.

Marie was following a big loop trail that started straight up the little mountain behind her house and a few kilometers later crossed a scenic plateau where in the distance she could see the white slopes of Mont Tremblant and the hills around St. Donat covered in hoarfrost.

She stopped in a little clearing where the trees parted helpfully, and a fallen log offered her a perfect natural bench. She sipped a bit of the hot tea in her thermos and took a few minutes to remove the ice balls frozen in Dog's paws. Just as she was putting her backpack on, she heard them. The sweet, two-note *fee-bee* of the chickadees, the first one higher-pitched. They were letting each other know that Marie was there—an intruder in their woods. A wave of relief and gratitude washed over her. For the past few months, Marie had noticed fewer and fewer birds singing in her forest. Many of the birds that stay for the winter in Quebec—the juncos, the nuthatches, and the chickadees had disappeared. She was terrified that climate change would bring the silent spring Rachel Carson warned against *in 1962*. The thought of an end to birdsong was to Marie, the end of the world. She was often too scared to admit her concerns to Roméo or her neighbors out loud—because if she did maybe it *was* really happening. Had really *happened*. When she heard those familiar little birds that could survive in 50 below zero temperatures chattering around her, she felt like weeping with relief and joy. They were back.

Marie began the sometimes treacherous descent to her house, dragging her ski poles between her legs when she picked up too much speed, watching for fallen trees across the trail, yelling at Dog to get out of the way, as he preferred to run in front of her skis on the way home. Just as she was about a minute away from her back door, Marie angled her skis into a snowplow and came to a stop. Meandering flakes of snow fell daintily around her—in stark contrast to the trees, their branches sagging with the weight of a foot of crusty, hardened snow. There was an absolute absence of anything human at that moment—no pain, no desire, no doubt, no fear—just the geophany of the wind playing in the swaying balsams. No matter how difficult her life was, no matter what abyss she sometimes found herself in, the effect of undistilled Mother Nature was magical. Marie always felt comforted and restored by it.

After the trauma of the events at the dog shelter, Marie had been exhausted. Finished. She could still feel the weight of the log she'd grabbed from the woodpile, the feral instinct that allowed her to bring it down hard on the man's shoulder, and when that didn't stop him, on his head. She had tried to block that sound out entirely, but it was impossible. The sound of Roméo just trying to breathe with one collapsed lung and broken ribs, the shock of violence in her life. Again. Marie closed her eyes and took a deep breath that she felt to the core of her body. When she opened them again, Marie could see her little house through the trees, nestled in a little dip in the topography, and looking perfectly self-contained. Marie loved her house. She loved this one place in the entire world that was hers. It was her home. The only one she had.

Marie was thinking about all this as she watched Roméo carefully place the last of the plates in the dish rack and begin the meticulous scrubbing of pots. It drove her crazy how he cleared the table often while guests of theirs were still eating. And how carefully and fastidiously he washed the dishes, which hadn't been as clean since the day she unpacked them from the box. But he did it all with no fuss and no complaint. Marie's best friend Lucy often talked about how romantic her husband was, even after thirty-eight years of marriage. How he showered her with flowers, and trips to exotic places, little unexpected gifts, thoughtful surprises. Roméo, Marie had to admit, did none of those things. But when Marie was in bed with the H1N3 flu for eight days, Roméo moved in, nursed her phlegmy, coughing, feverish, and smelly self back to health, while also walking Dog every morning at 6:30—in the winter darkness. Her other dog, Barney, had been so anxious about Marie being sick that he'd had diarrhea for several days. Roméo cleaned it up with no protest or complaint. When her mother, Claire, wandered away from the nursing home in Ste. Lucie and got lost for twenty-four hours, Roméo mobilized the local Sûreté cops and found her. If that wasn't romantic, Marie thought, then what was?

But he could be too quiet and withdrawn, and it often seemed like Marie had to work too hard to pull the words from him. Like tonight. She got up to stoke the fire which was threatening to extinguish itself, and then watched Roméo neatly fold the dish towel and give her kitchen counter one last thorough wipe. They had not discussed the case that morning at all, each tacitly agreeing to let it go for the weekend. They each knew that when—and if—Peter LaFlèche went to trial, they would both have to testify and revisit the horror again. They had of course already discussed it and him at length, asking themselves why some people with such damaged childhoods turn the rage inward and struggle with drugs and self-harm, while others (and, thank God, the overwhelming minority) direct that rage outward. It was like a light gets switched on or off. A sudden homicidal madness. A misplaced sense of justice.

Roméo himself had survived a horribly humiliating and abusive father. It had taken him a long time to tell her, and even when he did he kept insisting it was long ago, and he was long over it. But Marie knew better. She felt such overwhelming, crushing tenderness for Roméo when she heard his determination *to let it go*. The vulnerability in him that it revealed. After they learned that Peter LaFlèche had been admitted to the Pinel Institute, Roméo told Marie he remembered the case of the Boy in the Cage from when he was a child himself. He said that his story had made him feel better somehow—that someone had even had it worse than him. Then he felt the terrible shame of that.

"Would you like some tea?" Roméo held the kettle aloft.

"I would much rather have a scotch. That eighteen-year-old Glenmorangie I have stashed away? Let's open it."

But Roméo was busy with something in the fridge now. Would he ever stop and just *sit*? "There's a blueberry pie in the fridge, but I thought maybe we'd save it for the brunch tomorrow."

Ben, Maya, and Noah were driving up from the city the next morning, and amazingly, Ruby had agreed to drop the books for an afternoon and come along with them. They had planned a fancy brunch, followed by a ski on the gentler trails around the lake. Even more miraculously, Sophie had consented to join the family gathering. Marie did not know what that might portend, but she was very pleased anyway. Roméo had been cryptic about her troubles with her newish boyfriend—all Marie knew was that Sophie was coming alone, and Roméo seemed very relieved. Marie thought about Rosie Nukilik's family. How they would never see her have children and grandchildren. She thought of the other murdered Inuit women—who would never come home to their families. How lucky she was to have her children alive, and with the chance to choose the lives they wanted.

Marie watched as Roméo removed something from the fridge and clearly wince in pain. His ribs were healing, but even a deep breath could still hurt. She could just make out his softly whistling something complicated and classical to himself. Was it one of Bach's *Goldberg Variations*? Marie now recognized most of his favorites. He paused the tune briefly, straining with effort, and then resumed again. Suddenly, the issue that had dominated their conversations for months, that had hovered over them, like a storm cloud they couldn't escape—no longer mattered. The thought of Roméo not being in her life—what if that maniac had managed to kill him? What if something happened to Roméo? How many people got to fall in love again at fifty-nine years old, like she had? With a good, kind man who never bored her, even when he was doing the *dishes*? How many people got to feel *necessary* to someone else, and in turn, allow themselves to be necessary to someone again? Marie wasn't going to wreck that. Not now. Not ever. She knew that the journey was much deeper and better with Roméo on it with her. If it meant selling this house, this home, and finding a new place together, for them to build a life together. Then. Okay. Yes. She could accept that.

Marie rose to one knee and peered over the top of the sofa at the kitchen.

"Roméo? Could you, um…drop whatever you're cleaning in there—are you defrosting the fridge, or what? Could you just come here and sit by the fire with me a minute? I want to tell you something." Marie felt her entire body tingling, anticipating his reaction.

"*Une minute, s'il te plait.*"

Marie could hear the pinging of the crystal scotch glasses, one of the few things passed down to her from her father. And then Roméo was beside her, holding two champagne flutes in one hand, and a bottle of *Veuve Clicquot* in the other.

"Whaaat are you doing? What's the occasion?"

Roméo set the glasses and champagne aside on the coffee table. He folded his long body onto the sofa next to Marie, holding his ribcage ever so slightly. Marie picked up a sleeping Barney and moved him to the other end of the sofa to make room. Dog was dead asleep before the fireplace, his legs spasming from some squirrel-chasing dream, while the occasional muffled yip escaped his maw.

"I've made up my mind about The Decision."

"So have I—"

Roméo held his hand up. "I'd like to speak first." He took as deep a breath as his ribs allowed. "I would be honored to live here with you. It is your home. And you are my home. So. Here I am."

"Roméo—I…I decided I'd sell the place and we'd start fresh—somewhere between here and St. Jerome like we talked about. I'm okay with that. I am."

Roméo started to shake his head, like he was disagreeing with her. "I swore I would never do this again as long as I live…but…." Then he slid off the sofa, rested gingerly on one knee and faced Marie. From his pocket he removed a little box. He opened it. Inside was a thin gold band with a single stone—an emerald—Marie's favorite. It was understated and elegant, just like the man offering it.

"Marie Lapierre Russell, would you make a better man of me and agree to marry me?"

Marie was so utterly astonished by this turn of events, so completely gobsmacked—all she could do was laugh. Really laugh. A big belly laugh, the one Roméo knew so well and especially loved, because he himself so rarely was able to produce one. This time though, Roméo joined Marie, and they both laughed and laughed until they wept.

# ACKNOWLEDGMENTS

Thank you to the many people whose coverage of the several issues examined in this book provided so much crucial detail and information, and thanks to the people too many to name here who shine a brilliant and healing light in this world.

https://www.cinemapolitica.org/fr/film/qimmit-clash-two-truths (Sled Dog Shootings)

https://montrealgazette.com/news/local-news/mutual-respect-means-inuit-feel-at-home-in-city-of-dorval/ (Interview with Annie)

https://www.forbes.com/sites/debbikickham/2019/02/12/tahiti-is-a-hot-new-travel-trend-for-2019/#3b665f22230e (Gennifer reading Tahiti article)

https://www.cbc.ca/cbcdocspov/features/inuit-defend-canadas-seal-hunt (Roméo remembering seal hunt)

Chapter Fifty-Two opening lines ("When a Nunavik....")
are from: https://nunatsiaq.com/stories/article/65674
nunavik_communities_struggle_to_bring_
inuit_who_die_in_the_south_/

I consulted the above site and a few others:
https://www.nationalobserver.com/2017/10/16/news/
branded-how-inuit-women-montreal-end-street-or-dead

Wīcihtāsowin: Building Bridges to Understanding
| Nakuset | TEDxMontrealWomen
https://www.youtube.com/watch?v=chZ1NZednsA

Books consulted:
*Wild Blue: A Natural History of the World's Largest
Animal*, Dan Bortolotti, Thomas Allen, 2009

*The Whale: In Search of the Giants of the Sea*,
Philip Hoare, Harper Collins, 2010

To my early readers, thank you for your insight, kindness,
generosity of time and spirit:
    Alice Abracen, Isaac Abracen, Harriet Corbett, Michaela
Di Cesare, Lia Hadley, Debra Kirshenbaum, Anne Lagacé
Dowson, Michelle Le Donne, Maila Shanks, Rebecca Million,
Laura Mitchell, Richard Mozer, Susan Mozer, Michelle
Payette-Daoust.
    To Sasha Mandy for his expertise.
    To Cindy Woods for sharing her experience.
    To Kathryn Cole, Gillian Rodgerson, and all the people
at Second Story Press.

# ABOUT THE AUTHOR

During the course of her almost thirty years at Montreal's Dawson College, ANN LAMBERT has taught English literature to literally thousands of students. For the last twelve years, she has co-written, directed, and produced plays with the Dawson Theatre Collective. The Collective is proud of the fact that they welcome students from all backgrounds and abilities, often have casts as large as thirty-five, and play to enthusiastic and non-traditional theater audiences every year.

Ann has been writing and directing stage and radio plays for thirty-five years. Several of them—*Two Short Women, The Mary Project* (with Laura Mitchell), *Very Heaven, Parallel Lines, Self Offense, The Wall, Force of Circumstance, The Pilgrimage*, and *Welcome Chez Ray* have been produced in Canada, the United States, Ireland, Greece, Australia, and Sweden. Ann is the co-artistic director of Right Now! which produced her plays *Two Short Women, The Assumption of Empire, Jocasta's Noose* and *The Guest*, by Alice Abracen. From 2001–2005, Ann adapted and directed plays for The Roslyn Players, a children's theater company that specialized in performing Shakespeare's plays. From 2002–2004, Ann headed the Playwriting Program at the National Theatre School of Canada. In the spring of 2019, she launched a new theater company called Theatre Ouest End in Montreal.

Ann is also the vice-president of The Theresa Foundation (www.theresafoundation.com), dedicated to supporting AIDS-orphaned children and their grandmothers in several villages in Malawi, Africa.